The Surest Poison

Chester D. Campbell

To Sharon

[signature]

Copyright © 2009 by Chester D. Campbell

This book is a work of fiction. All names,
characters, places, and incidents are products
of the author's imagination or are used fictitiously.
Any resemblance to actual events or locales or persons,
living or dead, is entirely coincidental.

First Edition

10 9 8 7 6 5 4 3 2 1

All rights reserved. No part of this book may be used or
reproduced in any manner whatsoever without
the written permission of the copyright owner and
the publisher.

Cover design by

Printed in the United States of America

Library of Congress Control Number: 2008910323

ISBN 978-0-9799167-8-6

Night Shadows Press, LLC
8987 E. Tanque Verde #309-135
Tucson, AZ 85749-9399

Also by Chester D. Campbell

Greg McKenzie Mysteries:

The Marathon Murders
Deadly Illusions
Designed to Kill
Secret of the Scroll

1

IN A RURAL county fifty miles east of Nashville, Sid Chance turned his restless gaze to the front window. The rustic cabin perched like a stalking bobcat high on a wooded hillside. After the rain had moved on, a few slivers of moonlight revealed indistinct outlines of tall hardwoods that crowded the steep slope. Though small, only two rooms, the cabin provided everything he needed. He had found he could do without electricity or running water.

The odor of seafood and soy sauce lingered in the air. He had cooked supper on his camp stove around eight, a stir fry concoction fashioned from canned vegetables and shrimp. That was when the rain started. After eating and cleaning up the mess—though not the tidiest of cooks, he didn't like feeding bugs—he turned down the oil lamps and tried to relax in his homemade recliner. It wasn't easy. This return to the hideaway where he had enjoyed a peaceful life for nearly three years left him wondering if he'd made the right decision in leaving. Going back to the type of work he had pursued for more than three decades left him exposed to the same flawed humanity that had chased him up here in the first place.

The warmth of dying flames in the small fireplace soothed muscles weary from a day of lifting rocks and toting logs. Nature was unforgiving if you ignored her for long. Despite the doubts that plagued him, the fire's warmth and the lullaby of rain chattering musically on the roof proved more effective than a Valium. He soon dozed off. He awoke around two in the morning.

With the commitments he had made, he knew it was time to get back to the city. He lit the stove, put on a pot of coffee, gathered up the few things he had brought along and stuffed them into his duffle bag. After pulling on his boots, he donned a flannel-lined windbreaker, slogged out into the soaked underbrush and closed and locked the heavy wooden shutters over the windows.

Back inside, the zesty aroma of Colombian coffee pervaded the room. Filling a large mug emblazoned with a brown bear and the initials NPS, he drank slowly, like a condemned man savoring his final cup. And, like a condemned man, his thoughts slipped back to the source of his greatest agony, the false bribery charge that had tainted his good name, costing him the job he hadn't planned to give up until retirement. Lurking in the back of his mind was the unfinished business of putting a name to the person who had set him up.

Soon it was time to hit the road. He snuffed out the lamps and doused the smoldering logs, slung the duffle over his shoulder, grabbed a garbage bag and his battery lantern and trudged downhill to where he had parked his truck. Despite efforts to clear part of the meandering trail, it remained treacherous in the dark tangle that remained of late summer's erratic growth. Regardless of what it had or had not accomplished, this brief return to the basics was over.

THE PATROL CAR cruised slowly through the remnants of a chilling rainstorm. At the wheel was a bored Metro Nashville park policeman more concerned about winding up his shift without getting soaked than in looking for trouble. He found it anyway. As he watched the rain tap-dance on the asphalt up ahead, something odd caught in his peripheral vision. Off to one side, where everything should have been green or brown, lay a splotch of red. His eyes snapped open wide. He braked to a stop, backed up, swung his spotlight around. The bright beam picked out a sight that ruined his night. A body clothed in a bulky red jacket sprawled beside the road.

The officer shrugged into his raincoat, pulled on his cap, and trudged out into the shower. A young cop with more experience at changing diapers than confronting trauma on his beat, he approached the still figure with the caution of a hunter unsure if his target was alive. The man's cap had fallen off, leaving black hair matted against his head. When the officer's flashlight played over the jacket, he saw what appeared to be bullet holes in the cloth.

Not pausing to check for a pulse, he hurried back to his car and called in an apparent murder.

EAST PRECINCT Homicide Detective Bart Masterson stood outside the glow of portable floodlights set up beside the road in a secluded section of Shelby Park. Had it been daylight, he would have looked across at the railroad trestle that spanned the Cumberland River. Though the rain had passed, the clouds masked any hint of stars or moon and a musty dampness lingered in the air. The chill led him to poke slender hands into the pockets of his navy jacket. A six-footer with the tenuous build of a scarecrow, he wore a black mustache like an inverted V. It gave him the look of legendary Old West lawman Bat Masterson, who might well have been an ancestor. He turned away from the indistinct tree line as a hound bayed in the distance.

The detective stared at the prone figure lying face down on the soggy ground. What had been a living, breathing human being only hours ago now amounted to little more than deteriorating skin and muscle and decomposing organs of no intrinsic value to anyone but a forensic pathologist. It was a sight he had encountered way too many times, but, as with all the others, he wouldn't rest until he dug into every corner it took to find the killer.

The scene had been exhaustively photographed. A technician from the Medical Examiner's office, a short man with tousled hair and a pinched brow, knelt beside the victim, checking the random pattern of small holes in the red jacket still soaked from the rain. He rolled the body onto its back and studied the front of the jacket.

"I count five entrance wounds in the back," he said without looking up. "Don't see but three exits in the front."

"Good," Masterson said. "Maybe you'll find some lead."

"Hopefully. My guess is it was a .38."

"Let me know when you have something definite." The detective turned to a crime scene officer standing nearby with a large flashlight. "You got anything?"

"Negative. We'll check again in the daylight. There's definitely no brass. He was probably pushed out of a car."

Masterson shook his head. "Five slugs. Somebody damn sure had a grudge against him."

IT WAS STILL DARK when Sid Chance pulled off I-40 at the Old Hickory Boulevard exit. He turned his vintage brown pickup toward Madison, a rambling middle-class suburb on the northeast side of Nashville. A big man, every bit of six-six, he had a headful of black hair and a short beard to match, both laced with threads of silver. The last time he had glanced in a mirror, the glower he saw made him think of a troll. He recalled an old admirer saying he looked like a Hollywood hero when he smiled. He wasn't so sure. He hadn't done all that much smiling in recent times.

Though most of the area's workers remained asleep or just getting started on breakfast, traffic moved at a moderate pace on the circumferential highway. After crossing the Cumberland River, Sid took the cutoff north to Gallatin Pike, Madison's Main Street. His office, a grudging requirement of his new life, occupied a corner in a glass and stone building near RiverGate Mall, anchor for the community's primary shopping area. One strip center after another lined both sides of the street, deserted mini-cities at this time of day.

He glanced at his muddy boots and smudged jeans as he ambled toward the front of the building. He needed a shower and clean clothes, but that could wait. He figured his chances of encountering someone now little better than those of winning the lottery. Nobody was fool enough to come in at this time of day except a habitual early riser, something he'd been since service with Army Special Forces in Vietnam. That's where he learned to exist on a minimal amount of sleep. Inside, he turned toward his office and glanced at the "Sidney Chance Investigations" sign on the door. It brought one of his infrequent grins. How cool would it have been if they had named him Random instead of Sidney.

The answering machine chirped its practiced greeting as he walked in. Welcome back to what most people would call the real world, he thought. Maybe a few more months of civilization would rekindle his appreciation for the marvels of modern technology. Right now they seemed more an annoyance. A computer glitch that had gobbled up three days of painstaking work was the kicker that sent him back to the cabin for a cooling off period.

He found six messages on the machine. Two from Jaz LeMieux wanting him to return her calls, two from guys he didn't know and doubted he wanted to, one from a process server, and one from a lawyer seeking his help. He played that one again.

"This is Arnie Bailey, with the law firm of Bailey, Riddle and Smith. Jasmine LeMieux highly recommended you for a job I need done. She said you were good at finding missing persons. This is a little different, however. It's a missing company. My client faces a major financial disaster if we can't find the organization involved. It's a chemical pollution case around Ashland City. I'd appreciate your calling me as soon as you can."

He glanced at his watch. It was way too early to call a lawyer, even somebody who sounded as anxious as this one. He decided to go home and shower, eat breakfast, then come back and have another go at it. No doubt the calls from Jaz related to Bailey's problem.

Sid lived in the ranch-style brick house his mother had

called home for twenty-five years. She died around the time his career as a small town police chief crashed and burned. The house stood near the river at the end of a quiet street in a neighborhood of mostly young couples and a few retirees. The sky had begun to brighten by the time he pulled into his driveway, though dirty gray clouds seemed to hang within arm's reach.

He reveled in the soothing spray of the shower. It drummed against his back like a masseur's fingers, easing some of the troubled thoughts that had knotted up his mind on the drive back from his hillside retreat. Despite a lot of jury-rigging, he had never come up with a reliable way to get a hot shower in the backwoods. He dressed and settled into the compact kitchen for breakfast. As he poured milk onto his cereal, the phone rang.

"Glad you finally decided to answer." Jaz LeMieux's voice had an edge.

"I just got home a little while ago."

"From where?"

"The cabin."

"Don't you answer your cell phone?"

"When it's turned on."

There was a pause. "I think you're reverting to your mountain man persona, Sid."

He said nothing.

"Have all my efforts been wasted?"

"I did a lot of pondering last night," he said. "But I came back."

At first he had credited his financial mentor, Mike Rich, with the responsibility for luring him out of self-imposed exile. Lately he had begun to lean toward Jaz.

"Have you talked to Arnie Bailey?" she asked.

"I went by the office around 5:30 and got his message off the answering machine. What's the story?"

"You'll have to get the details from Arnie."

"He a friend?"

"He's a good guy. He's done legal work for us."

At forty-five, she served as chairman of the board of Welcome Traveler Stores, a lucrative chain of truck stops her father had founded. She was also a sharp, attractive, persuasive woman who knew how to get what she wanted. Sid wondered how much pressure she had put on the lawyer.

He settled back in his chair. "Bailey says you told him I was good at finding people."

"You are. You've navigated those databases like an old pro."

"Fine, if the computer would quit eating the results."

"I told you I could fix that." Jaz held a computer science degree as well as an MBA. She knew the inner workings of the machines as well as arcane methods of mining the Internet's secrets. "Is that why you went traipsing back up the mountainside?"

"Partly. There were other issues." Sid rumpled his brow. "Bailey mentioned a pollution case."

"There was a story in the paper, but I didn't get a chance to read it. Do you plan to call him?"

"Yes. But I doubt he'd be around this time of day."

"I know he gets to his office early. Maybe not this early, but he likes to be well prepared before court opens."

"Okay, Jaz, I'll talk to him. That's a promise."

"Good. Let me know what he says."

Sid placed the portable phone back onto its base. Despite occasional disagreements, he couldn't help but like her. She had no reason to continue pushing him other than a belief that it was in his best interest. Jaz had been the key to his entry into the PI business. With his background, he had slipped into the role as smoothly as pulling on a pair of comfortable sneakers. He found running investigations for private clients a convenient and, so far, profitable way to stay involved in police work. About the only drawback had been a feeling that sometimes Jaz's efforts skirted the boundaries of his independence.

After finishing breakfast, he realized a couple of days away from his exercise routine had left him sluggish. He settled on an abbreviated version of his morning run. He didn't want to have to shower again.

APPROACHING THE office a little later, he saw cars and pickups clustered around the mall's entrances like mice at a cheese shop, parked by mall walkers, mostly seniors, who swarmed the corridors before time for the stores to open. Considering his own exercise routine, Sid wondered if the lawyer might stop off at a place like this before appearing at his office. No matter, he called Bailey, Riddle and Smith at 7:30 and found the senior partner at his desk.

"Glad you called," Bailey said. "I've been on spikes and nails all night."

Sid translated that as needles and pins. Evidently Bailey liked to be creative with his clichés.

"You mentioned a pollution case," Sid said. "Before we go any further, you need to be aware of where I stand. I spent eighteen years in law enforcement as a National Park Service ranger. I do not like people who mess with the environment."

"Excellent. Miss LeMieux assured me you were the man for the job."

"You don't understand. What I meant was, if your client is responsible—"

"No, no . . . you've got it all wrong. My client is being saddled with a pollution mess another company created before he bought the property. It involves trichloroethylene that's polluted water in Cheatham County."

"I've encountered TCE before."

"It's bad stuff."

"Can be lethal."

"I'd like to talk to you in person before we get started, Sid. Okay if I call you Sid?"

"That's what my mother called me."

Bailey gave a slight chuckle. "I have a client due here in a few minutes, and I'll be in court until noon. Could you meet me here for lunch? I'll have my secretary order us some food."

With that settled, Sid called Jaz and related the conversation.

"Are you going to take the job?" she asked.

"Why not? The subject is one I'm somewhat passionate about."

"I thought it would be. Oh, I had a call from Bart Masterson. He wants to know if you'd like to host the poker club at your office Friday night?"

The poker club was a group of six people with present or past ties to law enforcement who got together occasionally for a friendly game of cards. Jaz had invited Sid to join them at their last session. She said it would give him an opportunity to make some good contacts in the field.

"Sure," he said. "Is everybody coming?"

"Bart's checking. He said he'd demand to be off. They called him out in the wee hours this morning, right after a messy rainstorm. It was a homicide in Shelby Park."

"What happened?"

"To quote Bart, it was a case of overkill. The man was shot five times with a thirty-eight."

"He find any clues?"

"Nothing. And what's weird is the guy worked on a Metro garbage truck. Who would do that kind of killing in that kind of place with a guy like that?"

2

SID SWITCHED ON his computer. While waiting for it to boot, he swiveled his chair, resting his gaze on the windowless beige wall beside him. It was covered with photographic memorabilia of multiple careers from Special Forces in Vietnam to policing various National Parks to providing law and order in the small town of Lewisville. Located a little over fifty miles to the southwest of Nashville, it was named after explorer Meriwether Lewis of Lewis and Clark fame. Lewis died nearby on the Natchez Trace. Some said he was murdered there.

When the Internet browser flashed on the screen, Sid checked his email. Jaz had engineered a website with the help of the Welcome Traveler Stores' webmaster, giving people a place to request on-line help. At the moment everything worked like a well-greased axle. He found two missing person search requests prepaid by credit card. That was easy cash.

Using Internet data bases and a few phone calls, he spent the next couple of hours tracking down people who had disappeared from friends' and families' radar scopes several years back. It helped that he'd had experience with missing person cases while running the Lewisville PD. He emailed results of his investigations, then returned to the computer with a stack of notes to try recreating the files that had been lost earlier in the week. He stayed with it until time to drive downtown to keep his luncheon appointment.

Sid pulled into the garage beneath the building that housed the offices of Bailey, Riddle and Smith around noon. As expected, the first parking floor was already packed like

The Surest Poison

dominoes in a box. Near the entrance, some character in a green VW Beetle had backed into a parking space for the disabled, making it impossible to tell if he had a special license plate. Since Sid was no longer a sworn officer of the law, it was none of his business. But as he passed, he glared at the driver, who still sat in the car. An NRA sticker graced the bumper, but no disabled parking permit dangled from the rearview mirror. Sid shook his head. Some people . . . .

Finally locating a parking spot two levels down, he crossed to the elevators and sped up to the twentieth floor.

"Mr. Bailey just called from the courthouse," his secretary said as she ushered Sid into the walnut-paneled conference room. A grandmotherly woman with neatly-coiffed white hair and an Aunt Bea smile, she pointed to an assortment of sandwich meats, cheeses, bread, lettuce, raw veggies and dips, potato chips, cookies and slices of cake that filled trays at one end of a long shiny table. "He said you could go ahead and start eating. What can I get you to drink?"

"A cup of coffee would do fine."

Sid looked out a broad window at the dwarf-like lunchtime figures scurrying along the sidewalk below. After several years as a small town police chief, followed by three years of isolation at his cabin in the woods, he found it difficult to adjust to Nashville's booming growth, both downtown and in the suburban counties. New skyscrapers had changed the skyline, and the planned 70-story Signature Tower would usher in a whole new wave of changes. Developments like Nissan North America's new international headquarters in Brentwood reshaped the suburbs. It was hardly the quaint Southern town he remembered from his youth.

Arnie Bailey arrived a few minutes later. The polar opposite of Sid, who had a solid frame, broad shoulders, and a modest waist, Bailey launched his short, chubby body through the door like a well-dressed groundhog storming out of hibernation. He pulled off his navy blazer and draped it around the back of a chair.

"Been waiting long?" he asked.

Sid held out his cup. "Long enough to get started on your version of Starbucks."

The lawyer headed for the food display. "Grab a plate and fill it with some of this grub. I have to be back in court by one-fifteen. We need to get busy."

Sid chose turkey and Swiss on wheat and assorted veggies. He grimaced at the pile of food that filled Bailey's plate. Though ten years older than his host, Sid flexed muscles where Bailey collected fat. Most guys had passed their prime by the time they reached their fifties, but most guys didn't take care of their bodies like Sid did. He followed a daily running routine. Workouts in the gym. He would never forget the gunshot wounds that halted his Park Service career, injuries received in a multi-agency drug case fourteen years earlier. He didn't intend to get caught short in a situation where physical conditioning could make the difference between life or death.

"How about giving me the particulars?" Sid said when they were seated at the table. "It took place in Cheatham County?"

"Right. My client is Wade Harrington. He's around forty, a veteran of the Gulf War. He runs a small company just outside Ashland City that makes specialty shipping boxes. They're designed for specific products."

"Like cartons for computers and such?"

"Exactly. He started the company—it's called HarrCo Shipping—about ten years ago, with money he'd been saving. He found an abandoned plant nobody seemed to want and bought it at a good price. An uncle loaned him the rest of the cash he needed to get it going. He's paid that back."

Bailey said HarrCo only occupied part of the plant at first, but as the business caught on, the operation expanded until most of the building was now in use. Everything looked great until people who lived in the area began to complain of headaches, nausea, and dizziness. Others reported bouts of clumsiness that made them appear drunk. Tennessee Department of Environment and Conservation inspectors found trichloroethylene, or TCE, in the well water. It had also seeped into streams that fed into the local water supply.

They tracked the TCE back to an area at the rear of the HarrCo Shipping plant. When the ground was tested there, they discovered it was soaked with the hazardous chemical. With no way to determine just when the spill occurred, the state came after Wade Harrington to pay the hefty clean-up bill, which could run into the hundreds of thousands. It would bankrupt a thriving small business with lots of promise for the future.

"Trouble is, Wade's plant never used TCE or anything like it," Bailey said.

"You're sure about that?"

"Dead sure. There's no need for that stuff in the shipping business. Besides . . . " He rummaged through a folder in his briefcase, emerged with a paper scrawled with barely decipherable letters and numbers. "Here's a list of every chemical they use. Right down to the carpet cleaners."

"So it was the previous occupant?"

"Had to have been. They went out of business a couple of years before Wade bought the plant. He heard it had something to do with the automobile business. They must've used TCE some way in the process. How that much wound up on the ground is anybody's guess."

"The people Harrington bought the place from should be able to tell him what he needs to know."

"The guy who handled the sale said he didn't know anything about the company that previously used the plant. Somebody else was involved with that deal. It wasn't local."

Sid reached for the coffee pot and refilled his cup. No doubt Harrington faced a real problem. Somebody created a bad situation behind his plant, one that did serious damage to the environment. It was a bit different from the concerns he had encountered in the Park Service. A few national parks suffered from water pollution, but the greatest problems they faced stemmed from air pollution, primarily acid rain.

"Harrington hasn't learned anything about the previous owner?" Sid asked.

"Wade is completely in the dark. He hasn't turned up anything about the company other than a vague hint. He can't find who owned it or managed it, or what happened to them. It seems nobody around there knows what went on. He's really between a boulder and a brick wall."

More cliché adaptation. "What was the company's name?"

"Don't have that either. Sounds like a phantom operation."

Sid's look flashed a caution sign. "You realize phantoms can be hard to chase down. That can get kind of expensive."

"Do whatever you have to. Just find the culprit. It'll be a lot cheaper than whatever he'd have to pay the state." Bailey reached into his file, pulled out a large photograph. "Here's something they gave Wade. It's just a sample of what some irresponsible asshole caused."

Sid stared at the face of a small girl with curly blonde hair. Her mouth twisted up on one side. Her right ear appeared only as a gnarled stub. Large hazel eyes gazed out as part of a grotesque smile.

Sid looked at the lawyer, then back at the disturbing image. The little girl could smile now, unaware of what was to come. A cousin of his had been born with similar malformations years ago, after her mother took thalidomide during pregnancy. Attempts to correct the defects proved unsuccessful. Unable to take the stares and ridicule, the girl had committed suicide as a teenager.

"If that little girl was mine," he said, "I'd be looking for somebody's scalp." He handed the photo back to Bailey.

"That's how I feel, too."

"Have you told Harrington about me?" Sid asked.

"I talked to him this morning right after you called. I told him I was meeting with you here for lunch. You'll want to get with him, of course, but he was headed out of town. He'll be back tomorrow."

"What sort of time frame are we looking at?"

The lawyer referred to a sheet among the papers in front of him. "They've scheduled a hearing in two weeks. I need everything you can give me before then."

"Okay, I'll head down that way and start shaking the trees."

Sid pulled out of the garage and turned up the hill north on Third Avenue. Nashville was built on a series of hills. Not as steep as San Francisco's, but steep enough to give anyone's legs a workout who chose to hoof it about town. He had just made the turn behind the Courthouse when he noticed a dark green VW Beetle in the rearview mirror. It looked similar to the one he had seen at the garage on the way in. Checking back as he approached the bridge, he spotted the NRA bumper sticker. That cinched it. He could think of no reason anyone would be tailing him, but he kept an eye on it as he crossed the river and turned toward Ellington Parkway. When he reached the Hart Lane exit, he veered off and watched as the VW followed. After swinging into the street leading to a Highway Patrol Driver Testing Station, he turned into the parking lot and drove up to the building.

Glancing around as he walked, he saw the Beetle had backed into a parking space in the last row toward the street. He strolled into the building, turned, and looked out to see if anyone got out of the car. No one did. After waiting a few minutes, he returned to his car and drove out of the lot. He looked back toward the green vehicle to check the license number, but it had already pulled out.

He headed toward Ellington Parkway and took the long, curving exit onto I-65. He threaded into the HOV lane on the far left and jammed the accelerator. It was only two miles to the RiverGate exit, where he cut across two lanes, hit the succession of traffic lights just right and swung into the parking lot entrance at his building. He saw no sign of the VW.

It had been years since he'd encountered anything like this. Why now? And who could it be? He walked across to his office knowing there was nothing he could do except keep an eye out for anything else that sounded a discordant note.

3

BACK AT HIS DESK, Sid started a computer file with his notes from the meeting with Arnie Bailey. Jaz had coached him into a new familiarity with the digital world. Not that he was a rookie. He had used computers with the Park Service, as well as during his tenure in Lewisville. He recalled the old days when he depended on his memory to store much of the information he gathered. Now, at fifty-nine, he had experienced the unreliability of that tactic.

To clear Wade Harrington, he'd need to locate the management of the company that occupied the plant before HarrCo. An alternative would be to find former employees who might tell how the spill took place. A check of property records at the Cheatham County Courthouse should provide the information he needed to establish ownership of the plant prior to Harrington's purchase.

As a police chief, he had designated someone else to do the grunt work, digging through old records and surfing the Internet for elusive information. In the short time he had been a PI, he'd become proficient at doing the job himself. Even so, he preferred going head-to-head, matching wits and muscle with characters who thought they were above the law, people who tried to use cunning to throw justice on its ear. His new career required more leg work, more tact, less physical threat. But the possibility of taking a twisted situation and making things right was the lure that kept him in the business. That and the prospect of uncovering the creep who had framed him in Lewisville, butchering his reputation and his self-esteem.

Thanks to Briley Parkway, a limited access route that stretched around a major portion of Nashville, the drive to Ashland City took little more than twenty minutes. He kept a close watch for a green VW, or any other suspicious vehicle, but saw none. Thinking about that strange encounter, one thing seemed clear. Somebody knew he would be in that parking garage at that time. He needed to find out who it was and how they knew.

He located the Cheatham County property records in a small but modern office building a couple of blocks down Main Street from the old brick courthouse. A helpful woman at the Register of Deeds office brought him a book that showed transfers of ownership for the property where the plant was located.

She pulled off her glasses and jammed them into an abundance of brown hair. "Isn't that the place that's been in the news lately?"

Sid took the book and nodded.

"There was a man in here yesterday," she added, "said some toxic chemical in the water had made his neighbors sick. He said they intended to demand the county mayor do something about it."

"The state pollution people are working on it," Sid said.

"That who you're with?"

"I'm doing an independent investigation, trying to track down how it happened and who was responsible."

"Well, good luck." She pushed the glasses back over her nose and pointed at the book. "I hope that helps."

He took the records over to a table and began reading through the documents. The last entry recorded a transfer from Henry Keglar to Wade Harrington, the current owner. The Keglar name sparked a dark memory. Sid had logged several encounters with a man named Henry Keglar, better known as Hank, during his days as police chief in Lewisville. There had been whispers, he recalled, that Keglar was involved in shady dealings regarding stolen property. That was shortly after Sid took the job. He couldn't turn up enough evidence to support an indictment, nothing stronger than the word of unreliable witnesses. He'd never doubted Keglar's involvement. The man was a disreputable character who provided plenty of other headaches during Sid's tenure in the small town. His bar had been a magnet for drunks and prostitutes and a variety of unruly characters. When Sid saw the deed had been filed by Bronson Fradkin, a slick country lawyer in Lewisville, he was certain this was the same Keglar.

Following the paper trail, Sid learned Keglar had taken the property back through foreclosure from a company named Auto Parts Rehabbers. Tracing backward, he found the auto parts business took over the plant in 1992. Considering the dates of occupancy, he felt sure this was the firm responsible for the TCE spill. He wondered if the operation had moved somewhere else or if it had closed as a result of bankruptcy. One thing was certain, any attempt to get information out of Keglar would be useless.

After leaving the Register of Deeds' office, he noticed a sign for the Cheatham County Chamber of Commerce on a small building a block from the courthouse. Cheatham was the smallest of the six counties that surrounded Nashville. While most of the others had populations well in excess of 100,000, Cheatham was home to less than 40,000 people. The Chamber, he reasoned, should have a record of Auto Parts Rehabbers.

The reception area featured racks filled with brochures on area businesses and attractions. Sid ignored the literature and introduced himself to a young woman with short red hair and a face sprinkled with freckles who stood behind a counter just inside the entrance. She shook her head after he explained what he was after.

"I wasn't here in the early nineties," she said, "and neither was our current executive director."

"Do you have any records that might cover that period?"

"Let me check." She walked over to a file cabinet and pulled out a drawer. After thumbing through the folders, she took one out and looked inside. "Here's a list of members for that period, but Auto Parts Rehabbers isn't among them. Sorry. Is there anything else I can help you with?"

"Who was the executive director back then?" Sid asked.

"That would have been Murray Estes. He's retired."

"Is he still around?"

"He was until a few months ago. He's living with his son, Murray Junior, in Nashville now."

"Do you have an address?"

She tapped a finger against her chin. "I don't know if I should give out that kind of information, but I'm sure it's listed in the phone book. Anyway, since you're a detective, I guess it's okay."

When he was a cop, there was never a question. She wrote the address and phone number on a card, which he pocketed along with a brochure on the town before heading out to his car. He decided to make one more stop before returning to his office. He drove around the courthouse and turned in at the building behind it. Several sheriff's patrol cars were parked in the lot. He walked up the inside stairs to a second floor, glass-fronted entrance.

The cream-colored block corridor had two open doors not far inside. The sheriff's office was on the left, the desk vacant. Various framed documents hung on the paneled wall behind it. On the right, a pleasant-faced young woman sat at a desk in an office little larger than a walk-in closet. An officer dressed in a tan uniform with sergeant's stripes stood in the doorway.

Sid smiled at the sergeant, who had "Meyer" on his name badge and several years worth of lines around his eyes. "You look like you might be the man I need to talk to."

"How's that?" the officer asked.

"I'm looking for a guy who would go back at least to 1995," Sid said. "That fit you?"

"I've been here longer than that. What can I help you with?"

"My name is Sid Chance," he said. "I'm a private investigator from Nashville." He showed his P.I. license and explained that he was working on the HarrCo chemical spill case.

Meyer folded his arms. "You a former police officer?"

"I was police chief in Lewisville for around ten years. Worked in law enforcement for the National Park Service before that."

The sergeant grinned. "Thought so. You've got the look."

To Sid, that indicated an expression of wariness, a tendency to check out the surroundings, a thin layer of tension just beneath the surface. Mostly it meant a look of take no shit off anybody. If that's what Meyer referred to, he was right.

The deputy's face sobered. "That mess up around HarrCo has been a real pain. I've heard some folks are planning a march on the courthouse. You working with the state on this?"

"No, I'm working for HarrCo's attorney. It seems the spill took place while the plant was occupied by a company called Auto Parts Rehabbers, somewhere around 1995. I wondered if you folks might have had any problems out there back then?"

Meyer stood several inches shorter than Sid, but he packed a much larger waistline. He leaned his bulky frame against the doorway and shifted the holster on his hip. "Problems? I don't recall any trouble with the management. They kept a pretty low profile. We picked up a few of their workers, as best I can remember. I know I handled one DUI. Seems like there were others. As I recall, the ones we arrested had records. Maybe it was some sort of rehab project."

"What about names?"

"I don't recall any, and I'm not sure I could find that kind of paperwork after all these years."

"What about the boss? Do you remember who was in charge?"

"No, afraid not. Wish I could help you, but that's been a good while ago. As I said, we had very little contact with them."

Another dead end.

4

THOUGH IT WAS not quite five o'clock when Sid turned onto his street, the dull gray overcast that had lingered throughout the day brought a premature nightfall to the neighborhood. What he saw switched on a frown. After years of watching people in situations that ranged from the ridiculous to the absurd, he had learned to be wary of subtle shifts in behavior. The porch lights were on at most of the houses. Some also had their eve lights on. Then he spotted a large, toothy orange grin in a window.

It was Halloween.

His first Halloween in four years. In Lewisville, it had been a night for cruising the town to make sure harmless pranks didn't mutate into vandalism. He had never been at home to entertain small spooky creatures. Now he had no idea how many kids might show up. Certainly not as many as in the old days before deranged creeps put a serious crimp in trick-or-treating. Though he hadn't thought to prepare for tricksters, he remembered an unopened bag of miniature candy bars in the kitchen. Something to test his will.

A strong gust sent yellow leaves cascading across the hood as he slowed near the big maple tree in the neighbor's yard. His own lawn resembled a churning sea of geometric shapes, billows of brown and yellow and red. His mother had told him the area was dense with hardwoods before developers invaded.

He hit the garage door opener as he headed down the driveway and pulled in beside his truck. Inside the house, he checked the answering machine in the small bedroom he used as a home office. No calls. Then the doorbell rang. He glanced at the clock. Twenty after five.

He detoured through the kitchen, grabbed the package of candy, emptying the goodies into a plastic bowl as he hurried to the front door. The nostalgic smell of wood smoke from the neighbor's chimney swept in on a chilling gust as he opened the door to find two small spooks standing on the porch, one dressed like Peter Pan, the other Tinker Bell. They flinched at the sight of what must have seemed a real giant, then reached out with tentative hands to choose morsels of candy and mumbled, "Thank you."

Sid looked down. "Happy Halloween."

He waved at the woman waiting in the driveway, huddled against the wind in a bulky leather jacket. He felt certain she lived at the other end of the street. Though he had seen the kids out playing, he had never met the mother or daddy. And considering he was not much of a social type, chances were he never would.

Back in the kitchen, he decided on a can of vegetable soup as the simplest solution to supper. He had just opened the can when the doorbell sounded again.

Grabbing the candy bowl, he strode to the door and pulled it open. He studied the odd figure bathed in the glow of the porch light. She stood a good head shorter and appeared at least a hundred pounds lighter than he did. Dressed all in black, hair flowing in long black tresses, she looked at him with the sultry eyes and blank stare of the old TV character Morticia Addams.

"Jaz," he said, shaking his head. "Where the devil did you get that long black hair?"

She gave a cackling laugh. "Trick or treat!"

He pulled the door open wide. "Get in here out of that cold wind."

"I was on my way to a party at an old basketball teammate's house in Hendersonville," she said. "You didn't call to tell me what happened with Arnie Bailey."

"Sorry. I've been busy." He waved at the sofa. "Make yourself at home."

She sat and glanced around. Sid followed her eyes as she took in the earth tones of the sofa and chairs, furnishings chosen to give the place a masculine look, despite a few touches left over from his mother, like a crisp white scarf on the table beside the window.

Jaz looked back at him, fingering the wig. "I got this at a costume shop."

"You make a great Morticia," he said from his recliner, "but I'm partial to the real thing." Her own hair was short and blonde. The tight black outfit revealed a shapely figure but hid the muscular structure that must have helped put her in the boxing ring, something he'd heard mentioned. She still drew men's glances wherever she went.

"Well, thank you, Mr. Chance."

Sid smiled. There was no way around it. Jaz LeMieux was one helluva woman. She had the looks and the brains to be whatever she wanted, and she had the money and the contacts to pull it off. But it hadn't come easy. Mike Rich told him about the struggles she'd faced after making an impetuous decision to leave college and go her own way. He admired what she had done, but he had too many issues of his own to go beyond that.

She cocked her head to the side. "Okay, Sid. What did Arnie have to say?"

"He wants me to find everything there's to know about the polluter. It was a company named Auto Parts Rehabbers."

He told her about his visit to Ashland City.

"And the company simply disappeared?" she said.

"Maybe not so simply, but it hardly left a trace. I'll see if the old Chamber of Commerce guy can give me something to get a grip on. I plan to check with him in the morning."

"Are you going to see Harrington tomorrow?"

"After I talk to Murray Estes."

"Do a good job on this, Sid. Arnie can throw you plenty of business."

He leaned back and tapped his fingertips. "You remember how reluctant I was to look into your employee problem."

"Sure." She waved a hand. "I had to twist your arm a bit. But you did a whale of job with it. You got a faithful employee reinstated and a crooked manager fired."

"But after that I intended to head back to the cabin. You kept pushing me into the PI business. Why didn't you let it go?"

She gave him an impish smile. "It was your scintillating personality."

"Bullshit."

She turned serious. "Mike told me a lot about you. After seeing the way you handled my case, I thought this was what you needed to be doing. Not sitting on a mountainside, living like a monk." She paused, as though wondering whether to go on.

Sid stared at her without comment.

"And, of course, there's more," she said, shifting to a lighter note. "You know I was once a Nashville cop."

"Right. Mike told me a bit about your wayward career."

"I guess it's still in my blood. I'm taking part vicariously in something I can't afford to do on my own. I have too much responsibility with the business. But I'd love to help you out on a case if there's something I could do."

"You're serious."

"Absolutely."

"You'd need a PI license to stay out of trouble."

"I'll let you in on a little secret. I've already put in for it and taken the test. I should be getting my license any day now."

He leaned forward in his chair. "I'll let *you* in on a little secret, Jaz. From what I've seen of this case so far, I may need a whole lot of help."

5

UP EARLY THE next day, decked out in gray sweat pants and a faded Yellowstone tee shirt, Sid got back to his regular morning run through the neighborhood. He covered four miles at a brisk pace, honing his powers of observation as he went. He noted the black van in the gravel driveway, the ornamental birdbath beside an oak tree, the red bicycle leaning against a fieldstone house, the large white mailbox with a bashed-in side. Last night's blustery wind had been replaced by a less turbulent breeze that rustled the trees, tingeing the chilled air with the scent of damp leaves. He watched the sunlight filter through baring limbs and paint slanted yellow stripes on the pavement. This was a special time of day that resonated with his love of the outdoors. He filled his lungs with air and sweated like a boxer in the ring and adored every minute of it.

Back home he showered, dressed, and fixed his usual breakfast of orange juice, instant oatmeal, cinnamon roll, and black coffee. He switched on the TV, sat at the kitchen table, and thumbed through the morning paper. When the phone rang, he walked to the counter and answered it.

"I've got a problem," Jaz said. "A missing person." Her voice betrayed a note of anxiety.

"Who's missing?"

"John and Marie's grandson, Bobby Wallace. He didn't come home last night."

She had told him about the couple, in their late seventies, employees of the LeMieux family for more than thirty years.

Since Jaz was a youngster. They were Uncle John and Aunt Marie back then. Time altered the way people addressed each other. Perceptions changed.

Sid carried the portable phone to the table. "Some guys make a habit of that."

"Not Bobby. He's in his early thirties, and he's never done it before."

"Where does he live?"

"Ashland City. He's their son's boy."

"How did you hear about it?"

"His wife, Connie, called Marie. She was frantic, didn't know what to do."

"They have kids?"

"A boy. Little Bob, they call him. He's nine."

"Any way I can help?"

"Maybe later. You have plenty to do now. I'll get back to you after I run down there and check on the situation."

Sid understood Jaz's concern. The Wallaces were like family. John handled maintenance, landscaping, whatever the need called for around the eight-acre estate, while Marie did cooking and cleaning chores and served as Jaz's nanny in the early years. They had lived in a smaller house behind the French Colonial mansion until after Mr. LeMieux died. Jaz worked hard to come up with a convincing argument that it was for her own benefit before they agreed to move in with her.

After Sid had dressed for work, he called Murray Estes, the former Cheatham County Chamber of Commerce executive. He explained who he was and asked Estes if it would be possible to drop by and chat for a few minutes about a business from the past in Ashland City.

"What was the company's name?" Estes asked.

"Auto Parts Rehabbers."

"Ah . . . I remember them well. As the saying goes, that was a tough nut to crack. Come on over and I'll tell you about it."

THE STREET WAS IN an upscale area of Old Hickory, a

northeastern suburb once known for its major industrial facility, the Dupont plant. The original factory produced gunpowder in World War I. After turning out a succession of products like cellophane and rayon that required large numbers of employees, the mix changed to an operation almost wholly automated. At night its illuminated towers loomed as a prominent landmark from the Old Hickory Boulevard bridge over the Cumberland River. Since the drive through the area took him past a station with cheap gas, cheap being a relative term, Sid took his truck. It needed a fill-up after the trip to the cabin.

He found the address among a row of large, fashionable brick homes fronted by well-manicured lawns. The Estes name appeared on a mailbox at a two-story house with windows and doors that reflected Georgian influences. Sid pulled into the driveway and parked beside a tan SUV.

A gray-haired man opened the door. He had heavy jowls and stooped shoulders and wore a yellow wool cardigan over a white dress shirt. Though a bit tall for the traditional image, he wore a mischievous grin that made Sid think of a leprechaun.

"Mr. Chance?" he asked in a lilting voice.

"Right. And you must be Murray Estes."

Sid shook the outstretched hand. Estes led him into a living room crowded with comfortable-looking modern furniture, where they sat in soft chairs, their backs to windows with drapes pulled to block the morning sun.

"Were you interested in anything specific about Auto Parts Rehabbers?" Estes asked.

"Any specifics you can give me. I'm not even sure what they did. It sounds like they remanufactured used auto parts."

"That's my understanding. I called on them a few times to try and recruit them for the Chamber. My efforts were about as effective as Bill Clinton trying to explain the meaning of 'is' to the Grand Jury."

With an election coming up, Sid figured a little political humor was to be expected. "I believe you called it a tough nut to crack."

"Indeed. I never managed to penetrate that hard shell. They were what I called unfriendly business neighbors. I encountered very few of those during fifteen years with the Chamber."

"In what way were they unfriendly?"

"The manager was a tall, thin fellow named Decker. He had slicked-back brown hair and a face out of a Viagra commercial. Maybe he was a ladies' man. He sure didn't cotton to me. He showed no interest in cooperating with other business people on anything. And he didn't want any part of community activities. When I asked to see their operation, he told me very plainly that visitors were not welcome."

Estes picked up a meerschaum pipe from the small table beside his chair. "Don't worry, I don't plan to smoke it," he said. "My daughter-in-law would have a hissy fit. I quit smoking sometime back, but I like to chew on this now and then."

"Chewing shouldn't cause any lung damage."

Estes laughed. "Don't suppose you smoke?"

"Not one of my vices."

"How'd you avoid it?"

"We lived with my grandfather when I was growing up. He was a Nashville cop and had a cigarette dangling from his lips most of the time. I don't know how he missed getting lung cancer. I suspect he was too ornery. Anyway, my mother detested the smoke and convinced me it was something I should avoid."

"Just as well. Not many places it's legal anymore."

"About this Decker," Sid said. "Do you remember his first name?"

He looked down as he tapped the pipe bowl against his hand. "It was twelve or fourteen years ago, and the old memory isn't what it used to be. Seems like it was Tommy, or Terry, or . . . wait . . . Tony. Yeah, that sounds right. I'm almost certain it was Tony."

"Would anybody else around Ashland City know more about him?"

"I can't think who it might be. I'd say talk to someone at the bank, but they didn't do their banking in Ashland City."

"Wasn't that a little odd?"

"Certainly made them seem more like outsiders. I wish I could tell you more, but that's about it. Did you get my name at the Chamber?"

"From a nice young red-head."

"She hasn't been there all that long," he said before clamping his teeth around the pipe stem. "I'm afraid they're going to have a public relations nightmare with this trichloroethylene situation."

Sid thanked him and walked out to his truck. At least he had a name and a description now.

JAZ LEMIEUX parked her late-model Lexus in front of the small frame house in Ashland City around nine. Lavender and white chrysanthemums bloomed in pots on either side of the front stoop. She walked to the door with a lively step, dressed in snug-fitting black pants, a long-sleeved black shirt with an open collar. Her red leather jacket matched the color of her car. A lean hound dog peered around the corner of the house next door, where a scarecrow sat between two grinning jack-o-lanterns. The street may not have ranked high on the social register, but its houses looked neat and well kept.

An attractive, thirtyish woman with smooth brown skin and large, troubled eyes still moist from crying answered her knock.

"Thanks for coming, Miss Jaz." Connie Wallace had a voice reminiscent of a young girl's. "Bobby's granny said you were on the way."

"Hi, Connie. It's just plain Jaz, remember? You're not old enough to talk like Marie."

She showed a faint smile. "So be it. Come on in."

The neat living room appeared as Jaz remembered it from a previous trip here with Marie. The mauve sofa and chair, low coffee table, large TV would have looked at home in any modest income area. The aroma of chocolate wafted through the kitchen door. A large framed photo on one wall showed the couple with a small boy. Dressed in their Sunday best, they appeared as in a pose for a church directory. The boy had the same playful grin as his daddy.

"Is your son in school?" Jaz asked.

She nodded. "Bob Junior's in fourth grade."

"Fine looking boy. Does he know about his dad?"

"Only that he wasn't here for breakfast. I didn't know what to tell him. I don't know what's going on myself." She gestured at the sofa. "Please sit down. Can I get you anything? I just put a pan of brownies in the oven. They'll be ready soon."

She twisted slender hands and brushed the corners of her eyes. "I had to be doing something."

Jaz dropped onto the sofa. "Mmm . . . that smell is delicious. I'll have to pass, though. Too many treats instead of tricks last night. I bet your brownies are as tasty as Marie's."

Connie shook her head. "I can't cook like Granny."

"Nobody can," Jaz said. "Now, tell me about last night. Everything that happened. Marie said Bobby went out for something?"

The young woman sat at the opposite end of the sofa. She wore well-washed blue jeans and a red and yellow striped sweater that accented large breasts and a small waist. She seemed unsure whether to bawl or go ballistic. Crossing one bare foot over the other, she rested her heel on the thick pile of the beige carpet.

"Nothing unusual at first," she said in a plaintive voice, tilting her head in thought. "Bobby came home from work in a good mood. He had talked to his boss about a raise and said it looked good. He wants to buy me a car. I fixed supper while Little Bob finished his homework. Fourth grade is a lot harder than when I was in school. I don't know if kids are supposed to be smarter or if they just push 'em harder."

Jaz swung her legs around to face Connie. "I suspect it's a little of both."

The Surest Poison

"Maybe so. Anyway, we finished supper around six-thirty. I told Little Bob to go get his costume on so his dad could take him trick-or-treating. He was dressing up as Batman. Then the phone rang and Bobby answered it."

"Did he say who called?"

"Somebody he knew. The man said to meet him at a burger place, he had some information that could make Bobby a lot of money. Well, we could sure use it. We're paying on this house, and there's the new car, plus we're facing braces on Little Bob's teeth . . . ." Her voice seemed to run out of steam.

"What sort of information was he talking about?" Jaz asked.

"Bobby didn't say."

"Did he tell you the man's name?"

"No."

"How did he know him?"

Connie's fragile look seemed ready to shatter. "I don't know. Bobby was in such a hurry he didn't say much."

Jaz folded her hands and tapped her thumbs. It sounded like somebody had lured Bobby Wallace out on a pretext. "So Bobby agreed to meet him."

"He said he'd get back as soon as he could so he'd have time to take Little Bob trick-or-treating." She blinked to hold back the tears. "That's the last we saw of him."

"I have to ask you something, Connie. It may sound crass, but it's a question the police will ask if we bring them in. Have you and Bobby had any marital difficulties?"

She shrugged. "We argue sometimes about how to spend our money."

"I'm thinking more in terms of problems like with another woman, or another man."

Connie's mouth dropped open as she stared. "Heavens, no!" After a moment, she gave a grudging laugh. "We don't have time for stuff like that. Bobby had rather watch sports on TV than go out. And between looking after Little Bob and working part-time cleaning houses, I stay busy."

Jaz dismissed it with a wave of her hand. "Sorry, but I had

to ask." She had developed a good sense for recognizing when people were lying, and the look on Connie's face was as sincere as any she had seen in a long time. But it didn't tell her anything about what had happened to Bobby Wallace.

He might as well have stepped through a looking glass.

6

NOT LONG AFTER Sid returned to his office, Jaz called. She spoke in a rush. "I don't like the looks of this at all."

"What did you find?"

She told him what Connie Wallace said about the phone call. She added that nothing had been heard of Bobby since he left for the fast food place around seven last night.

"Has she talked to the police?"

"I got her to call them. You know that drill. They're skeptical until he's been gone a bit longer. Anyway, they're all tied up with a big protest around the courthouse in Ashland City. It involves your new case."

"Arnie Bailey's chemical spill?"

"Right. The folks around here are raging mad about the water pollution."

"A sergeant in the sheriff's office told me yesterday he'd heard something like that was in the works. Did Bobby Wallace have caller ID?"

"It didn't tell us anything. I did a quick check. The call was made from a prepaid phone. No way to trace the owner. I looked into the fast food place where they were to meet, but the manager on duty last night won't be in until this afternoon. They wouldn't give me any information on how I could get in touch with him."

"Did you find Bobby's car parked there?"

"No. That was a problem for the cops, too. I think they would have taken more interest if we'd found the car."

"But did he ever get to the restaurant?"

"I have no idea."

Sid considered it for a moment. "What if somebody met him in the parking lot and coaxed him into another car? Then a confederate drives his car away. Does Connie have any idea what he was supposed to do after he met the guy who called?"

"No. I suspect it was all a ruse, but I have no idea why."

"No obvious enemies? What about problems with the marriage?"

"I checked all that out. He was a hard worker, well liked. A nice young guy. I first met him several years ago when he came to visit his grandparents."

"Okay, Jaz. Let me know if there's anything I can do. I need to head out that way to meet with Wade Harrington."

THE DETAILED directions provided by Bailey, Riddle and Smith took Sid through an area of wooded hills and flat valleys where determined farmers squeezed in the occasional cornfield or stretch of pasture. Jagged outcroppings of Middle Tennessee limestone reared their knobby heads along the roadside. He located HarrCo a few miles away on a narrow lane with no houses in sight. There was no shortage of activity, however. Cars and trucks, mostly pickups, lined one side of the road. A ragtag crowd carrying homemade signs protesting the TCE spill milled about a chain link fence that surrounded the property. It had the look of an early rehearsal for a labor dispute. Two sheriff's patrol cars sat in the parking area. Uniformed deputies stood at the gate, keeping order.

Sid drove slowly through the protestors, advising the officer that he was here on business. A new brick office structure had been tacked onto the front of the old plant, which was built of metal and concrete blocks. Though painted in the recent past, it resembled an aging parent to the modern office wing.

Sid parked in a visitor slot and walked inside. Samples of various-sized shipping cartons sat on display around the small reception area. Framed pictures of Cheatham County historic sites decorated the walls, including a shot of the Harpeth Narrows, location of one of the oldest manmade tunnels in the U.S. Slaves hewed it out of a limestone bluff in the early 1800's to make a shortcut in the Harpeth River that powered an iron forge. After a brief glance at the photos, Sid approached a young woman absorbed in a stack of papers on her desk.

"Looks like you may be in the midst of something big," he said. "Mind if I disturb you?"

She looked up and smiled. "I was just trying to get caught up after watching all that noisy mess out front. What can I do for you?"

He handed her a business card. "Sidney Chance to see Mr. Harrington. Arnold Bailey sent me."

She took the card into an adjacent office, then came back and ushered him in. A stocky young man in a shirt and tie, sleeves rolled up at the cuffs, rose from the desk. A family photo that included his wife and small son sat beside a plastic pencil holder with a child's drawing pasted around it. Wade Harrington had the ruddy, windblown look of an outdoorsman, something Sid appreciated. An attractive arrangement of wildlife prints covered one wall.

"Mr. Bailey told me about you," Harrington said, holding out his hand. "I'd sure like to see the last of those country folks with all their signs out front. I hope you can find who's responsible for this. Be awful nice to get everybody off my back."

He had a slow Southern drawl that did minor surgery on words like "ever'body."

Sid shook his hand. "A lot of those country folks probably buy products shipped in your boxes, Mr. Harrington."

He started to protest, then seemed to think better of it. "I guess you're right. I can't blame them."

"I'll do my best to put the blame where it belongs," Sid said. He took a seat and looked across at Harrington. "I noticed in the county records that you bought this place from Henry Keglar."

"That's right. It was around ten years ago."

"Had you heard that he lives in Lewisville, goes by the nickname Hank?"

"I know nothing about him except that he did live in Lewisville."

"Did you deal with him in person?"

"I'm not sure."

"He's a huge man," Sid said. "You would have remembered him."

"Come to think of it, you're right. Everything was handled through a real estate agent and a lawyer. As I recall, Keglar didn't even attend the closing."

"Did anyone ever mention Auto Parts Rehabbers?"

"I haven't heard that name."

"That's who occupied the plant before you."

Harrington ran a finger beneath his nose as if a mustache might have once dwelt there. "I had no idea who was here before. All the equipment had been stripped out when I bought the place. There weren't even any old papers around like you might have expected. Somebody did a thorough clean-up job. Except for the TCE, of course. The inspectors say it was dumped out in back. They think around 1995. I can't imagine somebody doing that."

"Hard to figure. It's a nasty chemical that affects the central nervous system and can cause all kinds of health problems."

Harrington arched a bushy eyebrow. "Any idea what it's used for?"

"I checked into it before coming out here. I understand the Rehabbers outfit was involved in rejuvenating used auto parts. They could have dipped them in TCE for degreasing or cleaning. Mind if I take a look at where it was dumped?"

"Come on, I'll show you. We can't get too close, though. The state put a fence around it."

Harrington led him back through the plant, which was filled with machinery for fabricating corrugated boxes and a press for printing labels. They exited through a loading dock.

The Surest Poison

A couple of large trucks were parked on an asphalt apron in back. A few yards beyond that, a high chain link fence had been erected. Large signs attached to it cautioned "Warning! Keep Out! Contaminated Area!" The barrier surrounded a rectangle about a hundred feet wide and two hundred feet deep with a gentle slope to the rear. Scrubby weeds and blackened soil covered the ground. Much of the area showed signs of recent excavation.

"When I bought the place," Harrington said, "there were several rusted steel drums back here. I had them hauled off and thought nothing more about it."

"Your employees never had any problems from the pollution?" Sid asked.

"We've never used this part of the property for anything. Since none of the employees frequent the spot, it hasn't been a problem. When it rains, the drainage carries the water downhill away from the plant."

"That must be where the people live who have the health problems."

"That would be my guess. There's a creek at the bottom of the hill and a road that runs alongside it. The street has a number of houses on the near side."

Sid gazed down through the trees beyond the fence. "I understand the Nashville newspaper ran an article about what happened to some of the people down there." He looked back at Harrington. "Have you asked your employees if they know anybody who worked here before you bought the place?"

"I asked the ones from Ashland City. They didn't even know the place existed until they came to work for me. A lot of my employees are from the Nashville area—Joelton, Scottsboro, Bellevue, places like that."

"And you never ran into anybody who talked about who used the plant before?"

"Most folks around here aren't too talkative with strangers, Mr. Chance." Harrington swung his gaze around the trees that clustered about the perimeter. "This is an out-of-the-way spot.

The only reason I found it was I got lost one day looking for another site. I saw the For Sale sign and decided to check into it."

"No doubt I'll have to do a lot more digging around Ashland City," Sid said. "Thanks for the tour. This gives me a better idea of what we're facing."

Harrington offered a wan smile. "If you can find who's responsible for this, you'll have my undying gratitude."

Sid walked out with a troubled look on his face. Solving Harrington's problem was his major task from a professional standpoint, but on a personal level he wanted someone to pay for the damage they had done to the people of this area. So far all he had was a company name and a manager's name. And no idea where to find either of them.

7

THE CROWD OF protestors had dwindled to a manageable swarm of sign-wavers by the time Sid eased his way out of the fenced area. A haphazard line of cars and trucks remained along the roadside. As he started toward Ashland City, his cell phone rang.

"What's your location?" Jaz asked.

Cop talk, Sid thought. Anybody else would ask where are you? He really was giving her a chance to relive her past.

"I just left the HarrCo plant on my way to Ashland City. What about you?"

"I'm in front of the burger place. I got word the manager from last night came in early. I shouldn't be here long. If you want to meet for coffee, I'll fill you in."

For Jaz that meant cappuccino. "You have some place in mind?"

She gave him the location of a small restaurant not far from the courthouse.

"I've been nosing around here and found something a bit weird," she said. "Somebody called the farm supply store where Bobby Wallace works and said he wouldn't be in this morning, that he was sick."

"If it was Bobby, sounds like he might have been up to no good."

"Not a chance. The person who took the call said it didn't sound like Bobby. She didn't have any idea who it might have been, though. I talked to a couple of his coworkers who confirmed he's a pretty straight guy, a devoted family man. He's a little gullible in money matters. They thought he'd jump at a suggestion he could make money by meeting with some guy."

The phone call had distracted Sid so he failed to notice the blue car, a small sedan traveling at the same speed a couple of hundred feet behind, until he snapped the phone shut. How long had it been there? Was it following him, or was it some protestor headed back to Ashland City?

He was on a narrow country road, reversing the directions that had brought him to HarrCo Shipping. It was also the most direct route back to the small town. He kept an eye on the car all the way. It turned off to the right when he turned left into the restaurant parking lot.

Nothing to be concerned about, he decided. But it reminded him he needed to find out how somebody knew he would be in the downtown garage yesterday.

JAZ PARKED IN front of a big poster hawking 99-cent specials, with colorful illustrations of artery-clogging delights. Inside, she introduced herself as Private Investigator Jasmine LeMieux to a slick-headed young man whose badge identified him as "Gordie." He had been the manager on duty last night.

"Hi, Miz LeMieux, what can I do for you?" Gordie asked.

Despite his hairless look, the kid was young enough to be her son. He had a cloying grin she found a bit much. More like the older guys who were always hitting on her. Those types she enjoyed putting in their places, which had been especially true with her fellow cops when she was a policewoman. This situation was different, though, necessitating a little diplomacy. She held out a photo of Bobby Wallace.

"Do you recall seeing this man here last night?" she asked.

Gordie stared at the photo. "I don't think so. What'd he do, like rob somebody, shoot his old lady?"

"Nothing of the sort. He was supposed to meet someone here, but he's disappeared. Did you see anything in the parking lot last night that might not have seemed quite right? Maybe someone urging another man into a car?"

"Sorry. Most of the time I'm, you know, too busy to check out the parking lot. What time was he here?"

"It would have been around seven."

He twitched his mouth from side to side. "Maybe I did see a guy switching cars, you know. I'm not sure. That would have been after dark. The lights out front are pretty bright. Whatever, I can't say for sure if it was this guy."

"Did you notice what kind of car he got into?"

"No. I wasn't paying that much attention. Sorry."

"Is there anybody else here who might have seen something?"

He looked around at the workers behind the counter, all teenagers. "I doubt it. They don't get out front much, except to clean the tables or empty trash cans. I'll ask around and give you a call if I learn anything."

Jaz gave him a business card and thanked him.

"How about a milkshake or something?" he asked with a silly grin. "It's on the house."

"Thanks, but I'm in a bit of a hurry." She smiled and turned toward the nearest exit. She wanted to be polite, but cradle robbing wasn't part of her repertoire.

She was about to open the door to her car when her cell phone rang.

Connie Wallace spoke in a hushed voice. "Bobby is back."

Jaz swung the door open and dropped onto the seat. "Is he okay? What happened?"

"He hasn't been beat up or anything, if that's what you mean. But he's acting awful strange. Something's scared him. I haven't seen him this shook up in years. Not since the time he almost drove off an embankment one night when somebody swiped a road sign."

"Where has he been?"

"He won't talk about it, and he doesn't want me to say anything to anybody, either. He doesn't know I'm calling you. Please don't mention anything about it. Oh, oh . . . I hear him. I've gotta go."

8

THE RESTAURANT sat a few blocks from the courthouse. It was a small, airy place full of chrome and white tile with a working jukebox, reminiscent of something out of the middle of the last century. Sid found a booth near the entrance. He ordered coffee for himself and a cappuccino for Jaz. After burning out on coffee during her Metro Police days, she had taken up the Italian concoction during visits to her truck stops. She didn't care for the fancy kind made with a noisy mixer but the commercial version produced with powder and hot water from a self-serve machine.

Jaz arrived shortly after the waitress brought their drinks.

"Guess what," she said. "Bobby Wallace is back."

"Back home?"

"Connie called and said he came home acting like somebody frightened of his shadow. He didn't want her to say anything about it to anybody."

"Where had he been?"

"He refused to tell her anything. But it sounds like somebody threatened to dump him in the fiery furnace."

"At least he's back home in one piece," he said. "Have you called his grandparents?"

"Yes. Marie was really relieved. I hope she can convince on him to come clean." She picked up the cup of cappuccino and took a tentative sip. "What did you learn at HarrCo?"

"Not much, except the crowd that picketed the courthouse moved out to Harrington's place. Looked like a bunch of Teamsters with all their signs. Harrington had never heard of Auto

Parts Rehabbers. I learned something useful from Murray Estes, though. The manager was a guy named Tony Decker."

"I can do a computer trace on him," Jaz said.

"Have at it."

"Auto Parts Rehabbers, too?"

"Sure. It'll save me some time." She knew a lot more about digging for such things than he did, although he had gotten a short course on skip tracing from a PI he once worked with in Lewisville. "Is there anything I can do for you on the Bobby Wallace situation?"

"Until he decides to tell us what it's all about, I don't know what anyone could do."

Sid watched in silence as she toyed with the cappuccino cup.

After a few moments, he asked, "Heard anything else about the poker players?"

That perked her up. "I talked to Wick this morning. Jack and the Judge are in. I guess that takes care of everybody."

Wick was Metro Police Sgt. Wick Stanley. The others included Jack Post, a retired newspaper crime writer, former Criminal Court Judge Gabriel Thackston, and Bart Masterson. Post, the word merchant, had dubbed them the Four Felons and Miss Demeanor Poker Club. Now, with Sid on board, they were Five Felons.

"I presume everybody includes you?" he said.

"Of course I'll be there. With rings on my fingers and bells on my toes."

"You going to try to jangle some nerves?" He drained his coffee cup. "Harrington told me about the area down the hill behind the plant, which is where the TCE wound up. I want to drive over there and take a look around."

"I have a feeling you're prepared to give this one all you've got."

Sid gave a slight nod. "Somebody, for some reason, made an awful mess that had terrible long-range consequences. Bailey showed me a photo of a little girl whose face was badly disfigured. It apparently resulted from the TCE contamination. Years ago, I had a cousin in almost the same shape. She ended up commiting suicide."

"That's terrible." Jaz shook her head. "I'd like to see that area, too. Why don't we take my car?"

He knew she didn't care for his truck, though for him it fit like an old glove. "Why not? You get cut-rate gas."

Since inheriting controlling interest in Welcome Traveler Stores, she kept a close watch on the business but took no active role in the day-to-day operation of the company.

They strolled out to Jaz's Lexus, and Sid directed her toward the HarrCo plant. They had gone only a short distance when he glanced at the mirror on his side. It felt like deja vu.

"See that blue car behind us?"

She turned her head. "What about it?"

"It looks like the same one that followed me into town when I left HarrCo."

"You're kidding."

"Yesterday, a green Volkswagen followed me when I left Bailey's office."

"Who would be doing that? And why?"

He didn't reply.

"Is there somebody from your past who might have a reason to come after you?" she asked.

He watched the mirror in silence before replying. "I'd have to pull off both shoes and count toes as well as fingers. But I don't know of any reason for it to happen now."

The car made each turn as they did, though it held back a little farther than before. When Sid spotted a farm gate set back from the road up ahead, he told Jaz to pull onto the graveled entrance and stop.

"We'll check his license plate when he passes," he said.

As soon as Jaz stopped, the other car did the same. The road was a bit wider here. The car suddenly swung into a tight turn. A cloud of dust boiled up from the shoulder. The blue vehicle disappeared around a curve back toward Ashland City.

"Shall we give chase?" Jaz asked.

"There were too many turn-offs back there where he could hide." He looked toward the road ahead. "I'll get another shot at him. He must have been watching the restaurant parking lot."

"You think somebody's just trying to be a nuisance?"

Sid shrugged. "He's being that all right. For now, let's go find that road on the other side of the hill and see what it leads to."

She drove past the last of the picketers up to the intersection beyond HarrCo and turned in the direction Harrington had indicated. They found the creek and followed the road beside it, soon reaching a spot where the land sloped away from a high wooded hill that appeared to be the one behind the HarrCo plant. Along the bottom of the hill, a hodgepodge of small frame or asbestos siding houses were sandwiched among a few single or doublewides. They saw one typical old two-story farmhouse. Most had battered pickups parked in front. A hayfield spread off to the other side of the road. Large, round bales lined a rickety fence.

"I imagine a lot of the people who picketed the plant live around here," Jaz said.

Sid watched a school bus heading in their direction. No doubt the area included families with children, too. That made it all the more tragic. From the looks of the houses, the people here clung to the lower rungs of the economic ladder. He had learned such people responded better to outsiders who left the impression of being more on their side of the financial divide.

He turned to Jaz. "I'd like to talk to some of these folks and see what they have to say. But I don't think a fancy Lexus would provide us with the kind of intro it takes. I'll come back in my pickup."

She cut her eyes toward him took a deep breath, looking ready to chew glass. "Next time I'll eat an extra helping of humble pie before we start out."

"Hey, what the—?"

"I'm damned tired of people implying I'm some kind of stuck-up socialite. I've gotten that from cops I used to work with. I expected better of you."

He looked at her and shook his head. Why did women get so touchy?

"I didn't mean to imply anything of the sort," he said, keeping his voice calm. "You can drive a Lexus or a Lamborghini, whatever you like. It's only logical that this isn't the right car to approach these people in. If they came to the door and saw it, they probably wouldn't talk to us."

She exhaled a noisy sigh. "Maybe so. But it sure struck a nerve with me. Do whatever you like. I need to get home and prepare for a board meeting in the morning. It may be contentious."

More contentious than this, he thought?

Jaz had little to say the rest of the way back to the restaurant.

"Good luck with your meeting tomorrow," he said as he got out of the car. "Thanks for the ride. Let me know if you hear anything else from Bobby Wallace."

"I will," she said.

And roared off like a NACAR driver coming out of the pit.

BACK AT THE ROAD behind the HarrCo plant, Sid made his first stop at the old white frame two-story. He had on his usual informal attire, black pants, knit shirt, and tan windbreaker, which seemed adequate for the task. The house had a wide front porch with a vintage swing and two wooden rockers. The dried brown remains of several large ferns zapped by a recent freeze dangled from hanging baskets. A dying odor of another sort lingered in the air, likely from an animal carcass nearby. The deep-throated bay of a hound echoed through the woods in back.

A short woman with stringy gray hair and the mournful look of a troubled past opened the door and stared out at him.

He gave her a gentle smile. "I'm Sidney Chance, a private

investigator. I've been hired to look into the pollution problem at the HarrCo plant just over the hill."

She grunted, then spoke. "You ask me, there's been enough lookin' into. It's high time somebody done something about it. My husband died last month from cancer. They said he probably got it from that stuff they put in the water at that plant."

"I'm sorry to hear that, Mrs. . . . ?" He paused.

"Jeffords. They ought to put that place out of business. They hire you to come down here and tell us we're just imaginin' things?"

"No, ma'am. I'm quite sure you've got real problems. And so does—"

"My daughter, Emily," she continued, "lives just down the road. She's been having headaches and gets real dizzy at times. The doctor says it's that tri-whatever-it-is stuff."

Sid gave a sympathetic nod. "Trichloroethylene. You're right, it's bad stuff. But the company that dumped it occupied the plant back before HarrCo came along. It was called Auto Parts Rehabbers. Do you remember anything about them?"

The lines deepened in her forehead. "That was a long time ago. How could it cause all this trouble now?"

"They say it takes several years for the chemical to drain down through the soil and the rock until it reaches the water supply. Do you remember anybody who worked for Auto Parts Rehabbers, or maybe who managed the plant?"

"They didn't stay all that long, seems like." She rubbed her brow with a wrinkled hand. "I didn't know anybody up there. They never came around here."

He gave her what he hoped was a comforting smile. "Well, I appreciate your talking to me, Mrs. Jeffords. You can be certain I'll do my best to find out who was responsible."

"I hope they burn in hell for what they done to us."

She had the eyes of a wounded animal. Her look of despair haunted him as he walked back to his truck. He always made a point of keeping a neutral stance on cases he participated in.

It didn't help to become too involved on an emotional level. But this interview left him troubled.

His next stop was a doublewide with a clutter of balls, ragged dolls, and various toys, including a battered Etch-a-Sketch, in the grass out front. A young woman with tousled blonde hair, toting a small girl in diapers on her hip, answered his knock. He introduced himself and explained what he was doing in the area.

"You talking about the stuff that came from that plant up on the hill?" she asked.

"Yes. Has anyone in your family suffered any health problems from it?"

"Look at this," she said, holding the baby out, turning it around to show her face.

The little girl's mouth twisted to one side. Her left ear appeared only a gnarled stub. It was the child in the picture Bailey had shown him.

Sid looked down at her. "That shouldn't happen to a pretty little girl like you." He glanced back at the mother with a pained look. "How old is she?"

"Almost two. Her daddy has headaches and gets real dizzy at times. He's had to miss some work."

"The chemicals causing the problem came when a company named Auto Parts Rehabbers occupied the plant. They were there until 1995. Did you live around here then?"

"No. We've only been here about five years."

After hearing similar stories and failing to turn up any helpful information at several other houses, Sid gave up and headed back to Nashville. The trip made him more determined than ever to find who had caused the problem, but he was no closer to the answer than when he'd left the office that morning.

9

JAZ'S OFFICE occupied a bookshelf-lined room her mother had called the library and her father *ma cachette*, French for "my hiding place." A framed photo of Jaques LeMieux sat on one side of the cluttered desk, a similar picture of his wife, Gwendolyn, on the other. Jaz had calmed down since accepting that Sid's comment about her Lexus was perfectly reasonable, not intended to make her sound elitist. But coming after an accusation of acting uppity by one of her old police colleagues, the remark had hit her like a slap in the face. Sure, she liked nice things now that she could afford them, but that wasn't always the case. Her exposure to the humble life had lasted several years after her mother effectively banished her from the family.

She needed to get to work on Sid's case. Turning to the computer, she began checking her sources. She soon had a long list of Deckers, more than 200 in Tennessee, but none with the name Tony or Anthony. Of course, she reasoned, he could have moved out of state. Then she had an idea. She ran a criminal check on the name and came up with a Tony Decker from Memphis, who had served three years for armed robbery. He was released from prison in 1989. At the Board of Probation and Parole, she learned he had reported living in Ashland City in 1993. That put him on the scene when Auto Parts Rehabbers was in business. He had been off probation for more than ten years now, so they had no information on his current whereabouts.

She put in a call to a Memphis contact and got assurance

that background on Tony Decker would be available in a matter of hours. Nothing got faster results than the promise of a bonus.

Turning to Auto Parts Rehabbers, she checked the Secretary of State's office and soon found the company was formed in 1992. It went inactive in 1995. Then she began to dig deeper. What she could add to Sid's arsenal of investigative techniques was hacker-strength computer savvy and contacts with people who had resources not available to most investigators. And, if need be, she also had a pretty face and a set of curves she knew how to use to her advantage.

After completing her search with the return call from Memphis, Jaz phoned Sid at his office. She told him about Tony Decker's record.

"I'm surprised he got a position like that so soon out of prison," Sid said. "I wonder if the Rehabbers shut down because he absconded with the funds?"

"Maybe. It's also possible he worked on a degree while doing time. Some do that, you know. It gives them a better shot at a decent job."

"What else do you have on him?"

"My Memphis contact says Decker lived there with his mother until he finished high school. His dad abandoned them when Tony was a baby. Apparently he was a good kid until he took up with an older boy who got him involved in armed robberies. His mother died a few years ago, and Tony hasn't been seen around the neighborhood since he got out of prison."

"I'm impressed," Sid said. "You did a great job on Tony. What about the company?"

She checked her notes. "Auto Parts Rehabbers was an LLC, a Limited Liability Company, organized as a partnership. The registered agent was a lawyer in Lewisville. I thought that might pique your interest."

"What's his name?"

"Bronson Fradkin."

"Figures. I remember that shyster well."

"Somebody you ran into in court?"

"There, among other places."

"What other places?"

"He's big in county politics, one of the sheriff's main supporters."

"Would that be the sheriff who accused you of taking a bribe?"

"It would. Sheriff Zachary set up the deal, but somebody else had to have been behind it. He's only capable of shooting at targets of opportunity. I never figured out who masterminded it. Could have been Fradkin, although he wouldn't have had much reason to. I seldom managed to get the best of him."

"Was he a criminal lawyer?"

"He was whatever kind of lawyer you had the money to pay for. Bronson Fradkin was an expert at sniffing out technicalities. Whenever I found out he was on a case, I cautioned my officers to re-read the procedures manual and work like Candid Camera was watching every move."

"I don't suppose he'd be a good candidate to ask for information about Auto Parts Rehabbers?"

"I doubt he'd give me the correct time of day. If it becomes necessary, though, I might consider sending you to put on the squeeze."

Jaz caught a flicker of movement and looked around to find Marie Wallace standing in the office doorway, a white apron tied at her waist. She was a small woman with abundant white hair and fine lines down her face. Large round glasses gave her an owlish look, but the expression in her eyes at the moment spelled trouble.

"Hold on a sec, Sid," Jaz said into the phone. "Let me see what Marie wants."

Jaz put her hand over the mouthpiece and turned to Marie. "What's wrong?"

"I didn't want to bother you, Miss Jasmine, but it's Bobby. Connie called about him. She's real worried. One of the boys he works with told her he was quiet as a dead man today. He acted like he was just watching for somebody to come into the store looking for him."

"It must have something to do with his disappearance night before last," Jaz said.

Marie nodded as she smoothed the apron with nervous hands. "I want to talk to him. Could you take me out there after supper? I'll have it ready in a few minutes."

It was already dusk. Jaz knew Marie didn't like her husband to drive after dark. "Sure. I'll be wrapped up here by the time you get things on the table. What are we eating tonight?"

"Salmon fillets. I fixed a nice caesar salad to go with it."

Jaz licked her lips. Marie had no formal training, but she had a natural talent for cooking. She could rival a gourmet chef. After high school, she had worked in a restaurant as a waitress, then a cook, picking up valuable tips on preparing food in quantity. She concocted delectable dishes for large groups back when the LeMieux's entertained. Jaz still called on her to prepare dinner for small gatherings of friends.

She returned to the phone. "Sorry for the interruption."

"A problem?" Sid asked.

"Bobby. Marie wants me to take her out to see him after supper. Getting back to Auto Parts Rehabbers, the LLC members were Tony Decker and First Improvement Corporation. I don't know anything about the percentages of ownership."

"But Decker was a part-owner. Hmm. What kind of name is First Improvement?"

"It's a Delaware corporation. I checked them out and found it was a wholly-owned subsidiary of First Patriots, Limited."

When she paused, Sid prodded. "And where the devil did First Patriots come from?"

"Anguilla."

"Run that by me again?"

"Anguilla is the northernmost of the British Leeward Islands, a small blip in the Atlantic that's a haven for offshore corporations. Lots of privacy."

The Surest Poison

"Great. Meaning you reached a dead end?"

"For the moment, but I have somebody working on it. I should be able to come up with an answer in a day or two."

"Hopefully we can keep Arnie Bailey at bay for a few days. You did a great job on this, Jaz. And a lot quicker and probably more thorough than I could have. Anything else?"

She closed the folder on her desk, smiling at his acknowledgment. "That's it for now. What's your next move?"

"I'm going to try a new tack in the morning. I picked up a brochure at the Chamber of Commerce that mentioned a newspaper in Ashland City. Maybe they can give me a lead."

"Mind if I tag along?"

"I thought you had a Board meeting in the morning?"

"There isn't too much on the agenda. We don't start until eleven. That should give me plenty of time. You'd better wear your gumshoes, though. Have you seen tomorrow's forecast?"

"No. What's on tap?"

"Cool, wet, and windy."

"Sounds like my kind of weather . . . 'Into each life some rain must fall.'"

"Who said that?"

"Longfellow."

She grinned. Mike Rich had told her his full name was Sidney Lanier Chance, a name chosen by his mother, an American literature major when she studied for her degree in education. "I'll come prepared."

Jaz hung up the phone and looked around to find Marie standing in the doorway, the worried expression unchanged. Was she prepared for what they might find in Ashland City?

10

JAZ AND MARIE arrived at the Wallace home a little before seven. The hound next door gave a loud, throaty bark as they strolled up the sidewalk. Clouds obscured what little moon there might have been, leaving the house in darkness, except for a bright glow around the living room window.

Marie knocked. After a few moments, the door opened just a crack, allowing a thin shaft of light to fall across their faces.

Connie pulled the door open wider, a broad grin spreading across her face. "Granny, Miss . . . uh, Jaz. Come on in."

The house was warm. The smell of spaghetti lingered in the air. Across the room, a somber news anchor droned on beneath a "Breaking News" banner.

"Where's my great-grandson?" Marie asked.

"In the kitchen with his dad. I was just cleaning up from supper."

She led them into the bright kitchen where Bobby Wallace stood with an arm around his son's shoulder. He looked like a football lineman too long out of high school to hold down any position but the end of the bench. A newspaper lay spread out on the table where he and Little Bob had been reading it.

Bobby turned to his grandmother and cut his eyes with a guarded look. "Hi, Granny."

"Say hello to Jasmine, too, Bobby," said the older woman.

He gave her a slight dip of his head. "Hello."

"Hello, Bobby," Jaz said. "Little Bob. You're getting almost too big to be called Little Bob any longer."

The Surest Poison

The boy grinned. "I'm not near as big as my dad."

"What's in the newspaper?" Marie asked.

"NFL, NHL, NBA," Connie said from the sink. "That's all Bobby reads in the newspaper. Or watches on TV."

"What brings you out tonight, Granny?" Bobby asked, his look still clouded.

"We need to talk." She looked across at the table, where two schoolbooks sat stacked beside the newspaper. "Come on in the living room and let Little Bob do his homework. That all right, Connie?"

"Sure. Go ahead, Bobby. I'll help Little Bob."

Jaz and Marie returned to the living room, with Bobby a reluctant follower. Connie closed the door behind them.

After they were seated, Marie folded her slender, wrinkled hands in her lap and gave her grandson a stern glare. Born in a poor home in the early days of The Great Depression, she had lived through years of shabby clothes and meager meals. It gave her a strong incentive to see that her family enjoyed their little slice of the American dream.

"Bobby, I want to know what's going on with you," she said, a note of disgust in her voice. "You disappear all night, then come back acting like a possum scared to cross the road. What happened?"

His dark, brooding eyes stared at his grandmother, then at Jaz. "I can't tell you, Granny. I'm sorry."

"What would happen to you if you told us?" Jaz asked.

A flicker of fear showed in his eyes. "I . . . I can't answer that."

"If somebody threatened you, you need to tell the police about it. You can get a court order to keep them away from you." She knew court orders did not keep people intent on harming others from carrying out their threats, but she hoped mentioning it might shake something loose.

Bobby slumped in his chair. "It would only make things worse. Believe me."

Marie sighed. She looked drawn, a woman in distress. "Is

it just you, or did they threaten Connie and Little Bob, too?"

At that, Bobby put his face in his hands and sat in silence.

After a couple of minutes, Jaz could stand it no longer. She got up and folded her arms. "Bobby, you have to contact the authorities. You can't fight this alone."

He stood, listless as a sleepwalker. "You don't understand," he said in a whisper. He walked into his bedroom and closed the door.

SID HAD JUST turned on the TV to catch the ten o'clock news when the doorbell rang. He flipped on the light and put his eye to the peephole. Two men stood on the narrow porch. One was thick and muscular, though not particularly tall. He had a straight scar on one cheek that looked like a knife slash. His jowly face sagged like a pair of shorts that had lost its elastic. He looked vaguely familiar. The other man, tall and thin, stood almost too straight, as though he might break if bent. Neither looked capable of winning much cash on a quiz show.

The shorter of the two appeared to be in his forties. The other might have been a bit younger. One thing was certain. They were looking for trouble.

Sid pulled open the wooden door and pushed the metal storm door outward, forcing them to move back to the edge of the porch. He stepped out onto the concrete pad, his six-foot-six, 230-pound frame towering over them.

"Isn't it a bit late for door-to-door salesmen?" he asked with a nonchalant incline of his head.

'We ain't selling," scarface said. "We're news carriers, and the news for you ain't good, Chance."

They wore light jackets, open in front. Sid detected no weapons. "I'm used to bad news," he said, showing no emotion. "What's the old saying, if it wasn't for bad luck I wouldn't have any luck at all?"

Scarface clenched his fists for emphasis. "You're pissing off our boss with your messing around where you don't belong. He wants it stopped . . . now."

Sid feigned a puzzled frown. "I don't understand. Where have I been messing around?"

"Ashland City."

Now Sid knew where he'd seen that face before. "You're the guys who've been tailing me the past few days."

"You noticed." A wide grin showed the guy's yellowed teeth.

Sid glared at him. "I did. And I don't like it. You can tell your boss, whoever he is—I'll soon find out—tell him threats only anger me. And you don't want to make me angry."

The man's face twisted into a grotesque scowl. "I'll show you angry." He telegraphed his intentions by cocking his arm.

They stood hardly a yard apart. He lunged at Sid, prepared to deliver a blow with all the strength he had. He was a barroom brawler, though, not a skilled fighter. Sid saw the punch coming and shifted his weight to his left foot. As Scarface began his move, Sid kicked his right foot out. His number 16 shoe caught the man in the crotch. Following through, he pushed off with his left foot, propelling his assailant off the porch, down two steps, where he wound up flat of his back on the ground.

The taller accomplice stared wide-eyed, in shock. Sid spun him around, grabbed him by the collar and belt and heaved him off the porch, too.

Sid stood there, breathing hard, the blood pumping through his veins, the rage tensing his muscles. His first impulse was to go after them and finish the job. He still had the skills to do it, he was sure. But he hesitated, recalling the words of a hand combat instructor from years ago:

"When you get older, remember, age has its advantages. You know what to anticipate, how to react. But the difference is in the timing. The longer a fight goes on, the more chances you'll have to screw up. All things being equal, the faster guy will come out on top."

The tall, thin man pushed himself into a sitting position. His partner pulled up his knees and groaned.

Sid reached for the storm door. "I'm going to call the

police," he said in a voice laced with disgust. "You two can stick around if you'd like."

He stepped inside and slammed the door.

11

THE MERCURY had skidded into the forties overnight. A steady patter of rain made the morning only a trifle short of miserable as Sid stepped out of his truck at the restaurant in Ashland City. He shivered despite his windbreaker. Though he arrived five minutes ahead of schedule, Jaz was already there. She occupied the same spot as the day before. A cup and a carafe of coffee sat on his side of the booth.

"I'm having hot tea," she said. "I ordered bacon and eggs for both of us."

He slid into the seat across from her. "Thanks. My morning run was a challenge. Too many crazies out on a slick, dark street. You worked out in your rec room, I'll bet."

"It comes in handy on days like this."

"I had no problem with exercise when I lived at the cabin."

She arched a well-drawn brow. "That cabin looked pretty impressive for a one-man job. Mike Rich said you built it yourself." They'd first met when she showed up at the cabin door looking for help.

He poured his coffee. "It took a while. I saw the plans in a magazine and ordered them by mail. I must have hauled tons of material up that hillside."

"It's a wonder you didn't break your back."

"Twisted it like a corkscrew a few times." He took a tentative sip. Fiery hot, just the way he liked it. "Learn anything from your trip last night?"

She told him what happened on her visit to Bobby Wallace's house with Marie.

"So he wouldn't listen to reason."

"The boy is almost a basket case."

"If I could get him into an interrogation room, he might change his tune."

Jaz stared into her cup as she stirred her tea. "I doubt it. He's determined to keep silent, no matter what. I feel like I should go to the cops myself, but if he won't cooperate . . . ?"

She left the question hanging as the waitress brought their plates. Sid buttered his biscuit and took a bite of eggs.

After sipping her tea, Jaz looked across at him. "Have you seen anything else of whoever it was that put the tail on us yesterday?"

"Yes."

"On the way out here?"

"No. A couple of guys knocked on my door around ten last night."

She put down her fork and stared. "What did they want?"

"Said they weren't door-to-door salesmen."

She squinched her eyes. "What did they want, Sid?"

"Seems their boss thought I had been messing around where I didn't belong. He wanted it stopped . . . now."

"Do you think they were talking about the HarrCo situation?"

"What else? It's the only thing I'm messing around in currently."

"What did you say?"

"I said threats only make me angry."

"How did they take that?"

"Not too well."

"What does that mean?"

"One of them came at me with his fist cocked."

She waited in silence as Sid returned to his eggs.

"And?"

"And he wound up on his butt in the front yard. Along with his buddy. I told them they could stick around if they wanted, I was going to call the cops."

"Did you?"

"No. I knew they would high-tail it out of there as fast as they could get back on their feet."

"Did you get their license number?"

His eyebrows went up. "I should have, but at the moment I was highly pissed. I wanted to get away from them before I did something I might regret."

"Did you ask what was behind their following you?"

"They wouldn't have known. They weren't smart enough to be the brains behind this deal."

"Who knew you were on this case, besides Arnie Bailey and Harrington?"

Sid put his fork down and pushed his plate back. "That's a question I've been asking myself. Bailey told Harrington about me yesterday morning. I can't imagine why he would have told anybody else."

"So who did Harrington tell?"

Sid pulled out his cell phone and checked the number he had previously used to call HarrCo Shipping. He pressed the Talk button and got Harrington on the line. "Did you mention my name to anyone after you talked to Arnie Bailey yesterday morning?" he asked.

Harrington was silent for a moment. "No. I don't recall having any reason to. Why?"

Sid thought of two other possibilities. Somebody at the law office had provided the tip, which seemed unlikely, or Harrington's phone had been tapped or bugged. With the TCE pollution making news in the papers and on TV, whoever was responsible would have good reason to want access to discussions between Harrington and his lawyer, or anyone else involved in the case. If they had intercepted Bailey's call to Harrington, they would have known about the lawyer's planned meeting with a private investigator named Sidney Chance. It would have been a simple matter to get descriptions and license numbers for Sid's car and truck.

"I'm going to send a guy out to see you," Sid told Harrington. "Hopefully I can get him there pretty soon. His name is Jackson. He'll explain things when he sees you."

"What's going on?" Jaz asked when he closed the cell phone and stuck it back in his pocket.

"I need to call my countersurveillance guy. I haven't used him since I left Lewisville. I'm afraid Mr. Harrington's phone has sprung a leak."

Her eyes widened with a knowing nod. "Did you call him before you came out here yesterday?"

"I did."

"And the blue car showed up."

"It did."

Sid checked Information and got the number for Jerry Jackson, a technical surveillance countermeasures pro. After he explained the situation, Jackson promised to call on the HarrCo owner that afternoon.

Jaz pushed her plate back on the table and looked across at Sid, biting gently on her lower lip. "You know you made a couple of guys very unhappy last night. Particularly after they had to report back to their boss."

"True."

"They'll likely be back looking for revenge, and loaded for bear."

"The bear will be ready."

"Are you carrying?"

"Private investigators don't usually go armed, Jaz. You know that."

"If I were you, I think I'd seriously consider revising the rules for this case."

He held out his cup to the waitress for a refill. "Okay, I'll give it serious consideration."

She looked across at him, her eyes brightening. "So you threw them both off the porch. I didn't realize you were that aggressive."

He sipped at his coffee. "I guess you haven't heard about my tender upbringing. I was always big, even as a kid. My dad left us when I was a baby, and Mom and I lived with my grandfather, who was a cop. One of the kids in the neighborhood had some boxing gloves. He put me up to fighting an older boy who always gave the little ones a hard time. When he started really coming after me, I put him down for the count. My Mom didn't like it, but Grandpa just laughed. He said, 'Boy, you'd better always fight on the right side.' I've tried to do that."

"I'd say there wasn't any question about last night." She pushed her plate back and checked her watch. "I still have plenty of time, but we'd better get moving."

Sid paid the check. He told Jaz they would drive to the newspaper office in his truck. Out in the parking lot, she paused as he held the door open. She cocked an eyebrow. "You sure this thing will get us there and back?"

"For your information, lady, this thing is a lean, mean motion machine. It may not be the prettiest pickup on the lot, but I assure you it will get us anywhere you want to go."

She grinned. "Okay. If you're sure."

A few minutes later they parked a short distance past the courthouse in front of a long storefront building that accommodated several small businesses. The newspaper occupied the end unit. They hurried through the rain to a glass door plastered with notices. Sid followed Jaz inside.

An aisle ran down the middle of the office, with partitioned cubbyholes on either side. At the first desk, a young woman with sharp-pointed cat-eye glasses glanced up with a smile.

"Are you interested in subscribing or advertising?"

"Neither." Sid handed her a business card. "We're investigating the chemical spill at the HarrCo plant that's been in the news. It appears the spill took place some dozen years back while Auto Parts Rehabbers occupied the plant. We're having no luck locating people connected with the company."

She tapped her pen on the desk. "I think you need to talk to our editor, Carl Norris."

She led them back to the last cubicle, where a young man wearing gold-rimmed glasses stared at a computer screen. Bristles of black hair stood straight like mini-antennas tuned to the community's pulse. Tabloid-size newspapers, notebook sheets, and several photos crowded for space on the desk.

"Carl," she said, "these people are investigating that TCE pollution at the HarrCo plant. I thought you'd want to talk to them." She handed him Sid's card.

Norris pulled up a couple of chairs and invited them to have a seat. "I'm working on a story about the TCE mess. What can you tell me about it?"

Sid chuckled. "We were hoping you could tell us something. We've run into the proverbial brick wall with a company named Auto Parts Rehabbers. It appears to have been the guilty party."

The editor's eyes widened. "Auto Parts Rehabbers? That's a new one on me."

"I'm not surprised. We've had a problem finding anyone who had a connection to the company."

"The people from the state didn't mention it. They don't seem interested in anybody but HarrCo and Mr. Harrington."

"It's his property now. He's the most convenient target."

"Look for the deepest pockets," Norris said. He glanced back at the business card. "What's your interest in it?"

"We were hired by Wade Harrington's lawyer to find how the TCE got there and who's responsible."

"According to my information, it happened several years back."

"The state investigators say it was probably around 1995."

"The results were horrendous," Jaz said. "Have you been out to the plant to look at the site?"

"Yeah. Somebody really screwed up. I interviewed a few of the people who live in the area. They had some shocking tales to tell."

"I heard some of those yesterday," Sid said.

He shifted in his chair for a better view of the office. At the next desk, a young woman twisted her finger around a curl as she talked on the telephone. Beyond her, an older man who appeared to have cut his typing teeth on a Remington or an IBM Selectric pecked on his keyboard with a three-or-four finger system.

Sid looked back at Norris. "We would appreciate it if you could write something about our problem. Maybe ask anyone with information about Auto Parts Rehabbers, or their employees, to contact us."

The editor scratched his chin. "I might do a sidebar about your search. I have your numbers on the card."

"Is yours a daily paper?" Sid asked.

"Weekly. This will be in the issue that comes out next Wednesday."

Sid glanced at Jaz, who frowned. That would only leave a week before the hearing for Wade Harrington. Not a comfortable margin. He turned back to Norris.

"Do you have any suggestions on where we might look in the meantime? We really need to come up with some answers as soon as possible."

The editor reached for a green water bottle on his desk and took a swallow. His mouth widened into a smile as if triggered by a sudden thought. "If I were you, Mr. Chance, I'd go over to the Citizens Bank and talk to Miss Sophie Bright."

"Who's she?"

"As far as I'm concerned, she's Miss Cheatham County. It wasn't long after I took this job that I found out about her. She can tell you who's doing what to whom, and why. She's a walking encyclopedia of people and things that go on in this county."

Jaz stared. "How does she manage that?"

"I don't know. She must have a network of spies. When I asked her about a minor political hack, she gave me a complete *Who's Who* biography. She's unbelievable."

Sid smiled. Sophie Bright just might be the silver lining to this clouded search. He recalled a man in Lewisville with similar talents. It had been a godsend for a rookie police chief. He suspected you could find one in every small town. "And where is Miss Sophie's office?"

"The bank is just up Main Street on the right. You can't miss it."

"Thanks, Mr. Norris. It was a pleasure meeting you. I'll be looking for next Wednesday's newspaper."

"I'm sure we'll be seeing you again," Jaz said as she shook his hand.

Sid struggled to repress a grin as the young editor's eyes brightened. He hadn't been around Jaz all that long, but it always amazed him the way her looks and natural charm could hook guys of all ages.

Sid was about to get up when the phone on Norris's desk rang. The editor turned to answer it.

"They found what?" He grabbed a pencil and started jotting notes on a pad. After a few "uh huh's," he dropped the pencil. "Keep me posted on what happens. Okay?"

Sid stood as Norris put down the phone. "Sounds like you got yourself a story," he said.

"That was my contact in the sheriff's office. They found a body along Little Marrabone Road around the Davidson County line. He'd been shot five times. They're trying to decide if it's in Cheatham or Davidson."

"I had to investigate an accident along there once when I was with Metro," Jaz said. "It's a pretty lonely place at night."

The editor cut his eyes toward her. "I've driven that way a time or two. As I recall, there aren't any signs to tell you when you enter or leave the county."

Sid smiled. "I know one guy who hopes the murder is in Cheatham County."

"Why's that?" Norris gave him a puzzled stare.

"It's a friend who's a Metro homicide detective. I'm sure he has his hands full already."

"Maybe we'll both be lucky. He'll get to stay home, and I'll get a story for the newspaper."

After they hurried out to the truck and climbed in, Jaz looked across at Sid. "If that body is in Davidson County, you can be sure it won't be Bart's case."

"Why?"

"There have been a lot of changes in Metro during the past few years. They split up homicide and assigned all the detectives to the precincts. The only thing downtown now is a small cold case squad. This end of the county is part of the North Precinct."

"And Bart's in East."

"Right. And from what I hear, they don't always talk to each other about what's going on in their areas."

"So if this murder is the same MO as the one he's investigating, Bart might not know about it?"

"You've got it."

Sid pulled out his cell phone. "I can take care of that."

He dialed Bart's number and told him what they had heard at the newspaper.

"Thanks for the tip, Sid," Bart said. "I used to partner with a guy in North. I'll give him a call."

12

THE BANK LOBBY reminded Sid of one he had patronized in Lewisville. It had the usual glass-topped table with slots for checking and savings deposit slips, the wait-here-for-the-next-teller sign, and four windows with smiling young women behind them. Not that much different from what you'd see in Nashville, he thought. But there was a small town feeling about the place. Perhaps it was the fresh-cut flowers, the coffee and doughnuts on the table, the easy way they greeted each other by their first names.

"We'd like to speak to Sophie Bright," Sid told the diminutive woman with long brown hair who occupied a desk in the lobby.

She glanced around at one of the small glassed-in offices off to the right. "Looks like she's on the phone. Have a seat over there and I'll tell her you're waiting. Would you like a cup of coffee?"

Sid gave a slight shake of his head. "Thanks. We're fine."

He and Jaz moved over to a couple of comfortable chairs that faced a coffee table piled with magazines. A sofa sat across from them, flanked at each end by large green plants. Jaz shifted her gaze about the security cameras while Sid eyed Sophie Bright, who sat at her desk with a telephone cradled at her ear. A large woman with short white hair, she accompanied her conversation with hand gestures the listener could only imagine.

A few minutes later, she walked out of her office and crossed the lobby toward them. "I'm Sophie Bright," she said

The Surest Poison

with a pleasant smile. "Did you folks want to see me?"

"Sidney Chance." He handed her a business card. "This is my associate, Jasmine LeMieux. We're from Nashville."

The banker's lively blue eyes gave Jaz a quick appraisal. "I met your father, once. A most interesting gentleman. It was one of the few occasions when I had an opportunity to practice my French."

Jaz's expression turned pensive. "I still miss him like it was yesterday."

"I understood you had become board chairman of Welcome Traveler Stores, Miss LeMieux. When did you get into the private investigation business?"

Sid spread his hands. "She's just helping me on a volunteer basis. We're both former police officers. She got me some work for her company recently and found she couldn't resist the lure of the chase."

"Come on in and tell me what you're chasing now, what I can help you with," Miss Bright said.

They followed her into the small but neat office and took chairs facing her tidy desk. Sid was impressed by the way she had linked Jaz to Jaques LeMieux without hesitation. It looked like Carl Norris had her pegged correctly.

"I'm sure you're familiar with the TCE spill behind the HarrCo Shipping plant," he said. "I've been retained to find out the cause and who is responsible."

She leaned on her elbows, hands folded. "So how can I help you?"

"A company named Auto Parts Rehabbers occupied the plant back in the mid-nineties and appears to be the culprit. We haven't found anybody who knows much about them. The only name I've picked up is Tony Decker."

"Oh, yes, Mr. Decker. A handsome fellow," Miss Bright said. "I called on him to try and get his business for the bank. I found him very cordial, although some others I've talked to, men, I might add, thought otherwise."

"You didn't get his business, did you?"

"No. He said his financial backers had an arrangement with an out-of-town bank. That was understandable."

"Did you meet anybody else while you were there?" Jaz asked.

"Mr. Decker introduced me to his Director of Operations. His name was Pete Rackard. I remember a pair of shifty eyes as his most prominent feature. That and a limp."

"Anyone else?"

"No. I wasn't there very long. They were polite, but they let me know they were very busy. I'm sure I was in the way."

Sounded a lot like Murray Estes' experience, Sid thought. He looked up from his note pad. "Have you heard of anyone else who worked for the company?"

Hands folded in a steeple, she tapped two fingers against her chin. "Mabel Urey once told me a boy who lived down the street from her worked at that plant. She was surprised because she'd never even heard of the place until then."

"We've been out there," Sid said. "Even if you were looking for it, it would be easy to miss."

"Mabel never was one to do much traveling around."

"Where does Mrs. Urey live?"

"I'm sorry. Mabel died two years ago. She had breast cancer, and they didn't catch it in time. She was the nicest person, made the best pecan pie I've ever tasted."

"Is there a husband or somebody else living in the house?"

"No. She was a widow and had no children."

"Could you give me the address where she lived?" Sid asked. "We'll knock on some doors around there and see if we can find the person she mentioned."

He wrote down the address she gave him and stuck the pad in his pocket. "We appreciate the information, Miss Bright. You've been a big help. Do you mind my calling if I think of anything else?"

"Please do. What happened with that chemical pollution was a terrible tragedy for this community. I'll be happy to help any way I can." She stood and walked them to the door. "By the way, I remember someone mentioning they had seen Mr. Decker in Nashville. It was a year or so after the plant closed."

13

THE RAIN HAD changed to a light drizzle, just enough to be a nuisance and make a mess of the windshield. They sat in Sid's truck in the bank parking lot and discussed what Sophie Bright had told them. The fact that Tony Decker had been seen in Nashville a couple of years after Auto Parts Rehabbers closed didn't mean much. That was at least ten years ago.

Sid thumbed through his notes. "Maybe we'll have better luck tracking down Pete Rackard than we've had with Tony Decker."

"When I get back from my Board meeting, I'll get busy on him," Jaz said. She glanced at her watch. "Right now you'd better take me to my car. I need to head downtown."

He started the truck and headed for the restaurant. "Glad you came along this morning, Jaz. I may need more help down the line. After I drop you off, I'll take a run over to where Mabel Urey lived and see what I can learn about that employee Sophie Bright mentioned."

The address was not far off Highway 12, Ashland City's Main Street. Sid found a stretch of neat houses, most of them brick, lined up like a row of squares on a checkerboard. It was an older neighborhood, the street a narrow two lanes on a slight grade. Mature trees, missing most of their leaves, dotted the yards. He pulled off and parked in a space near Mabel Urey's former home.

Sid donned his rain cap and headed for the house beside the former Urey residence. He counted on his waterproof windbreaker to keep him dry in the slow drizzle. After several

The Surest Poison

punches on the doorbell button, plus multiple knocks, he concluded there was no one home.

The next house had a high-peaked roof over a small porch. It looked a bit friendlier, with a sheaf of cornstalks leaning against a post. A wreath fashioned of straw, dried fall flowers, and small gourds hung on the door.

A woman he judged to be in her late forties answered his knock. She wore a blue sweater and jeans, plus a questioning look in her dark eyes.

Sid introduced himself and showed her his P.I. license, a practice he had learned to follow whenever an interviewee showed any reluctance. He explained his investigation of the TCE spill and asked if she had lived on the street back in the mid-nineties.

"We're from Birmingham originally," she said. "My husband's job brought us here in 1995. He works for American Universal."

"The big plant over by the river?"

"Right. He's in transportation. He's responsible for scheduling and maintaining the trucks."

"Did you ever hear of anyone along the street who worked for Auto Parts Rehabbers?"

She brushed back a stray lock of brown hair. "I've never even heard of the company. Are they in Ashland City?"

"They were, but I guess they went out of business around the time you moved here. Do you know if any of your neighbors has lived here at least the past fifteen years?"

She thought for a moment, tapping a finger against her chin. "Try Ethel Gardner. She lives the third house down on this side of the street. She's up in years and hard of hearing, but I think she's lived here forever."

After his fruitless effort next door, he thought it best to ask about other prospects. "Can you think of anybody else?"

"No. I hate to admit it, but I don't know all my neighbors that well."

"I can understand that," he said. "Anyway, thanks for your

help." He handed her a business card. "If you should hear anything about Auto Parts Rehabbers, I'd appreciate your giving me a call."

"I'll ask my husband tonight. If they handled truck parts, I'm sure he'd know something about them."

"Just for the record, could I have your name?"

"Vickie Thomas."

He walked on down to the third house, an older white frame with tall, narrow windows. Noting the wrinkled look of the woman who answered his knock, he could believe she had lived here forever. She wore a faded yellow housedress and had her scrawny arms wrapped around a fat black cat.

"Ethel Gardner?" Sid asked in a voice a bit louder than normal.

She looked at him wide-eyed. "My, you're a big 'un. I'm Ethel. Who are you?"

"Sidney Chance. I'm a private investigator looking into the chemical pollution at the HarrCo Shipping plant. You may have seen about it on television."

"I don't watch the news. It's too depressing. Come on in out of the rain, young man. You'll catch your death of cold."

He smiled at the "young man" comment. She sounded like his mother. Stepping inside, he looked around. The room was crowded, but not with furniture. Rows of brown paper grocery bags filled with an assortment of mail, magazines, and newspapers filled most of the space. He hoped that was not an indication that he faced some sort of weird eccentric. You never knew how much to believe from one of those.

Ethel Gardner lowered herself onto the sofa, still clutching the cat. She waved Sid to the chair. "Private investigator sounds exciting. Is it something like CSI?"

"It's more like Jeopardy, figuring out the right questions to ask."

"I used to watch Jeopardy. Is that Alex Trebek fellow still on it?"

Instead of waiting for an answer, she proceeded to tell

about all of the celebrities she had seen on the program over the years. She appeared to have a decent memory and didn't sound too kooky. Sid listened as long as he could, with an occasional polite nod. Deciding it was time to nudge her back to the business at hand, he broke in when she paused for a breath.

"That's very interesting, Miss Gardner. But if you don't mind, I'd like to ask about a boy who once lived on this street and worked for Auto Parts Rehabbers."

"Auto what?"

He spoke a little louder and slower. "Auto Parts Rehabbers. It would have been around fifteen years ago. Does that ring a bell with you?"

She sat in silence, her brow rumpled, for a full sixty seconds. "You know, that sounds like something I ought to remember. My old mind doesn't function like it used to, but seems like there was a boy staying down at the end of the block. Was maybe a nephew, or something. I don't remember his name, but I think that auto parts place was where he worked."

"What's the name of the people he lived with?" Sid asked.

"Oh, they're not there anymore. They left some time back, about five years ago."

His expectations deflated like a punctured tire. "Do you recall their name, where they went?"

She reached both hands up to rub her forehead and the cat leaped to the floor, stretched its legs, sauntered into the next room. "That was about the time my husband died. My life was a confused mess back then. Talk to Vickie Thomas up the street. I'm sure she could tell you."

Right back where he started. Sid thanked her and, after some lingering chatter, broke away.

Vickie Thomas came to the door, obviously surprised to see him back so soon. He told her about his conversation with Ethel Gardner. She said the people down the block who had moved away were named Owens. The Hershel Owens family. Owens had been a teacher in the county schools, but she couldn't say for sure where they had gone. It might have been Murfreesboro, she speculated, a fast-growing town in the county just to the southeast of Nashville.

14

THE MAN SPOKE in low, conspiratorial a voice. "A friend in Ashland City gave me some unwelcome news today. Our former police chief is meddling again. Private Investigator Sidney Chance is asking questions around Cheatham County. He's interested in Auto Parts Rehabbers and the TCE dump at the old plant site."

"I thought you knew," the man on the other end of the line replied. "Our friends gave me the word. They've been checking on his travels around Ashland City."

"Why wasn't I contacted? You need to keep me in the loop. I want to know what he's up to."

"He's working for Harrington's lawyer in Nashville. The man has a bad habit of sticking his nose where it doesn't belong. Some day it's gonna get chopped off. Some day soon. He roughed up a couple of guys who were sent to see him last night."

"My advice is to be careful. Chance has an associate working with him named Jasmine LeMieux. I believe she's also an ex-cop. Plus she's got tons of money. Owns majority interest in the Welcome Traveler Stores chain."

"Yeah. I've heard about her. I understand She drives a bright red Lexus. I wasn't aware she was involved in this business, though."

"You'd better tell your people to keep their heads up."

"Don't worry. We have a few aces up our sleeves."

"Overconfidence is a recipe for disaster."

"You take care of your end. I'll handle the rough stuff. Mr.

Chance didn't learn his lesson the last time, but you can bet your ass he won't forget this one."

SID RETURNED to his office after lunch and took up the search for Hershel Owens. One of his databases provided a man by that name in a small town not far from Murfreesboro. It identified him as a teacher in the Rutherford County Schools. He checked with the school system and learned that Owens taught math in a middle school not far from his home. He had been on the faculty there for four years.

Sid punched in the number listed, got an answering machine, and left a message to return his call.

Afterward, he contacted Arnie Bailey to report on progress in the investigation. He thought it best to stay a step ahead of the client. Call him before he calls you.

"Think you can find this Decker fellow?" Bailey asked after hearing the details.

"We'll find him. If he's changed his name and gone into hiding, it'll be more difficult. You know the old saying, the difficult we do immediately, the impossible takes a little longer."

"By next week?"

Sid rolled a pencil between his fingers. That was a question he couldn't easily answer. He felt confident in his ability to locate the man, but at this point he had no idea how long it would take. Rather than give a reply that might be misleading, he said, "I'm waiting to hear from Jaz on Pete Rackard. I'm hopeful he can lead us to Decker."

"Okay. Keep me advised."

Not long after finishing his call to Bailey, the phone rang.

"I see you have a substantial new client," Mike Rich said in the same jovial voice he always used. Four years younger than Sid, he had a carefree attitude that masked the intensity he displayed in pursuing the financial markets.

"Who told you?" Sid asked.

"I saw you made a nice deposit from the law firm of Bailey, Riddle and Smith."

The Surest Poison

"You've been checking my bank account."

"That's what you pay me for, my friend."

It was true. Mike handled all of his funds. A financial consultant, he was, in Sid's opinion, the best in the business. In high school, Mike had been a star student of Sid's mother, Mary Virginia Chance. After he became a successful stockbroker, Mike went to Mary Virginia and offered to help with her finances. He got her into the house Sid now occupied and did such a great job managing her money that she recommended Sid use him, also.

Sid drummed his fingers on the desk. "I suppose you know how Arnie Bailey happened to look me up."

"I know he does some work for Welcome Traveler Stores."

"Right. Jaz pointed him in my direction."

"You're not complaining, are you?"

"I'm not sure. Was this idea of getting me into the PI business yours or hers?" It was a subject that, for whatever reason, they had never discussed.

Mike paused. "You're aware that I was a friend of her dad's, and that I also handle her portfolio. We were discussing things one day when she mentioned her problem with old Frank Hartley. He had come to her after getting fired for stealing expensive items off the store's shelves. She was inclined to believe his innocence but wanted it investigated outside company channels. I thought of you up on that hillside and told her I knew someone who had all kinds of investigative experience he ought to be putting to use."

Sid rocked back in his chair, remembering. "That's when she showed up at the cabin." She was accompanied by a deputy sheriff Sid had met when he first moved there. Otherwise it's doubtful she could have found the place.

"She told me you had assured her I was the man to take care of her problem," Sid added, "that I was dedicated to finding justice for the little guy."

Mike laughed. "I don't think I put it exactly like that."

Sid scratched his beard. "Well, I told her after what happened in Lewisville, I no longer had any faith in the human race. I was quite comfortable out there with my creature friends."

Mike was the one who had found the hillside property and negotiated the purchase for Sid. When he replied, there was a smile in his voice. "She flattered you, didn't she? Charmed you, cajoled you."

"She did all that, even offered to pay for my private investigator license."

"Jaz can be more persuasive than a TV evangelist."

"She claimed you told her I needed to get back into the real world and do what I'm good at."

Mike answered slowly. "I may have said that."

"Okay, I guess it was equal parts you and Jaz. What I can't figure is why you put her onto me, knowing what a charmer I am. I recall hearing that you two were an item."

Mike laughed. "How many did you charm up on your mountaintop? Anyway, that's ancient history. Jaz and I are just friends now. You two, though, you'd make a great pair. I'm sure I told you about her experience in the ring. I remember your mom telling me what you did to a kid once with boxing gloves."

"You're stretching things, Michael. You only mentioned she'd been a boxer."

"Not just a boxer. She was tops in her weight class. The only problem was women professional boxers didn't make enough to live on. Since she'd been with the Security Police in the Air Force, she joined the Metro Police Department so she could pay her bills."

Sid smiled to himself. "She's something else, all right."

"Just wait till you get to know her a little better." Mike chuckled. "Now tell me about this new case."

Sid gave him a quick rundown on the TCE spill and its aftermath.

"And you don't have a clue where this Decker guy is?"

"Not really."

The Surest Poison

"Well, good luck, buddy," Mike said. "The good news is you're in great shape financially. Just don't go out and buy any airplanes."

A little later, Sid got a call from Hershel Owens, who had just arrived home from school.

"What does a private investigator want with me?" he asked.

Sid explained that he was investigating a case in Ashland City and asked if Owens had once lived there.

"We left about five years ago," he said.

"I'm trying to locate former employees of Auto Parts Rehabbers. I was told a boy stayed at your house when you lived there, perhaps a nephew, who worked for the company. Is my info correct?"

"Referring to Larry Irwin. He wasn't a nephew, though. He was the son of a cousin I was close to while growing up. The boy'd had some problems, gotten into serious trouble. But he had made a real effort at getting straightened up. We agreed he could live with us if he found a job. Turned out he knew somebody at the Parts Rehabber place who helped him get on out there."

"Was he working for them when the plant closed?"

"Sure was. It happened without warning. One day he went to work and they told him they were closing. No advance notice."

"What did he do after that?"

"He'd studied automotive maintenance in high school and got a job as a mechanic in Ashland City. His mother died, and I haven't been in contact with him in a while. I'm sure he still lives in Ashland City, though."

"Do you have an address and phone number? I'd like to talk to him."

"Hold a second." Owens was back moments later and read out the information.

When Sid tried the phone number, he got an answering machine. Still at work, he thought. He left a message asking for a callback.

After tearing off the sheet with Irwin's contact info, Sid stared at the blank page on his note pad. It stared back like a silent challenge. He decided to try an exercise he sometimes used to generate fresh ideas. The scheme involved jotting down random thoughts about the case as they flashed through his mind. First came Hank Keglar, a known shady character, who sold the property to Auto Parts Rehabbers and took it back. Sid had tangled with Kegler on many occasions during his time in Lewisville. A grotesque hunk of humanity—make that inhumanity—Keglar was the godfather of the town's unruly element. Below that he made an entry about Tony Decker, the ex-con who had managed the company. Decker was an intriguing question mark, either polite and cordial or brusque and uncooperative, depending on who you asked. Pete Rackard? Sid looked up from his notes and wondered if Jaz had returned home yet.

He picked up the phone and called her cell number. When it went to voice mail, he knew she was still at her Board meeting.

JAZ GOT THE MESSAGE on her Bluetooth headset an hour later after leaving downtown. She decided to wait and return Sid's call when she got home. She wanted to check on Rackard first. Driving out I-65, she took the Brentwood exit and turned to the north on Franklin Road. This was a fashionable area that housed business leaders as well as up-and-comers. It had once been home to country music legends like Hank Williams and Eddy Arnold. She slowed as she approached the stone entrance that bore what she called, with tongue lodged firmly in cheek, the LeMieux coat-of-arms. It was a stonecutter's impressionistic version of an eighteen-wheeler with "LM" on the trailer. She flashed an infra-red beam at the sensor, and the heavy wrought iron gate rumbled open.

Jazz navigated the winding driveway lined with stately oaks and maples and saw John Wallace riding up on a small tractor with a trailer in tow. Large and stocky, with muscular arms and an almost expressionless face reminiscent of a figure chiseled on a mountainside, he had always impressed Jaz as a man at peace with his surroundings. She parked in front of the house, got out, and waited for him to turn off the engine, which raised a din rivaling that of a jackhammer.

"What have you been gathering?" Jaz asked.

"Getting some dead limbs out of the way, Miss Jasmine. That was a pretty strong wind the other night. Oh, there was a man stopped by asking about you around lunchtime."

"At the gate?"

"Yes, ma'am. I answered when he buzzed the house."

"What did he want?"

"I suppose he just wanted to know if you were here. That's all he asked. I said who should I say is calling, but I guess he'd already pulled away."

"Did you notice what kind of car he drove?"

"No, ma'am. You could check the tape and find out."

A motion-detecting surveillance camera kept track of visitors. She wouldn't have thought much about it except for what had happened to Sid. Still, she could think of no reason for anyone to connect her to his investigation. He hadn't mentioned her name while Harrington's office was bugged.

She thanked John and went inside. After calling to Marie in the kitchen to say she was home, she went to her office. Pete Rackard was her first priority.

It didn't take long to track him down. She called Sid's office to give him the information.

"Chance Investigation Agency," he answered.

"Ah, I got the CIA," she said.

"Funny." His voice lacked any hint of humor.

"Just checking in. I'm back from the Scar Wars."

"That bad?"

"I exaggerate. Except for a few disagreements with the chief financial officer and the director of marketing, I thought everything went as smooth as a well-tuned engine."

"Nice to hear."

"What did you learn today?" she asked.

Sid filled her in on his interviews in Ashland City and his talk with Hershel Owens. "Have you had a chance to check on Pete Rackard?"

"I have. Very interesting fellow. Item number one, he was Tony Decker's cellmate in prison. After several minor brushes with the law, he was sent up for beating a man half to death in a fight outside a bar. Item two, he grew up on a farm near Lewisville. He worked as an auto mechanic there."

"Item three?"

"He now runs an auto repair shop in Franklin."

That put him in Williamson County, a few miles down the road from where Jaz lived. A recent census report listed Williamson as one of the wealthiest counties in the nation. The former convict had moved into the middle of the high-rollers.

"What's the name of his shop?" Sid asked.

"Rack's Auto Repair. According to my information, it's doing quite well."

Sid paused. "With the rush hour traffic, I'd have a rough time trying to get down there before they close."

"I can talk to him," Jaz said. "It won't take me long to get over there."

"Okay. See if you can get any line on Decker, or the TCE spill. But you'd better get a move on. Don't be late for the Felons game."

She snickered. "Don't worry, I've got the bells out, ready to strap on."

15

SID WAS LOOKING over the notes he had scribbled about Pete Rackard when Jerry Jackson, the electronic countermeasures expert, called.

"I found your client's problem," Jackson said.

"How bad was it?"

"Did you go by his office and talk to him?"

"Yes."

"Then somebody knows whatever you told him."

"You found some transmitters?"

"One in the phone, one on a shelf behind his desk. I have them if you'd like to add to your gadget collection."

"Thanks, I'll pass."

"It wasn't a very sophisticated operation, but good enough. Probably monitored from a setup nearby that would be checked every few hours. They must have pulled it out. I did a search for the receiver but couldn't find anything."

"Any idea who's behind it?" Sid asked.

"It has all the earmarks of a guy I've run into before. Same equipment, same M.O. He's a PI out of Atlanta. There's no way to tell who the client was."

Sid thought about the two hoods who had knocked on his door last night. "I have another job for you, Jerry. I want you to set up an alarm system and some cameras at my house."

THE RAIN HAD ended, but clouds shrouded the early evening. Headlights glistened in long streaks on the wet pavement as Jaz drove through Old Hickory Boulevard toward

Hillsboro Road. It would be a less hectic route this time of day, bringing her into Franklin near the location of Rackard's repair shop. She drove through an area of homes and pastureland that had supported a thriving plantation economy until the Civil War reared its ugly head. Now the peaceful scene of rolling countryside populated by horse farms and high-ticket homes, Williamson County had attracted the headquarters of several major corporations.

Jaz parked her Lexus in front of Rack's Auto Repair, located in a brick building with tall, arched windows that resembled old-time structures in the historic downtown area. Cars pulled in through overhead doors on one side. Dressed in jeans and a matching blue shirt, she walked up to the high-topped counter in the small lobby area. A young man in coveralls, his red ball cap turned backward, grinned at her.

"What do you need, ma'am?"

Jaz smiled back and leaned her elbows on the counter. "I need to talk to Pete Rackard."

His eyes took in her face and as far south as he could manage. "Sure. He's in the back, just finishing up, I think. You'll have to leave your car overnight if you want anything done, though. We're about to close."

Jaz handed him a business card, a plain one she'd just had printed with her name, phone number and Private Investigator. "Just get him for me, okay?"

"My pleasure," he said. He glanced at the card as he walked into the open area of the garage.

Typical young, over-sexed male, she thought. While he's back there, he'll be working on a good opening line to find out if I'm available. Dummy ought to know I'm old enough to be his mother.

He was back in a couple of minutes with a big grin on his face. "Pete'll be with you in a minute. He told me to see if I can help you. Can I get you a Coke or something?"

"What flavors does something come in?"

That put a wrinkle in his forehead. "'Scuse me?"

The Surest Poison

She laughed, folding her hands, showing a large diamond on her right ring finger. It had belonged to her mother. "Just kidding. I'm fine. I'll check out the décor over here."

She turned to a wall half-covered with kids' artwork, showing their ideas of cars in different locations and situations. One imaginative youngster had placed a long green car up on the back of a smaller blue one. Good ad for a repair shop, she thought. A sign identified the display as the work of third graders at a local school. Rackard was attempting to appear civic-minded, a bit of a change from Auto Parts Rehabbers.

A couple of minutes later, Jaz turned as she heard someone approaching. She saw a large man whose bulging belly hung over his belt like a sack full of Jello. He wore grease-smudged jeans and a dark gray work shirt, and he walked with a slight limp. He looked her up and down with wary eyes.

"I'm Pete Rackard," he said, folding his arms. He gripped a faded shop cloth in one hand.

"Nice meeting you, Mr. Rackard." She gave him a congenial smile. "I'm looking into a situation that occurred at the place where you worked about a dozen years ago, where you were Director of Operations—Auto Parts Rehabbers."

She paused.

Rackard stared at her in silence.

She waited, watching his face begin to twitch. She knew she could out-stare him.

After a long pause, he said, "So what's your question?"

"You worked for Tony Decker. I'd like to talk to him. I'd appreciate your giving me his address or phone number."

"I don't know where he is."

"You haven't been in touch with him?"

Rackard gritted his teeth. "I just said I don't know where he is."

"So you did. However, I'm sure you remember when a lot of trichloroethylene was spilled or dumped behind the plant. How did that happen?"

He sucked in a deep breath, pulled the business card from

his shirt pocket, and glared at it. "This little chat is over, Miss LeMieux." He pronounced it "Lee Mewcks."

Jaz kept her cool, businesslike demeanor. She wasn't about to let him rattle her, or so she thought.

"I know, it's closing time," she said. "I can come back tomorrow."

"Don't bother. I'll be under a car."

He spun around and started back into the shop. She saw another mechanic looking at them, a grin twisting his odd-looking mustache.

"Maybe I should come back with a police escort," she said.

Rackard stopped, glanced over his shoulder. His dark eyes bored into hers.

"Yeah. You do that . . . bitch."

16

THE MISS DEMEANOR and Five Felons Poker Club convened at eight o'clock. Sid ate teriyaki chicken at a nearby restaurant and made it back to the office by seven. He set about arranging his reception area for the "meeting." The room contained a two-seat sofa, four metal chairs with cushions, a coffee table, and a small end table with a lamp. To accommodate the players, he pushed most of the furniture against the wall, brought in two additional chairs from his office and a round folding table he stored in the supply room. Mike had sent it to him to use for conferences, but up to now he hadn't found a need for a conference. He also brought in a cooler filled with iced beer.

Jaz arrived as he sat at his desk going over information about a deadbeat dad he had retrieved using data recovery software she had suggested. When he saw the disgusted look on her face, he guessed a different kind of recovery program was in order.

"What's the problem?" he asked.

"Mr. Pete Rackard is an SOB."

He leaned back in his chair. "That must mean he wasn't real cooperative."

"In spades. As soon as I mentioned Decker, he threw up his defenses. Said he didn't know where Decker was. And when I asked about the TCE dump, he suggested I get lost."

"We need his phone logs. You can bet he put in a call to Decker after you left."

Jaz sat in the remaining chair.

"I'd be surprised if he didn't," she said. "I have a friend who can check it out."

Sid noticed the frown continued to tug at the corners of her mouth. "What did he do to get you so bent out of shape?"

"He threw the B-word at me. I hate that."

She wasn't easy to upset, but he knew the so-called B-word was one thing she couldn't stomach. "So who just called whom an SOB?"

"That was only payback. Anyway, just repeating initials doesn't sound all that bad." Her features softened into a contrite smile. "I'll get him."

He didn't doubt that. She had the training to handle herself in any situation and the determination to pull it off. Mike Rich had shown him a video shot by a television cameraman back during her time as a Metro policewoman. It showed her taking down a robber who was attempting to flee the scene of a convenience market holdup. The guy had made a terrible choice of time and location. Not only had Jaz just gotten out of her police car in front of the store, a TV news crew was setting up nearby for a remote feed. The video showed the robber, a bulky, bearded man, coming out of the store with a large paper bag in one hand. He had stuck the gun back in his belt. As Jaz walked toward him, somebody opened the door and yelled, "Stop him!" The fleeing robber took a swing at Jaz. She blocked the blow and whacked him a good one with her nightstick. He went down hard. She was right on top of him with her Glock drawn.

At the sound of the outer door opening, Sid glanced up at the small monitor mounted on the wall facing his desk. "Wick is here," he said. He walked out to the reception area.

"What's up, Sidney?" Wick Stanley asked. The patrol sergeant, a fifty-year-old version of Joe Average in after-work denims and a blue Titans jacket, stuck his hand out.

Sid grinned as he shook it. "I feel lucky tonight, Wick. Hope you brought plenty of quarters."

Wick shifted his eyes as Jaz came out of the office swinging

The Surest Poison

a small handbag. "Man, you'd better be lucky if you want to beat that gal. I never saw a woman play poker like her."

"All in the technique," Jaz said.

She was a smiler at the poker table. A lot of players tried to maintain a neutral look, but she smiled all the time, good hand or bad. She slipped around to take her traditional spot at the table. Each of them gravitated to the same chair whenever they met. Wick insisted it would be bad luck to do otherwise.

"Have you heard from Bart today?" Wick asked.

"Sid talked to him this morning," Jaz said. "We heard about another murder victim shot five times with a thirty-eight."

Wick moved across to his chair. Without a feature unique enough to stand out in a crowd, he would have made a great undercover man, Sid thought. Wick had no interest in detective work, though. He liked to be out on the street, dealing with the rough and tumble of everyday life.

"I heard about that new victim," he said. "Got some of the guys speculating serial killer. We don't need one of those around here. The crackheads and pushers are making things miserable enough for everybody."

Sid pulled out a couple of beers and passed one across. "I heard Bart say ninety percent of the murders involve drugs in one way or another."

"The victim that got shot in Shelby Park Halloween morning was a Metro employee," Wick said. "He worked on a garbage truck. I hauled him in five or six years ago for fighting outside a bar."

Wick had been on the force for twenty-five years, his father a cop before him. Sometimes it seemed that he knew everybody in town. He liked to say he hadn't heard an original excuse from a lawbreaker in twenty years.

"What was his name?" Sid asked.

"Gillie Younger. He was a crusty character, not too bright, but not as old as he looked. I wasn't the first cop to pick him up. As I recall, he had a drinking problem."

Sid gave a shrug. "Doesn't everybody?"

"Surely not you," Jaz said.

"Not any more, thanks to Mike Rich. I was headed in that direction after the fiasco in Lewisville. I'm a big guy, but Mike has a bigger voice. He read me the riot act. That's one reason he thought it was a good idea for me to build my cabin out in the sticks. It was a long way to the nearest liquor store. After three years, he must have figured I was over it. Anyway, now I even go easy on the beer."

"You can count on my wife to coldcock me if I down too many of these," Wick said, popping the tab on the can.

The door swung open and two more players strolled in. Jack Post, short and stocky, wore a felt hat right out of the thirties. You could picture him going out on a story with a card saying "Press" stuck in his hatband. He had a round face marked by a beard that always made a quick comeback despite a morning shave. He was at least seventy, though he wouldn't admit to anything beyond that. After a long career of covering every kind of crime story imaginable, and some difficult to imagine, he wore the look of a confirmed cynic.

Gabriel Thackston, known to everyone as Judge, had an abundant thatch of prematurely white hair. He said it gave him more respect on the bench. However, it didn't provide enough respect to get him re-elected when an upstart assistant district attorney leaked information about Thackston's habit of sleeping around with ladies of questionable reputation.

Post's gaze swept the room like a football referee counting heads. "Where's Homicide Harry?"

"He's probably still out chasing down the bad guys," Wick said.

"We must be it, then," Thackston said. "Shall we get down to business?"

"Get a beer first," Wick said. "We can wait a few more minutes for Bart. Meanwhile, we need to interrogate the private eye on what he's up to these days."

The Judge raised an eyebrow. "Sergeant Stanley, you, of

all people, should be aware of the doctrine of confidentiality."

Sid came over and took his seat. "There's not much confidentiality involved in this case. Jaz is helping me track down the owners and management of a defunct company called Auto Parts Rehabbers. We'd be happy to have any of you brilliant people contribute your sage advice."

"What did they do to warrant devoting your high-priced talents to the chase?" Post asked. He still wore his wide-brimmed fedora, now pushed back to show an expanding forehead.

"They drenched the ground behind their Ashland City plant with trichloroethylene," Jaz said. "Ruined a lot of people's health downstream."

"Oh, that one. I saw the stories. I thought the plant had something to do with shipping."

"The current owner is HarrCo Shipping." Sid slipped a napkin under his beer. "Auto Parts Rehabbers did the dumping."

"And you don't know who owned the company?" Wick asked.

Sid told what they had learned about Tony Decker and the limited liability company. He also detailed Jaz's unsuccessful attempt to get to Decker through the garage owner, Pete Rackard. "I've only come up with one employee, a guy named Larry Irwin who lives in Ashland City."

The Judge toyed with his necktie. He always came dressed as if ready for the bench. "Surely you've attacked the case from other angles. What additional interesting facts have you unearthed?"

"Well, the property's original owner was Hank Kegler, a shady character I ran into during my tenure in Lewisville. He also took the property back when Auto Parts Rehabbers bowed out. And the company's registered agent was Bronson Fradkin, a lawyer in Lewisville."

"I've heard of Fradkin," Thackston said. "A friend of mine was once in partnership with him. He and Fradkin were in law school together, but he couldn't take much of the man in practice. He said Fradkin didn't seem to comprehend the meaning of scruples. It sounds like you have a definite Lewisville connection."

"Right. I think that's where we'll need to concentrate our efforts if things don't start developing around here."

The door opened and Bart Masterson walked in. He glanced around at the players. "Sorry I'm late."

"Hey, Bat," Wick greeted him. "Have we got a serial killer on the loose?"

"The chief doesn't want to admit it if we do. Same M.O., though. I talked with an old buddy from North Precinct. The new guy also had five thirty-eight slugs in the back, was left on the side of the road."

"When did this one happen?" Wick asked.

"Estimated time of death is Wednesday night. He'd been in the brush from thirty to thirty-six hours."

Jack Post tipped his hat a little farther north, exposing a bit more leathery skin. "I read where some forensic psychologist said there are hundreds of these psychos out there, a lot more than you hear about. Most of the time they look and act like Joe Nobody next door."

"Well, this Joe Nobody enjoys stitching patterns on guys backs," Bart said.

"Who was the victim?" Post asked.

Bart brought over a beer and took his seat. "White male, thirty-three. Guy named Larry Irwin."

17

Sid AND JAZ glanced at each other like doomsday had just been announced.

"What's going on?" Bart asked.

"Larry Irwin?" Sid stared at him. "What was his occupation?

"Auto mechanic. He worked for American Universal in Ashland City."

"Looks like your bad luck just got worse," Jack Post said.

Bart's dark eyes took on a semi-dazed look. "Does somebody want to clue me in on what's going on here?"

"Larry Irwin was the guy I hoped would give us a line on what happened at the Auto Parts Rehabbers plant."

After Sid told about his investigation and how he had identified Irwin, Bart pulled out his cell phone. "Let me call in about that cousin. They hadn't been able to turn up much on Irwin. The company didn't have a next-of-kin listed."

"Any connection between Irwin and that body in Shelby Park?" Jaz asked when Bart snapped the cover shut on his cell phone.

"Not that I've found. The park victim was Gillie Younger, a garbageman for Metro. He lived in a rooming house in East Nashville."

Sid leaned his chair back. "Wick arrested him once. He sounds like an older guy than Irwin. I don't see any similarities that might attract a serial killer."

"Perhaps the perpetrator had issues with both men and used the five-shot method to make the police think serial killer," Thackston said, his hands folded on the table.

Good idea, Sid thought. After fifteen years on the bench, no doubt the Judge had heard enough murder scenarios to write a series of mystery novels.

Bart turned, his forehead rumpled. "You may have something there, Judge. I haven't bought into the psychopath thing, and not just because the chief doesn't want it to be that way."

Wick turned to the old newspaper reporter sitting at his left. "You got any cases that need solving, Jack? Bart has two murders, Sid and Jaz have a chemical spill. This astute group should be able to tackle any number of situations that stump the experts."

"I left all my cases back at the newspaper," Post said.

"No problems we can tackle?"

"The only problem I have is keeping my ex-wife from telling me how I should spend my money. She thinks I'm getting rich off a newspaper pension and Social Security. What a joke."

That brought a laugh. Then Jaz began to drum her fingers on the table. "Unless somebody has some specific ideas on how to track down the baddies plaguing our fair city, I suggest we get to the business at hand."

She reached over and spread out the deck. "High card deals."

Bart snickered. "I just may have to take you down a notch, Miss LeMieux."

IT WAS AFTER nine o'clock, with the pile of coins growing in front of Jaz, when her cell phone rang. She checked the caller ID, saw it was her home number. She got up and moved to the side of the room.

"Marie?"

"Miss Jasmine, I hated to bother you, but I'm worried sick. I've been trying to call my grandson. Twice nobody answered. The last time, somebody picked up the phone, then hung it right up again."

The Surest Poison

Jaz knitted her brows. "Were you calling for any particular reason?"

"I asked Connie this morning about the play Little Bob has been practicing at church. She said to call her back tonight and she'd let me know the time."

Did Bobby hang up the phone, or somebody else? Jaz wondered. And why?

"Just hang tight, Marie," she said. "I'll go check it out."

She broke the connection and looked up Bobby Wallace's number in her contact list. She listened to the ring tone after pressing the Talk button. No answer. She knew they had Caller ID but no answering machine. She stuffed the phone in her purse and walked back to the table.

"I hate to put a damper on things, but I have an emergency. You guys can split my quarters and keep on playing."

Sid's eyes narrowed. "What's the problem?"

She told him about Marie Wallace's call and her own unsuccessful try to reach Bobby or Connie. "Something's wrong. After what happened the other day, I'm afraid it could be serious. I'm going down there."

"Going where?" Mitch asked.

"Ashland City."

Sid pushed up from the table. "I'll go with you."

"No need to ruin your night," she said.

"A good cop doesn't head into a potential hot spot without backup. I'm going."

"Sorry Bart and I can't help," Wick said. "Cheatham County is out of our jurisdiction. Of course, if you get in some real trouble, you know who to call."

Sid clapped a hand on his shoulder. "Thanks, Wick. I'm sure the Dynamic Duo can handle the job. Judge, I'll leave you in charge. You can lock up when the game is over."

Thackston stared at him. "You'd trust these questionable characters in here with your confidential files?"

Sid smiled. "I trust them without question. As long as the files are locked away."

"Bart is the best lock-picker in the business," Wick said.

Sid pointed to his office. "Judge, you're authorized to jail anybody who goes through that door."

On the way to the parking lot, he and Jaz agreed that since this mission was her responsibility, they would go in her car. She drove past RiverGate Mall to I-65 and headed south toward Briley Parkway, where they joined the evening traffic that zipped along at its usual hectic pace.

"Have you had any new thoughts about the nature of Bobby's problem?" Sid asked.

"No. Connie hasn't been able to pick up any clues, and Bobby won't say beans to Marie."

"What about a gambling problem? If he's big into sports, that could be a possibility."

"I hadn't thought of that. This sounds like the sort of squeeze a loan shark might put on."

Sid glanced back at the headlights behind them. None appeared close enough to have any interest. He looked back at Jaz. "If something new has happened, I suggest we notify the police or the sheriff's office. I haven't liked the implications of this deal from the start."

"I agree, for the most part," Jaz said. "But let's get a reading on the situation first. Whoever is responsible must have threatened to do something drastic if Bobby talked to the police. We need to break down the barrier and get to the bottom of this."

"Reminds me of the situation I got caught in during the Vietnam War. People were making threats if anybody talked."

"Mike told me you served over there."

"Yeah. I went in right out of high school, took Ranger and Airborne training and was sent to Vietnam as a Special Forces replacement."

He told her how it started when he was assigned as liaison with a detachment of Military Intelligence personnel operating under the guise of a Special Forces unit. Their mission was to plan and direct cross-border intelligence operations into

Cambodia, using South Vietnamese civilians as agents. The operation gathered valuable information on enemy movements and supply routes, allowing U.S. commanders to thwart several Vietcong attacks. But key agents started disappearing like balloons around a dart board. An investigation showed the problem occurred in an area managed by a particular Vietnamese agent. The man was interrogated, administered truth serum, and given a lie detector test. The results showed him guilty. He soon vanished, never to be heard of again.

"What happened?" Jaz asked.

"After an investigation, the Army charged several officers and enlisted men with murder. I got caught up in the hysteria. They interrogated me for hours. I heard some of the guilty parties whispering threats against anybody who talked to the investigators, but I couldn't tell them anything because I hadn't been clued in on the plot."

"How did it wrap up?"

"The charges were dropped when the CIA refused to testify, but a lot of careers came to premature ends. Although I was exonerated, `it helped me decide to get out of the Army, get a degree, and become a National Park Ranger."

"Sounds like you got caught in a bad spot."

"Yeah." Sid tried to stretch his long legs as best he could. "It reminds me too much of my experience with the shooting that ended my Park Service career, and that abortive drug sting in Lewisville. You think maybe I have a talent for being in the wrong place at the wrong time?"

She turned her head and smiled. "You were in the right place at the right time for me. But I know the feeling. According to my mother, I spent several years in the wrong place."

"Was that when you quit college?"

"Right. I was playing basketball, and they brought in a new coach who changed everything. I no longer felt that I fit in. I got angry, quit and joined the Air Force. It's not the best choice when your mother's an aristocratic snob."

Sid watched her face in the glow of the dashboard lights, the pique in the curl of her lip, the rigid set of her jaw. "Mike said your family disowned you."

Her eyes cut toward him for an instant, then returned to the road. "I was persona non grata at the mansion. To make it even worse, as far as they were concerned, when I left the Air Force I went into boxing. My former sergeant was a Golden Gloves champion. He became my trainer. As you may have noticed, I'm pretty independent."

"Agreed. But things obviously worked out in the end."

"The issue involved my mother more than my dad. After she died in the early nineties, he was nearly killed in a car wreck. I quit my job as a policewoman and moved back home to take care of him. After he was well enough to work again, I returned to college to get my degrees. I served as his assistant until he died."

Sid thought about what she had said as the conversation wound down. Now that he knew the whole story, he found a lot to admire about her, not the least her tenacity.

A few minutes later, Jaz swung into a parking spot in front of the small house in Ashland City. Bobby's car sat in the short driveway. In the yard next door, the jack-o-lanterns grinned as though nothing was amiss. Jaz killed the lights and they walked up to the house. Only a soft glow behind the draperies in the front window gave any indication of life beyond the walls.

Noting a peephole in the front door, Sid covered the lens as Jaz knocked.

After a minute or so, the door opened a few inches. Bobby's eyes, large and distrustful, appeared in the gap.

"Hello, Bobby," Jaz said. "We need to talk."

"I can't talk, Miss Jaz. And please don't come back again."

He started to shut the door, but Sid jammed his foot into the narrow space. "I'm Sidney Chance, Bobby," he said, pushing the door open. "I'm a friend of Jaz's. I operate a private investigation agency. It's time for some answers, son."

Bobby stepped back, fear twisting his face. He looked a bit

The Surest Poison

cowed by Sid's size. As the visitors stepped into the room, Connie and Little Bob appeared at the entrance to the kitchen. Jaz closed the door behind her.

Bobby turned to his wife and son. "Get back in the kitchen."

"Stay." Sid spoke in a commanding voice, holding up a hand for emphasis. "It's time for a family conference. Let's all sit down and get comfortable."

Though he looked anything but comfortable, Bobby moved over to a chair. He seemed unsure how to handle this new large, dominating presence in the room.

Sid remained standing after the others were seated. He had been playing it by ear up to this point, but the ploy seemed to be working. Jaz sat in silence beside Connie, appearing engrossed in his performance.

Sid stared into Bobby's eyes. "Something happened today. You refused to answer your grandmother's calls, even hung up on her once."

"I told him he shouldn't have done that," Connie said, her voice like a whisper.

Bobby sat with his arms folded, his lips sealed.

Sid let his gaze move around his audience. "Okay. Here's the deal. All the indications are that this family is in big trouble. Jaz and I are both private investigators and former police officers. We can't ignore the situation. If you don't explain the problem, we'll have to report it to the police and let them take over. I can't predict how they'll handle it." He was quiet for a moment. "It's your choice."

When Bobby said nothing, Connie spoke up. "They grabbed Little Bob off the street this afternoon."

A shocked look crossed Jaz's face. "Who did?"

"I don't know. They drove him around for about an hour, then let him out up the street."

Sid looked at the boy and asked in a gentle voice, "Could you describe the car?"

He shrugged, his face somber. "It was sort of new. Maybe a Dodge or something, I think. It was black."

"Did you see the license plate?"

"No, sir."

Bobby finally spoke. "The man called when I got home. He warned me not to talk to anybody. Next time they take Little Bob, we'll never see him again. He said don't talk to Jasmine LeMieux. He knew she'd been here."

Jaz's eyes widened. "How did—?"

"Somebody's been watching, or they have a contact around here." Sid turned back to Bobby. "Have you been borrowing money to pay gambling debts? Did they demand the money and you couldn't pay it back?"

Bobby's mouth dropped open. "No, no," he protested. "I don't owe nobody. Honest, I don't."

Sid wasn't sure whether to believe him, but he decided to let it drop. "Look, the only way we can fight this is to find the perpetrator. You must know who he is."

"I'm not sure," Bobby said, hugging his shoulders.

"What did he tell you not to talk about?"

Bobby shook his head, his eyes downcast. "I won't sign my boy's death warrant."

Sid saw his chances for coming up with anything useable fading like a morning fog. But he decided to make one more try. "You must have seen the man when they picked you up at the hamburger shop."

"I didn't know the one who met me. They blindfolded me before they took me to the man who made the threat. I'm sorry, Mr. Chance, I won't give them an excuse to hurt my family."

18

WHEN THEY WERE back in the car, Jaz called Marie to tell her everyone was okay, she could relax and go on to bed. Little Bob's experience was left out of the conversation.

She turned to Sid. "I appreciate what you did in there. It was a super job. He paid a lot more attention to you than he would have to me."

"I just wish it had produced some positive results. We still don't have anything to go on. Bobby is a scared, confused young man. He's a bit naïve and not sophisticated enough to realize his best hope is to get police protection."

In the glow of the dash lights, he could see the doubt on her face. "This is a small town and a small county, Sid. How much protection would he get? What would it take to get it?"

Sid stared into the darkness as she turned toward Ashland City's Main Street. "We need more background on Bobby. Where do his parents live?"

"His mother left them when he was twelve. His dad died several years ago. That's one reason Marie has always been so protective of him."

"Check with her when you get home and see if she recalls anybody who had a grudge against Bobby, anybody who might have a reason to threaten him."

"I'll try, but I'd think she would have said something by now."

As they headed down Ashland City Highway, Jaz slowed the Lexus and backed off from a car that swerved just ahead of them.

Sid stared at the taillights that now hugged the shoulder of the road but pulled away fast. It was a late model Chrysler. The light over the license plate was out, but he saw a bumper sticker with the sabertooth tiger logo of Nashille's NHL hockey team, the Predators.

"That character is either drunk or stupid," he said. "He almost clipped us."

"I vote for both." Jaz's tone mirrored her disgust. "He came up beside us moving really slow, then gunned it."

Sid considered that for a moment. The man who called Bobby at home mentioned Jaz by name. He knew she had been a visitor at the house. Could this guy be somebody who had followed them from Bobby's street to see where she was headed, or who was with her?

"Did you get a good look at who was in that car?" he asked.

"No. The windows had a dark tint. Why?"

He told her the question that had crossed his mind.

"You think they're following me now? Could it be the same people who tailed you?"

"Not the same car, for sure. And it may be nothing. I don't want to start getting paranoid, but I think it's time you started watching your back. Wouldn't be a bad idea to start carrying your piece."

She pointed to the handbag on the floorboard beside her foot. "I never leave home without it. Well, rarely. Are you going to start taking your own advice?"

"Probably."

"Maybe we'd better take a closer look at this guy," Jaz said.

She sped up in an attempt to catch him, but the suspect car had already disappeared down the southbound ramp into a stream of traffic by the time Briley Parkway came into view.

"If it's somebody interested in us," Sid said, "I'm sure we'll meet again."

Jaz swung onto the northbound lane toward Madison.

IT WASN'T UNTIL she got home that Jaz thought about the

man John mentioned who had asked if she was in that morning. She got out the surveillance tape from the front gate camera and ran it back until she found the car involved. Normally, the tape would have provided a good image of the driver, but in this case he had a black cap pulled low on his forehead and large sunglasses. The only identifying feature was a dimple in his chin.

Since the car backed out of the driveway entrance, the license plate was not visible. One fact struck her, however. The car was a green Ford. It could have been a twin of the one that followed them out of Ashland City on Thursday.

19

SID BEGAN HIS run Saturday morning at sunrise, although he'd been in bed hardly long enough to call it a night. A book of fascinating cases written by a veteran PI had kept him turning pages way past the time he should have given up. After his usual routine of shower, breakfast, coffee and newspaper, he set out to follow through on what he and Jaz had agreed. He called the farm supply store where Bobby Wallace worked. The woman who answered told him it was Bobby's day off. As soon as Jerry Jackson arrived to beef up his security system, Sid climbed into his pickup truck and headed back to Ashland City. He kept an eye out for any sign of a tail but saw no one.

The store fronted on Main Street not far beyond the center of town. Small tractors lined up at one side of the parking area like race cars awaiting the checkered flag. Sid walked inside. He took in the artful display of power tools and small farm implements, then approached the counter where a young woman with boyish brown hair and a pixy smile greeted him.

"Is the manager in?" Sid asked.

She pointed to the rear of the store. "The fuzzy one in the hunting cap."

Sid followed her directions back to where a short, stocky man stood. He had a full beard that would have made him look like Santa Claus except there was much less hair on his head than on his chin. Sid introduced himself.

"Bobby Wallace's grandmother, Mrs. Marie Wallace, asked me to see if I could help him out. He's got a difficult personal

The Surest Poison

problem he's reluctant to talk about. It involves somebody he used to know, but he won't open up so I can help him. I wondered if anyone has been asking about him around here?"

"Does this have something to do with Thursday morning when somebody called in sick for him?"

"I think so." Sid didn't want to say too much and get Bobby into any more trouble.

The manager pushed his lips out almost in a pout. "He was evasive when I asked him what the problem was."

"As I said, he won't even talk about it with his grandmother," Sid said. "Have you seen or heard anything that would lead you to believe somebody had a problem with him, maybe was out to put a hurt on him?"

The man shook his head slowly. "Nothing like that's happened since Bobby's been working here. I have no idea what it could be. If you want to look back further, I can check his records and see where he worked before he came with us."

"I'd appreciate it," Sid said.

After spending a few minutes in his office, the manager came back and handed Sid a card with the address of Norton's Food Mart, a small grocery not far away.

"That's where Bobby worked before he joined us. It's been nearly ten years ago. I hope you can find out what's his problem. He's been a good worker for me."

Sid found the store in a weathered brick building that appeared to have been around for about as long as he had. Posters in the windows advertised specials on bread and eggs. A handful of customers wandered about the shelves. One stood at the counter where a girl with long blonde hair ran items past a scanner.

Sid used his disarming smile approach. "Good morning. Is your manager in?"

She waved toward the rear of the store, where stacks of staples—flour and sugar and large bags of rice—were stacked along the narrow aisles. Sid wondered if an influx of Asians had moved into the area. He had been indoctrinated into the rice culture during his Army tour in the Far East.

"He's in the storage room. Back through the swinging door."

Sid spotted the door and walked to it, noting prices along the way and marveling at how little guys like this managed to stay in business in competition with the supermarkets. He pushed the door open and saw a man dressed for the golf course checking labels on a row of boxes.

Sid introduced himself. "I was told that Bobby Wallace worked here around ten years ago. Do you by chance remember him?"

The manager leaned against the wall, arms crossed. "Can't say I do. But that was around the time I bought the place."

Sid frowned. "Who did you buy the store from?"

"Old fellow named Higginbottom. He died a few years ago. Sorry I can't help you."

That phrase had begun to sound like a mantra from those he interviewed.

Sid returned home around lunchtime and fond Jerry Jackson wrapping up the job.

"I checked out your existing alarm system and added a few things," Jackson said as he packed up his tools. "The eve lights are on motion detectors. You have cameras facing each direction, also with motion detectors. It's set up so you can monitor the system from your computer at the office. If there's a breech, it will call your office and cell phones. Of course, when you're at home, you can monitor everything on your TV."

"Thanks. Sounds like Fortress Chance."

Jackson grinned. "You realize you're going to get a pretty hefty bill."

"Yeah. The HarrCo part will go on Arnie Bailey's tab."

When Jackson left, Sid checked his answering machine and found a call from Bart Masterson. Before returning it, he dialed Jaz to report on his trip to Ashland City.

"Did you learn anything interesting from Marie about Bobby's past?" he asked.

"Nothing you don't already know. She couldn't think of

anybody who might have reason to make such threats."

"Okay, I think I'd better start spending a little more time on Arnie Bailey's case. We'll have to play the Lewisville card come Monday."

"Back to your old stomping grounds?"

"It's almost unbelievable, but I still have a few friends around there. I'd like to turn you loose on Bronson Fradkin."

"The lawyer?"

"Yeah. You'll have a much better chance of getting something out of him than I would. I'll drive us down."

"In the truck?"

Sid laughed. "We'll take the car this time."

"I'll put it on my calendar," Jaz said.

"By the way, what was Marie's response to last night?"

"Oh, God. She's been in a tailspin since I told her the full story. I've thought about bringing Bobby and Connie and Little Bob over here to stay a few days."

"Might not be a bad idea. You may have to hog-tie him, though."

Jaz gave a loud sigh. "I'm going to have to do something. I don't want to go through another morning like this one."

"Sounds like a real bummer. Last night was bad enough."

"Have you heard what happened to the Felons game after we bugged out early?" Jaz asked.

The office had been dark, the door locked, when they arrived back in Madison. Sid glanced at the number on his desk pad. "I had a call from Bart on the answering machine when I got here. I'll return it and see what happened."

"Give him my apologies, will you?"

"Don't worry about it. They understand."

After he hung up, Sid was about to call Bart when the phone rang.

"Mr. Chance?" It was a casual male voice.

"This is Sid Chance."

"I hear you're looking for people who used to work for Auto Parts Rehabbers in Ashland City."

His pulse kicked up a beat. "That's right."

The caller ID listed an Atlanta number. Perhaps it was someone visiting Nashville with an Atlanta cell phone?

"I happen to know a guy who was involved in the operation back around 1994 and 1995," the man said. "His name is Gordon Gracey."

"Do you know where I can find him?"

"He's in Nashville. Try All-Brand Parts on Lebanon Road."

Was this too good to be true, Sid wondered? "Did you get my name from the newspaper guy in Ashland City?"

"No."

"Where did you hear that I was looking for former Auto Parts employees?"

The man laughed. "Via the grapevine."

"How do you know Gracey?"

"We go back a long way. That's enough to say."

Sid was about to ask the caller's name when he heard a click and the line went dead. He did a quick check on the number and found it was a prepaid phone purchased in Atlanta. He recalled Jackson's comment about his suspicions regarding an Atlanta PI but couldn't figure how that would tie in.

He looked in the phone book and found All-Brand Parts in Donelson, a suburb near Nashville International Airport. Like most of the city, this area had seen its share of change over the past few years. The core of the community, however, looked about the same, with clusters of small businesses along Lebanon Road where it intersected with McGavock Pike. Judging by the street address, Sid figured that was the location of the All-Brand store, an automotive parts retailer.

Face-to-face encounters were always preferable to phone calls. He decided to follow up with Bart Masterson, though, before heading for Donelson. He found the homicide detective at his office on Trinity Lane.

"I thought you were off today, Bart."

"I might get off once in a while if people around this town would quit killing each other."

"What this time? Another drug shooting?"

"Had a drive-by on Gallatin Road. Twenty-year-old student at the Auto Diesel College. A witness got the license number. We picked up two kids, one sixteen, one eighteen."

Sid pulled a drawer open, propped his feet on it. "Having any luck with Mr. Thirty-eight Five-shot?"

"Crime scene boys didn't find a thing at the park. It looked like the killer stopped on a graveled area beside the road. Didn't leave any marks. We placed the victim at a beer joint in East Nashville late that night, but nobody saw him leave."

"Hear anything else about Marrowbone Road?"

"They got a little bit of a tire impression. The ground was soft around there. It appeared to be from a tire used on luxury cars. I talked to the cousin you told me about down in Rutherford County. He says he hasn't had much contact with Larry Irwin in the last couple of years. North Precinct detectives are questioning people around Ashland City."

"Got anything to link the two cases?"

"Yeah. The TBI lab said the bullets found in both victims were fired from the same gun. That's the only reason I'm able to get information out of North."

Sid often wondered how many crimes went unsolved because of the lack of cooperation between rival law enforcement groups. He was familiar with the Tennessee Bureau of Investigation crime lab, though, and wasn't surprised that they could link both victims to the same weapon. "What kind of gun?" he asked.

"A Smith and Wesson Model 642."

"Isn't that the revolver they came out with a few years ago to mark S. and W.'s hundred and fiftieth anniversary?"

"Yeah, it's a light-weight snub-nose. It was fired at close range in both cases."

"That sounds ominous. Have the newshounds jumped onto the serial killer angle yet?"

"No!" Bart almost shouted, then softened his voice. "And I shouldn't have said what I did. Don't breathe a word of this,

Sid. We don't intend to release the TBI findings just yet."

"No problem. I suppose your next move is to try and find a common denominator."

"We need to bore in a lot deeper on both of the dead guys."

"Good luck. Say, what happened last night? Everybody was gone when Jaz and I got back."

Bart's voice took on a note of annoyance. "Jack's ex called with some cockamamie sob story and he left. He might as well marry that gal again the way he caters to her. The Judge pulled out his handkerchief and started blowing. Said he felt like he might be catching a cold, so we folded up and went home. Mitch promised to take the pile of quarters to Meals on Wheels Monday. What happened with Jaz's problem?"

Sid told him about confronting Bobby with no success.

"It sounds like a criminal case," Bart said, "but if he won't cooperate, it would be difficult to pursue."

"I agree."

"I'd say he was into something pretty deep, though. She'd better get that boy straightened out before Cheatham County finds itself stuck with another homicide."

"Jaz talked about bringing them to her house until she can figure out what's going on. I may have to help her pound some sense into his head."

"Well, if you need any help from me, you know where to call."

20

THE ALL-BRAND Parts store occupied a building on Lebanon Road just beyond McGavock Pike. An unimpressive two-lane street, McGavock traveled north through a heavily-populated residential section that included the stately McGavock home known as Two Rivers Mansion, started just before the outset of the Civil War.

Sid parked in front of the store, strolled in with the casual air of a weekend shopper, and stopped at the checkout counter.

"I'm looking for Gordon Gracey," he said to a slim clerk with wavy hair.

"I saw him a few minutes ago." The young man craned his neck, looking around the store. "He may be in his office."

"Where's the office?"

"I'll call him. What's your name?"

"Sidney Chance."

The clerk picked up the phone, punched a number and spoke to someone. He turned back to Sid. "He'll be with you in a few minutes. You can wait over at the service counter, if you'd like."

The clerk pointed to a few barstools in front of a long counter at the rear of the store. Sid strolled back and slid onto an unoccupied stool. He leaned an elbow on the counter and gazed about at the merchandise displays. Judging by the steady flow of customers, the store did a good business. From the office mention, he took it that Gordon Gracey was the manager.

"Mr. Chance?"

Sid looked around to find a stocky man with black hair that had the clipped look of a toupee. His ingratiating smile appeared to be no more genuine.

"You must be Gordon Gracey." Sid held out his hand. "Nice to meet you."

"What can I do for you, Mr. Chance?"

"Nice store you have here. Isn't it new?"

"We've been open for about six months."

"From the looks of the customers, you have a good location. How long have you been with All-Brand Parts?"

"I started with the company about ten years ago, worked my way up. Why?"

Sid leaned against the counter. "That must have been shortly after Auto Parts Rehabbers in Ashland City closed."

A look of annoyance replaced the smile. "I have no idea what you're talking about."

"I was told you worked there."

"Who told you that?"

"He said he was an old acquaintance."

"Who?"

Sid spread his hands. "I didn't get his name, Mr. Gracey, but he said you worked there back in the middle nineties."

Gracey motioned to Sid and turned to the door he had come out. "Let's go in my office."

A small room in the back of the store, it had space for little more than a wooden desk, a file cabinet, and a couple of chairs. Gracey sat behind the desk while Sid took a chair facing him. The wall held a display of colorful posters from a variety of parts manufacturers and distributors. A snowy winter scene above the month of November on the calendar didn't reflect the experience of recent winters in Nashville, where measurable snow was little more than a distant memory.

"So what's your interest in my employment history?" Gracey asked, his tone less cordial.

Sid handed him a business card. "I'm investigating a situation at the old Auto Parts Rehabbers plant."

The Surest Poison

"So what's it to me?"

"The ground behind the plant was soaked with trichloroethylene. It's a dangerous chemical that causes lots of health problems. We've determined that it happened back during the time Auto Parts Rehabbers occupied the plant. What can you tell me about how it got there?"

Gracey tugged at his ear and shifted his eyes to the side, rumpling his brow as if in total ignorance. "How would I know anything about that?"

"You worked there."

"Yeah, I know, some stranger told you. And you believed him."

Sid had been exposed to a world of lies during his career in law enforcement, some subtle, most blatant. The body language he saw came through loud and clear. "You're right, Mr. Gracey. I believed what the man said, and it's time to cut the bullshit."

Gracey folded his arms and sat there in silent defiance.

Sid stared into his eyes as though able to see into the dark recesses of his brain. He continued to stare until the man looked away. He knew he had him.

Gracey's chest sagged as he seemed to deflate. "Yeah," he said, "I worked there."

"What was your job?"

"I was the quality control inspector."

"What did that involve?"

"You look like an intelligent guy, Chance. What do you suppose I did? I checked reconditioned parts to be sure they were ready for the market." He leaned back in his chair. A smirk had slipped across his face.

Let him have his fun, Sid thought. Maybe I'll get the last laugh. "Did you work under Pete Rackard or Tony Decker?"

"Rackard. He was in charge of production."

"What did Decker do?"

"He was general manager. I think he was part owner, too."

"Let's get back to the trichloroethylene that was found out

back. It's obvious that you must know how it got there."

"I don't know anything about TCE. There was none around where I worked."

Sid watched him closely. The answers sounded casual, but his hand moved frequently to stroke his face or pull on his ear. The tension showed in a look that had turned brooding.

"And you never noticed that smelly, discolored area out behind the plant?"

"I don't remember anything like that." He looked away as he spoke, a classic symptom of a lie.

"When was the last time you talked to Tony Decker?"

His eyes made an abrupt shift as he straightened up in his chair. "I haven't talked to Decker in years. I heard he left the state."

"Where'd you hear that?"

"I don't remember. It's been a good while ago." He glanced at his watch. "This has been a busy day for us, Mr. Chance, and I have a lot to get done. Sorry to rush you off."

He stood behind the desk.

Sid rose also and fixed him with an icy stare. "Mr. Gracey, I think you're lying through your teeth. I think you know about the TCE and you probably have an idea where Tony Decker is. The State Department of Conservation and Environment is also investigating this affair. If your memory improves, give me a call. Otherwise I may be back with some state inspectors."

Gracey listened in silence, his lips clamped tightly.

Sid knew he'd have to run a thorough background check on the man. Maybe it would produce something useful for prying information out of him later.

For now, though, his last laugh had turned out to be little more than a feeble grin. He left with nothing new

21

STYMIED, HE returned home, put on a pot of coffee, strolled into the living room, and plopped down into his favorite recliner. He had a gut feeling that Tony Decker was hiding somewhere just out of sight. He could sense his presence, but he couldn't touch him. Before long the guy would make a misstep, Sid thought. They all did sooner or later. Maybe there were a few criminal masterminds around, but most of those lived between the pages of crime novels. The majority of criminals were dumb. It was a matter of watching until they showed a fatal flaw. Trouble was, in this case, he didn't have the luxury of time to wait and watch.

Sid walked into the kitchen, poured a cup of coffee, prepared to return to his thoughts. Then the telephone rang.

"This is Herschel Owens, Larry Irwin's cousin."

Sid slid into a chair at the table. "I was shocked to hear about Larry's death, Mr. Owens."

"It gave us quite a jolt, too. We hadn't been close in recent years, but we were happy that he seemed to be doing well. I helped make his funeral arrangements."

"Have you learned anything about what he'd been doing lately?" Sid asked.

"That's why I called. I heard from one of Larry's close friends. It was a young fellow who lived in Ashland City until a year or so ago. He knew we were related."

"What did he have to say?"

"He talked to Larry Wednesday evening, the night he died. He remembered Larry mentioning a phone call that had him pretty disturbed. Larry didn't say what it was about, but his friend got the impression somebody had been harassing him. Larry said he'd thought about calling the police."

"Do you have the friend's name and phone number?"

"Hold on and let me check the caller ID," Owens said. A few moments later he was back with a number in Clarksville, a city on the Kentucky border near the Fort Campbell Army post. "I don't have a last name, but he called himself Reggie."

Sid had been on the go since his run early that morning. He was beginning to feel the effects of having slept little the night before. After a couple of jaw-steching yawns, he decided to relax a few minutes before calling Jaz. He wanted to tell her about his trip to Ashland City and the Gordon Gracey interview. He also needed to contact Larry Irwin's friend, Reggie, but he made the mistake of closing his eyes to ease some of the tension that had been building over his lack of success with the case. The warm air pumping up through the floor vent nearby proved more soothing than a rocking cradle. A few minutes later he was sound asleep.

JAZ SPENT MUCH of Saturday afternoon trying to console Marie Wallace. The elderly grandmother, distraught after hearing that Little Bob had been snatched off the street, quickly used up a box of tissues. The only solution Jaz could come up with was the one she had mentioned to Sid—bring the young man and his family to stay at the LeMieux house. She contacted the local Welcome Traveler Store manager. He agreed to provide a van to transport the Wallace family, their clothes, and whatever else they chose to bring along.

Since Bobby still refused to answer his telephone, Jaz loaded John and Marie into her car and drove to Ashland City. After several chilly days, Saturday had turned out pleasant, with temperatures in the upper sixties. Slanted rays of the afternoon sun cast a golden glow over the neighborhood as Jaz parked in front of the Wallace house. From where Bobby's car sat in the driveway, she was sure it hadn't been moved.

The Surest Poison

As she followed her passengers to the front door, Jaz took a careful look at the nearby houses. Cars or pickup trucks sat in most of the driveways. Down the block a couple of kids in short sleeves rode in circles on their bicycles. Her red Lexus was the only car parked along the street. It appeared as normal as any residential neighborhood on a warm fall afternoon.

Bobby answered the door and, with considerable reluctance, invited his grandparents in. Jaz followed them and took a chair in the living room. Marie hugged Little Bob, then sat on the sofa beside her husband.

Bobby flashed an insincere smile. "You're looking good, Granny." He spoke like a man trying to appear nonchalant while feeling the exact opposite. "Everything going okay for you?"

She gave him an icy stare. "No, Bobby, everything is not going okay. You've had me almost in a state of panic."

"I'm fine," he said, twisting his hands. "Everything's cool. Really. There's no need to worry."

"My grandson is kidnapped on the street and hauled all over the place by strangers and there's no need to worry? Everything's cool?"

"Nobody hurt him."

"This time."

John Wallace was a large, gentle man who seldom expressed his views. When he did, he demanded attention with a deep, sonorous voice reminiscent of James Earl Jones. Graduating from high school in Pennsylvania shortly after the end of World War II, he bucked the trend and headed south, where he met and married Marie. A public school maintenance man before attracting Jaques LeMieux's attention, he had always taken whatever steps were necessary to see that his family got the care they needed.

"Bobby, you're putting your family in danger," John said in a clear, forceful tone. "I don't know what your problem is, but it isn't worth what you're doing to Connie and Little Bob. Your daddy wouldn't have sat by and let this happen, and neither will your Granny and me. Miss Jasmine has offered to let you stay with us at the mansion until you can get this straightened out. The three of you will be safe there."

"But . . . but . . . " Bobby stammered.

"No buts, Bobby," Marie said in a voice as firm as a judge's verdict. She turned to Jaz. "Tell him what you've done."

"There's a van coming from my company to take you and whatever you want to bring along."

"What about my car?"

"One of the drivers from the van will bring it. You and Connie can use one of the guest rooms, Little Bob another. Or you can stay in John and Marie's old house out back. This way we'll know all of you are safe until we can work out a solution to this dilemma you're facing."

Bobby tried more protests, but his grandparents and Jaz had an answer for everything. *What about my job?* Jaz said his boss told her he had vacation coming. He could take some time off. *But Little Bob doesn't need to miss school.* He wouldn't. A large uniformed guard would deliver him to the schoolhouse door and pick him up in the afternoon.

Connie added her insistent voice to the chorus. The former high school cheerleader had also been a candidate for the debate team. Her arguments were clear and decisive—she and Little Bob were ready to move. Bobby's look soon made it clear he knew the game was over. Democracy would rule. He'd been outvoted.

Jaz summoned the van crew while the Wallaces packed enough clothes for a few days, and Little Bob gathered his toys.

The caravan arrived a little after six o'clock and pulled up to the sprawling mansion, which was bathed in the ghostly glow of floodlights at the corners. They parked Bobby's car in front of the smaller house in back and unloaded the bags. At first Bobby insisted he wanted to stay there, but after the Welcome Traveler Stores crew left, Marie convinced him it would be better in the main house where they would have access to more bathrooms and her large kitchen.

22

THE RINGING SOUND woke Sid with a start. He reached over and grabbed the phone from the table beside the recliner.

"Hello."

"Did I catch you at a bad time?" Jaz asked.

"I don't know. What time is it?"

"Nearly seven. Did I wake you?"

He pushed himself up from the chair. "Yes, thanks. I need to get moving. I don't know why I dozed off. I sat down here a couple of hours ago with a cup of coffee, closed my eyes, and that was it."

"I haven't had time for napping. I just did what we talked about this morning."

"What's that?"

"I brought Bobby and Connie and Little Bob over here. Bobby wasn't very happy about it. He raised some strenuous objections, but John and Marie wouldn't back down."

"How long do you think you can keep them there?"

"Long enough to find out what the devil his problem is, I hope."

"Any idea how to do that?"

Her voice took on a lighter note. "I thought I could count on you to come up with something. How would you like to join us tomorrow for one of Marie's signature Sunday dinners?"

Sid had heard her talk about Marie's cooking, but he'd never been to her house. "I haven't had an invitation to a home-cooked dinner in ages, but I can't promise any miracle solutions to loosening Bobby's tongue."

"I'm sure you'll think of something. Mike said I should have faith in you."

"Mike's a flatterer. Sometimes it takes more than faith. I thought I had made a real discovery this afternoon, but it turned out another might-have-been."

He told her about his interview with Gordon Gracey at the All-Brands Parts store.

"You think he lied about everything?"

"Maybe not everything, but we'll have to do a thorough check on him. I'm certain he knows a lot more than he let on. I also had a call from Hershel Owens, Larry Irwin's cousin. He'd heard from a friend of Larry's in Clarksville I need to talk to."

"At least you're getting some leads. Did you ever get through to Bart?"

"Yeah. He wasn't too happy about last night. I think it's just as well we left." He related the situation with Jack Post and the Judge.

"I'd have to agree with Bart," Jaz said. "Jack seems to have a real dilemma. What about the homicides? Did Bart mention them?"

He told her what the TBI lab had found and Bart's caution to keep it away from the news media.

"You know I'm not a big fan of the media. They haven't been too kind to my company over gas prices. Tell you what, I'll get onto Gracey and check out his pedigree. You can follow up on Larry Irwin. Don't forget to give some thought to how we might handle Bobby."

Sid hung up the phone and glanced at the clock. Seven-fifteen. Might as well give this Reggie guy in Clarksville a call, he thought. He dialed the area code 931 number and an answering machine picked up. "The University Automotive Maintenance Shop is closed. Please call back during normal business hours. We are open Monday through Friday—"

He ended the call. The only alternative would be to go through the school's personnel office, but they would be closed as well. No, not personnel. Human Services. He always got a chuckle out of those modern PC designations. It made him wonder, did they also have Inhuman Services, maybe Robotic Services? Anyway, talking to Reggie was out until Monday.

He debated whether to head out to one of the Rivergate area's many restaurants, but on a Saturday night it would be a mob scene, with long waiting lines. He checked the fridge. He found lettuce, a bit wilted around the edges. Also several dabs of leftover vegetables, though he recalled seeing them in the same spot several days ago, prior to his trip to the cabin. Something long, wrapped in foil, caught his eye. No doubt it was the remains of mahi mahi he had cooked a day or so before he left. That would have to go for sure.

He gave up and decided to do the restaurant scene. Before he could head out to the garage, though, Judge Thackston called.

"How's the cold?" Sid asked."

Thackston grunted. "Bad news travels fast."

"I talked to Bart earlier. He told me about Jack's summons and said you might be catching a cold."

"I've been taking zinc pills and vitamins and lots of other useless remedies all day. If it's any consolation, I doubt the condition is terminal."

Though he hadn't known Thackston for long, he had noticed that the Judge usually tended to take a dark view of things. "That's nice to hear."

"Thanks, I think. How did the trip out to Ashland City go? I trust Jazmine got everything resolved."

"Not exactly resolved. She finally took things into her own hands though."

He told how Jaz had arranged to take Bobby Wallace and his family to her house for a few days.

"That young woman is always full of surprises," the Judge said. "However, I digress. The real reason for my call is a conversation I had this afternoon with the attorney friend I mentioned. The one who was once in practice with Bronson Fradkin."

"Something new on the shifty barrister?"

"Not exactly."

"What then?"

"He mentioned a name you used last night—Decker."

"Tony Decker?"

"Trent Decker. It sounded close enough that it caught my attention. It seems that Fradkin represents him in a lawsuit involving his business, Dixie Seals. My friend is the lawyer for the plaintiff."

Could Trent Decker be a brother? Or had Tony changed his name? "What kind of company is Dixie Seals?"

"They make door and window gaskets for automobiles. The plant is located off I-24 out near the county line. My friend tells me they do a good business with auto plants in the area. You had mentioned something about an automobile parts operation. I thought this might be of interest."

"Thanks for the info, Judge." Sid's mind started spinning. With Trent in the auto parts business, there were all sorts of possibilities. "I'll check out Mr. Decker."

He drove to a popular seafood restaurant not far from his office. The place was crowded, but by now the waiting list had dwindled. He found a solo table with no problem. A couple of acquaintances stopped briefly to chat, but he spent most of his time thinking about where to turn next. He had picked up some techniques skip tracers used to get information by phone, using what was known in the trade as "pretexting." It involved pretending to be the person whose information you were after. If Jaz and her computer couldn't come up with what he needed, he would use the phone to chase down some leads.

It was close to nine when he left the restaurant. He stopped by his office to see how the remote surveillance system worked. He logged onto his computer and punched in the code to access his control panel. He activated the front view

The Surest Poison

camera and watched as the picture filled the screen. With no streetlight nearby, the area had a ghostly look. A small tree in the distance resembled a shadowy scarecrow. He checked the rear view and both sides. All worked fine.

He detoured by the restroom to get rid of some of the coffee he'd drunk during dinner. When he returned to his office, he checked the computer again, fascinated by the new surveillance system.

He clicked a button on the screen. As his front yard appeared, the lights flashed on.

A familiar face stared up at the camera, eyes glaring. Scarface from Thursday night. He wore black pants and a black jacket. The shocked look on his face disappeared as he turned away and hustled out of view.

Sid shut down the computer, dashed out to his car, and raced toward his house. He slowed on reaching his street. He kept his eyes moving from side to side, like watching a ping-pong match. He saw no cars except those parked in driveways. He spotted no one on foot.

When he turned into his driveway, it triggered the motion detector and the lights flashed on. He circled around the back and hit the garage door opener. Easing the car in beside his truck, he glanced about the garage but saw nothing that sparked any concern.

As he stepped out of the car, two soft popping noises froze him.

The sharp clang of metal against metal followed instantly.

Having fired suppressed weapons, he recognized the sound made by a silenced gun. What had they hit? He ducked beside the car. He heard what sounded like air escaping from tires. If somebody was shooting at him, he realized, he'd already be dead.

He reached over to the door opener controls and switched off the light. Hugging the wall, he moved toward the open door. The eve lights angled outward toward the lawn, leaving the garage mostly in darkness. When he reached the back, the faint glow was enough to show the pickup's rear wheels resting on a flat bed of rubber.

Sid stared out across the darkened lawn but could see no one. The shooter may have slipped through the yard behind to the next street or escaped along the riverbank. He had no doubt it was Scarface. It made him mad as hell. Shooting his truck was almost as big a sin as shooting at him. He took another careful look around, then accepted there was nothing he could do about it at the moment.

Sid closed the overhead door, entered the house, and shut off the alarm. He walked into the living room and turned on the TV. Switching to camera monitor mode, he watched the succession of pictures showing the view from each side of the house. The lights were off now. All quiet.

The phone rang.

He picked it up and was about to answer when a voice he recognized as scarface said, "You're lucky, Chance. This time it was just tires."

The line went dead. He looked at the unfamiliar number on the caller ID. He'd check it out, though most likely it was another untraceable phone. He could call Metro and have them recover the bullets, but after striking the steel core of the wheels, they would likely be too disfigured to be of any forensic value. He'd search the backyard for clues tomorrow in the daylight.

Jaz called a little more than an hour later. "It appears that your All-Brand Parts man is a soul brother of the other rehabbers," she said. "Another ex-con."

"I suspected as much." Sid glanced at the clock. "What are you doing working so late?"

"I find maneuvering around with the computer a lot more fun than getting caught in the Wallace's verbal crossfire. I've also discovered I'm not at my best trying to entertain a nine-year-old boy."

"I'm sure I wouldn't be any good at it. So what's Gracey's background?"

The Surest Poison

"Shoplifting, petty theft in his early days. He's been straight since Auto Parts Rehabbers. I'm getting the feeling that your sheriff's sergeant had it right about the company's employees. Everybody seems to have a criminal record."

"I'll have to find a way to use that."

"Did you get in touch with Larry Irwin's friend in Clarksville?"

"No, but Judge Thackston called me with an interesting tip." He told her about Trent Decker and Dixie Seals.

"That man definitely needs looking into. Why don't I do another sweep and see what turns up?"

"Okay. Have you been able to get anything on getting Pete Rackard's phone logs from Friday night?"

"My telephone contact doesn't work weekends. I'll get onto it first thing Monday morning."

"You keep this up I'll have to pay overtime."

She laughed. "This isn't work, Sid. I thrive on challenges."

Knowing her background, he wasn't surprised. "Okay," he said. "Let's see how many challenges you thrive on tomorrow when we tackle Bobby Wallace."

"Spoilsport." She made a hissing sound. "Incidentally, have you heard anything else out of your friends from Thursday night?"

"Yeah. About an hour ago."

"Really? What happened?"

He told her.

"My God, Sid. They shot out your truck tires? Did they shoot at you?"

"No, it was just a threat. A warning. But if I get hold of that guy—"

"And you didn't call Metro? You should at least tell Bart about it."

"He's got enough trouble on his hands."

"What do you plan to do?"

"I'll be carrying my nine-millimeter Sig wherever I go until this thing is solved."

23

AS SOON AS Sid finished his morning run, he headed for the backyard and began a methodical search. The wind was not as strong as during the past few days, but it ruffled the leaves enough that any small item dropped by an intruder could have been hidden. He spent a couple of hours criss-crossing the area and kicking leaves to no avail.

Back in the garage, he surveyed the damage to his truck. The tires had a lot of miles on them and were no great loss, but just the thought of what the lowlife had done made him boil. He worked off his anger by dismounting both wheels and tossing them in the trunk of his car.

He took a shower, sat down with the Sunday newspaper, and ate breakfast. The TCE spill and its aftermath rated extensive coverage, but there was only one small mention of Auto Parts Rehabbers. A reporter quoted Attorney Arnold Bailey as saying a preliminary investigation indicated this was the company responsible for the pollution. The newspaper was unable to unearth any further information about the firm.

After breakfast, Sid sat at the computer in his home office and checked out the phone number from Scarface's call the night before. As expected, it turned out to be untraceable. He cursed himself for failing to get more information out of the pair while they stood on his front porch Thursday night.

He drove around looking for two new truck tires, an exercise that only increased his anger at scarface and his boss. He discovered it was almost impossible to find a place open that sold tires on a Sunday morning. No doubt his mother would have told him it served him right. He should have been in church rather than out shopping for tires.

He arrived at the LeMeiux gate around one, dressed in an open-collar white shirt and a brown plaid wool jacket. When John Wallace opened the barrier, he drove until the mansion came into view. The house sat on a small knoll that likely would have provided picturesque views from the upper story windows except for all the towering oak and elm trees that surrounded it. The mansion looked like an import from the Louisiana countryside with its four gables highlighting the second floor roof and a wood-floored veranda that crossed the front and ran halfway back on both sides. Jaz met him at the door with a Chessy-cat grin.

"The background I unearthed on Trent Decker is quite a shocker," she said. "Come on back to my office."

Crowded bookshelves stretched around the room. A large metal globe mounted in rich, dark wood sat in one corner. A wheeled ladder on a track stood beside a wall of books, reminding Sid that she had spoken of her dad as a short man. He would have needed the ladder to reach the upper shelves.

"Take a look," she said, pulling a chair next to hers in front of the computer monitor, a twenty-four-inch screen. "One of my most reliable sources just came through. I haven't printed it out yet."

She clicked the mouse a couple of times and brought up a page headed "Trent Decker — Age 43." Sid leaned forward and caught a whiff of Jaz's perfume. She looked particularly elegant today. Concentrating his attention on the screen, however, he read:

"Trent is the twin brother of Tony Decker, who served time in Tennessee for armed robbery. Their father, Virgil Decker, ran off to South America with Trent when the boys were babies. Tony's mother raised him in Memphis. After the father died in Argentina in 1996, Trent came back to the States. He settled in Nashville and bought a five-year-old business named Dixie Seals. The firm has done quite well. Trent now lives in a fashionable section of Brentwood. Tony's location could not be established."

Sid sat back and looked at Jaz. "So what do you make of Trent Decker's relationship to Bronson Fradkin?"

"Quite a coincidence, isn't it?"

"If you believe in such things. I'd say it indicates Trent has been in touch with his brother."

"Ergo, he should be able to put us in touch with said brother."

"Correct. It's a pretty day out. Maybe we should take a little Sunday afternoon drive and pay a visit to Mr. Decker."

Jaz turned away from the computer. "Agreed. And I know something you should do tonight," she said.

"What's that?"

She took a newspaper clipping from her desk and handed it to him. "There's a TV program on Channel 8 that includes a biography of the poet you were named after."

"Sidney Lanier?"

"Right. Have you read much about him?"

"Not in a long time. Maybe I'll learn something."

First there was Marie's bountiful Sunday dinner to indulge in. They ate at the large family table in the dining room, set with the LeMieux's fine china and silverware. The menu was traditional Southern, fried chicken, mashed potatoes, green beans, corn, peas, a green salad. Chocolate pie with a thick meringue topped it off.

After Jaz all but ordered her to, Marie joined them at the table. Sid tried to draw Bobby into the conversation with little success, sparking nothing but one-word replies. With all the questions from Little Bob and his great-grandparents, Sid became the center of attention. He told tales about his tenure as chief of police in Lewisville, including some of the dumb things criminals did.

"One of the funniest cases I remember involved a young man and his girlfriend. They wanted to get married, but he didn't have enough money for a honeymoon. He had seen bank robberies on TV and thought it looked easy. He borrowed a pellet gun he thought looked pretty fierce and drove to the bank. Before he went in, he remembered they always handed the teller a note. He looked around and saw an envelope on the seat. He grabbed it and printed 'HAND ME YOUR MONEY!' Then he went inside and walked up to the teller. He gave her the note and showed her his gun. He scooped up the stacks of bills and shoved them into his jacket, then ran out. As soon as he turned around, the teller looked at the front of the envelope. There was his name and address. It was a bank envelope with a letter saying his account was overdrawn."

After they all laughed, Connie asked, "Did you retire from that job?"

Sid frowned. "Afraid not. I resigned."

"Why?" Little Bob asked.

Connie scolded him. "Don't be so nosy. He doesn't have to tell you why he did anything."

"No, it's a fair question." Sid looked down at the boy. "It might be a good lesson for you, Little Bob. Be very careful who you get involved with. One of my officers had arrested a young man for possession of drugs. I was more concerned about where the drugs were coming from, so I offered to go easy on him if he would help us catch the dealer."

"What's a dealer?" the youngster asked.

"A man who sells drugs. They're bad folks who get teenagers and other people in trouble. Don't ever have anything to do with them. Anyway, the man we had arrested agreed to cooperate. I didn't want to put him in any danger, so I asked him to tell the dealer he had a friend who wanted to buy some crack—that's crack cocaine. Bad drugs. We set up a time and place for him to deliver the stuff to me."

"Weren't you afraid he would recognize you?" Connie asked.

"I had worked with some theater people in town, and they created a great disguise. My own mother wouldn't have recognized me. I met the guy in the parking lot behind a restaurant. I had a couple of my officers out of sight for backup. As soon as I walked up to the man, he handed me a fat envelope. I hadn't expected to get drugs delivered that way. I looked at him and said, 'What's this?' He smiled and said, 'The five thousand bucks you asked for, Chief. Now keep your cops off my back.'"

"A setup," John Wallace said in his deep bass.

"Exactly. The sheriff and several deputies swarmed around us. Turned out they had wired the dealer and recorded what he said on tape. There I stood like an idiot with an envelope full of hundred-dollar bills in my hand."

"What did they do?" Connie asked.

"They put me under arrest and charged me with taking a bribe from the dealer. I had been causing trouble for some of the county bigwigs, and they'd been looking for a way to get rid of me. It seems the man we arrested had confessed to the dealer about our plan. The dealer went to the sheriff with a tale that I had asked for a bribe. Instead of checking into the guy, the sheriff jumped at the chance to get back at me."

"Sid was exonerated," Jaz said. "He had said nothing incriminating on the tape, and his officers stood behind him. The dealer and the man they had arrested for possession both had records, including lying under oath. The district attorney threw out the case."

Sid wiped a hand across his face as though attempting to rid himself of a painful memory. "The publicity was devastating. I didn't feel I could accomplish anything further down there, so I resigned and came back to Nashville."

Marie spoke with a solemn face. "I appreciate what you did and the way you handled it." She turned and looked straight at Bobby. "I just hope my grandson will find some of the same courage to stand up against whatever he's facing."

The young man averted his eyes and said nothing.

Sid looked across the table at him. "She's right, Bobby. If you don't stand up against these people, it will haunt you the rest of your life."

"But I'll still have my family," he said. He got up and left the room.

The Surest Poison

IT WAS AROUND three o'clock when Sid and Jaz left in her Lexus for Brentwood, which straddled the county line a few miles up Franklin Road. Trent Decker's home sat in a neat subdivision with designer street lamps and patterned brick crosswalks. A large single story structure with a high-peaked roof that likely meant a cathedral ceiling, the house was brick except for stonework around the entrance. Jaz parked in the broad driveway, and they walked across to the front door.

After Sid rang the bell several times, Jaz threw up her hands. "I guess we should have called first."

He gave a final rap with his knuckles. "We'll hit him tomorrow morning at the business."

As he was turning away, he heard the door open. Looking back, he saw a tall, handsome man with sandy hair, a smile tugging at the corners of his mouth. The man wore jeans and a white dress shirt with thin blue stripes. When he tilted his head, Sid noticed his hair was pulled back into a lush ponytail.

"Hi," he said. "Were you looking for me?"

"Trent Decker?" Sid asked.

"Right. Are you the new folks up at 2231?"

"No, we're trying to locate your brother, Tony. We have some information for him."

Decker gave him a curious look. "You know, I haven't heard anything of my brother in years."

"Not a letter, a phone call?"

"Nothing. Not a lot of people know about my brother. How did you happen to know?"

"We don't know him personally. But a friend familiar with your background suggested you could help us find him."

"Then you must know I grew up in South America. When I came back, my brother resented the fact that I had done so well down there. And he wasn't real happy that neither my Dad or me had made any contact over the years. I planned to let him take part in the business here after I took it over, but he didn't want anything to do with me."

"Do you have any idea where he might be?"

"Nope. He left about the time I bought Dixie Seals. He never said good-bye or good riddance. One day he was here, the next day he was gone."

Sid pulled out a business card and handed it to him. "If you should get any inkling of where we might find him, I'd appreciate your giving us a call. It's very important."

Decker looked at the card. "Private investigator. What did Tony do?"

"I'm not sure that he did anything, but we'd like to talk to him."

Sid thanked Decker and walked back to the car with Jaz. She paused as she started backing out of the driveway and looked at Sid.

"I don't like that man," she said. "I watched him carefully as you talked. Something about the way he acted, a bit too blasé for the circumstances. Other than 'What did Tony do?' he never asked what we wanted with his brother, what sort of information we had for him. I had the feeling he knew perfectly well what was going on right from the start."

Sid shrugged. "I didn't read him quite the way you did, but you may be right."

"I think he knows a lot more than he admitted. If he and his brother were all that estranged, how did he get linked up with Bronson Fradkin?"

"Good point."

"We need to keep a close eye on Mr. Trent Decker. He gave my car a thorough going over the minute he stepped out. And what was he doing with that ponytail, trying to look like a rock star or a fugitive from Music Row?"

Sid noted the dour look on her face as she spoke. He wondered if some of it stemmed from the way Decker had ignored her during the conversation. Jaz was not a woman to be dismissed without peril.

24

IT WAS AROUND dusk, the sky stained with broad strokes of dark red by the fading sunset, but light enough to make out most details on the ground. The black Lincoln cruised up Franklin Road, pulled onto the shoulder, and stopped. With the engine running, the driver stared across at the entrance to the LeMieux estate. He sat there for several minutes, observing the gate and its surroundings, including the picturesque old dry stone wall that ran along the front of the property.

Moving on, he drove toward downtown, swung onto the interstate, and headed north. Twenty-five minutes later, he turned into the parking lot of the building occupied by Chance Investigation Agency. Noting Sid's car parked near the building entrance, he drove past it and took Gallatin Road south to the middle of the Madison business district. He turned onto Neelys Bend Road and followed its curving path through a mixture of old and new houses, past a rehab hospital and two schools. Following the directions provided by his GPS, he turned toward the river on the street where Sid lived. The detective's was the last house on the block. A dull brown pickup truck with two new rear tires sat in the driveway.

The Lincoln turned around at the corner, paused briefly across from Sid Chance's, then drove on.

SID SAT AT HIS DESK, wrapping up an on-line missing person search. The fact that it was Sunday evening made no difference. He had always been a workaholic. During his time in the woods, he often worked from dawn till dusk, then read by candlelight or an oil lantern. He finished the search and returned to his notes on the Auto Parts Rehabbers' case. Thinking back on Jaz's experience with Pete Rackard, he wondered if the auto repair shop owner might be the best prospect for locating Tony Decker. They worked together at the Ashland City plant for around three years. If he could find a way to put pressure on Rackard, maybe he could shake something loose.

He called Bart Masterson.

"You still trying to get Jaz's boy straightened out?" Bart asked.

"We haven't figured out the details of his problem, but we're working on it. Jaz brought him and his family over to her house last night. I had to get back onto my Auto Parts Rehabbers case, though. I'm staring at a short deadline. We found one of the top people, a guy named Pete Rackard, did time for attempted murder before the company came along. In prison, he was a cellmate of Tony Decker, who became the company's general manager."

"Is he in trouble again?"

"Not that I know of. I suspect he was involved in that chemical dump, though. I'd like to lean on him to find out where Decker is. Can you check into whether he's been charged with anything recently?"

"Sure. Give me the info."

Sid read him Rackard's name, address and Social Security number. "I'm heading home. You can call me there."

"Let you know when I have something."

Sid checked his watch and realized he was running late for the show Jaz had alerted him about. It was on the Public TV channel. The program titled "Poets of the Late Nineteenth Century" was in progress when he arrived home. Walt Whitman and Emily Dickinson got the first and foremost coverage, however, so he had missed none of the Lanier story.

The segment began with shots of Macon, Georgia where the poet was born in 1842. A natural musician, he learned to play the flute, violin, organ, piano, and guitar about the time he learned to read. Sid nodded, recalling his mother's insistence that he master the keyboard. He still had a piano but seldom went near it. At nineteen, young Lanier enlisted in the Confederate Army, serving during the Civil War as a scout and in the signal service. Another parallel, thought Sid.

From there, their paths diverged. After working a few years in his father's law office, Lanier abandoned the legal profession to pursue music and literature. He settled in Baltimore, where he played first flute in the Peabody Symphony Orchestra. He also concentrated on his writing there, publishing his most celebrated poem, "The Symphony," in 1875. Sid was familiar with that one. It ended with Ellie Virginia's favorite line from Sidney Lanier:

"Music is Love in search of a word."

The telephone ended Sid's TV watching.

"Mr. Rackard is clean as far as Metro's concerned," Bart said. "However, he's been involved in a couple of scuffles in Franklin. One in 2003, another in 2005. But no jail time."

"Doesn't sound like anything I can hold over his head."

"Sorry. If you can lure him to Nashville, I'll find something to bust him on."

"Thanks. Jaz and I plan to pursue the Lewisville angle tomorrow. Maybe we'll hit on something down there."

"That would make the Judge happy. He thinks you're some kind of miracle worker."

Sid leaned back in the recliner. "I'm afraid I've been a bit short on miracles lately."

"Wouldn't hurt to find one to keep in your hip pocket. Friend of mine from the next county tells me your old sheriff is riding high."

"He's going to fall off his high horse one of these days, and I'd like to be the one to give him the push. Take care, Bart."

Sid hung up the phone and walked into the kitchen to fire up the coffee maker. Monday should be an interesting day.

25

SHORTLY BEFORE nine the next morning, Jaz called Sid at his office.

"I just talked to my telephone man," she said. "He promised to get the information on Rackard's Friday night calls sometime today."

"Great. Did you get Little Bob off to school?"

"It was a hoot. He thought he was a celebrity, having a uniformed escort. We told the school no one else was authorized to pick him up."

"What about Bobby? Did he go to work?"

"No. He called in and arranged to take a few days of vacation. He's still as sullen and agitated as an old wet hen, but Marie fed him, and he's gone out to work with John."

"I've been thinking about your situation there," Sid said, his voice taking a serious turn. "We know the people who threatened Bobby are keeping tabs on him. We have to assume they know you brought him to your house. What if they should decide to come after him there?"

"We'd know if they tried to come through the gate."

"What about a back entrance?"

"There isn't any. The road behind us is pretty far back. There's a fence, and the lawn is full of trees."

"What if they came in on foot?"

"The alarm system would warn us if anybody attempted to break in."

"Have you thought about hiring security guards?"

"What for?"

The Surest Poison

"To patrol your property."

Jaz's sigh sounded a note of agitation. "Wouldn't that be a bit of overkill? If they're watching my house, they know there haven't been any police around for Bobby to talk to."

Sid preferred to err on the side of caution, but he decided to drop it for now. "Are you ready to head for Lewisville?"

"Shouldn't we call ahead to make sure Fradkin isn't in court?"

"They don't hold court in Lewisville on Mondays."

"Okay. I'll be ready by the time you get here."

It would be his first visit to the small town since leaving in disgrace nearly four years ago. Disgrace might seem too strong a word since the district attorney had vindicated him, dropping all charges. He thought the term appropriate, though, since his reputation had been tarnished almost beyond repair. People tended to focus on the original headlines rather than the less dramatic story of his exoneration. He had learned recently that a few old friends and supporters had wanted to invite him back but couldn't find him. This wound would take a long time to heal. Today, however, the trip was all business.

He picked up Jaz and headed down I-65 to Columbia. There they took a state highway west through rolling farmland, now bare of crops. A few miles beyond the two-lane memorial highway that tracked the historic route of the 1800's trail known as the Natchez Trace, clusters of homes began to appear. A little farther on they saw a Lewisville welcome sign, followed by one of billboard proportions that proclaimed:

"Support Law & Order. Re-Elect Sheriff Zachary."

"Is that your old nemesis?" Jaz asked.

"Yep, looks like Zack is back."

Beyond the grounds of a new high school, older houses lined the highway. That soon gave way to commercial buildings, the usual dotting of fast food restaurants and service stations, and, at the center of town, a typical square housing the old red brick courthouse. A statue of the famed explorer,

Meriwether Lewis, stood on a pedestal in front of the building.

"Where was your office?" Jaz asked.

"In the City Hall. It's just up the street off the square."

He circled the courthouse and pointed out a couple of white patrol cars parked on the side street.

"Where do we start?" she asked.

"One of my oldest friends runs a restaurant down in the next block. It's almost lunchtime. Let's stop in there and get a reading on the community's pulse."

He found a spot in front of a real estate office with a two-hour parking sign beside it and pulled in.

"Can you get a parking ticket fixed around here?" Jaz asked with a grin.

"If you're a friend of Sheriff Zack. I think he owns the current police chief."

Behind a big sign proclaiming City Café, the restaurant had a dining area floored with white tile squares and a lunch counter at one side. As soon as they walked in, a chubby woman with Shirley Temple curls ran out from behind the cash register and threw her arms around Sid.

"Chief Chance," she shouted, "where in the world have you been? I don't believe you've changed a bit, except for the beard, of course. I'm used to those, though."

Sid hugged her and untangled himself. "You haven't changed either, Maribeth." He leaned back and gave her the once-over. "Except maybe you've gotten a little bit prettier."

"Pshaw. You're still as full of it as ever. Who is this with you? You're not married?"

"No. This is my business associate, Miss Jasmine LeMieux. Jaz, meet Maribeth Lewis."

Smiling, Jaz stuck her hand out. "They must have named the town for you."

The woman shook hands and straightened her apron. "Did Sid teach you how to lay it on?"

"Where's Jeff, Maribeth?" he asked. "I need to talk to him."

"He's back in the kitchen. Let me get you a table and I'll go tell him you're here. What a treat seeing you again."

"How about putting us somewhere over there near the wall," he said. "I don't want to attract any attention."

She turned to Jaz as they started across the room. "This man attracts attention like sugar attracts flies. I know what he means, though." Her smile dimmed a bit. "Things haven't gotten any better in this town since you left, Sid."

After they were seated, she shuffled off to the kitchen, and Jaz looked up. "What do you suppose she meant by things haven't gotten any better?"

"My guess is the old courthouse bunch is still ruling the roost and stirring up trouble."

The lunchtime crowd was just beginning to gather. Sid kept an eye out for anyone he might know. While Jaz looked over the menu, a man with rust-colored hair and short beard to match came out of the kitchen, pulled off a white apron and folded it as he walked to their table. Sid jumped up as soon as he saw him.

"Jeff, you old devil. You're looking great." He gave his friend a hug and turned him toward the table. "Jeff Lewis, Jaz LeMieux. She's a business associate and a very special friend. And, yes, Jaz, he's the one they named the town after. Meriwether was a long lost cousin who happened to cash in his chips along the Trace."

"I'm sure you know better than to believe anything this guy says." Lewis grinned. He reached over to pat Sid's arm. "Boy, it's good to see you. I sure wish you were still around here."

Sid dropped into his chair. "Join us if you have a minute, Jeff. I'm interested in Maribeth's comment that not much has changed since I left."

"I can't stay long. They'll start backing up the orders." He took the chair beside Sid. "As for the situation around Lewisville, I'd say things have changed a little bit, but not for the better."

"We saw the sign on the way in where Sheriff Zack is running for re-election."

Lewis gripped the apron in both hands and twisted it in a show of disgust. "He bragged how he got rid of you. Now he thinks he can do anything he wants. He takes his orders from Bronson Fradkin, though. That man is pure evil."

"Well, he's in for disillusionment." Sid leaned his elbows on the table, something his mother would have frowned on. This town brought back memories of her. She was the one who had insisted he take the chief's job.

"Why would he be disillusioned?" Jaz asked.

"'He who is pregnant with evil and conceives trouble gives birth to disillusionment.'"

She tilted her head and stared at him. "Who said that?"

"David. Psalm Seven."

She turned to Jeff Lewis. "Did he do this when he lived down here?"

Lewis laughed until his cheeks turned the shade of his beard. "I used to call him the poet. Some of the names other people gave him were a little less complimentary."

"People like Bronson Fradkin?" Jaz asked.

"Probably," Sid said. "And if we find what I'm beginning to suspect, Mr. Fradkin is likely to become even less complimentary."

"Be very careful with that man, Sid," Lewis said.

"Jaz is going to talk to him. I'm convinced I couldn't get anything out of him."

Lewis gave her a somber look. "I'll give you the same advice. Take care when you deal with Fradkin. He's powerful and he's ruthless. Is this a confidential matter?"

"No, we're looking for the people responsible for that chemical spill at an Ashland City plant that's been in the news."

"I read about that. Sounds pretty bad for those people up there. And you think Fradkin was involved?"

Sid nodded. "There's a good possibility. I found his name associated with the company that used the plant at the time."

"If there was a scheme to make money, you can bet our boy Bronson was behind it."

The Surest Poison

Maribeth came across the dining area and called, "They need you in the kitchen, Jeff."

He jumped up and unfurled his apron. "Gotta go. Nice meeting you, Jaz. Drop by after a while if you can. I'll have more time to talk."

Maribeth sidled up to the table. "You guys going to eat with us?"

Sid opened his menu. "We sure are. What strikes your fancy, Jaz?"

"How about the vegetable soup and salad?"

"Good choice," Maribeth said. "The soup's to die for."

Sid winked at her. "I think I'll live awhile yet. Bring me the salad and a Reuben sandwich."

"And black coffee."

"You remembered."

"How could I forget?"

"Tea for me," Jaz said.

Maribeth collected the menus and headed for the kitchen.

"They're nice people," Jaz said.

"Hank was a rock when I hit my lowest point. He still has a lot of influence around town. His dad was county judge years ago. That was before Bronson Fradkin and his ilk took over."

Sid and Jaz were eating a short time later when a big man swaggered into the restaurant like some Old West gunslinger. He was dressed in a pale blue uniform, a large semi-automatic swinging from his hip. Jaz saw him first.

"Who's the cop?" she asked.

Sid looked around. "Trouble."

"That his first or last name?"

"Both. He's double trouble. The sheriff's chief deputy, Richard Tracy."

Jaz stared, her mouth half open. "Dick Tracy?"

"Unbelievable, isn't it?"

He followed her gaze and saw Chief Deputy Tracy coming straight toward their table, a crooked smile on his face. He stopped in front of them.

"Well, as I live and breathe, if it ain't our old police chief. What are you doing down here, Chance? I heard you was a big city dude now."

"Where'd you hear that? Till recently I lived a long way from the big city."

"People tell us things."

Sid stared into his eyes, displaying no emotion. "Tell your people I still get nostalgic for the small town atmosphere."

"You do, huh? Well, our atmosphere is dong fine without you."

"We're just visiting. I thought tourists were welcome in Lewisville."

"Some are, some aren't. We don't welcome folks who think they're above the law."

"How about the law of entrapment?"

The deputy's face twisted into an evil grin. "I'll bet you're down here looking for a new dealer."

Sid had to restrain himself from jumping up and taking a swing at the guy. Instead, he gritted his teeth and said, "You shouldn't believe all you hear on that wrist radio, Dick."

"You'll think wrist radio if I catch you doing anything out of line, like the last time."

"Like the last time? How many false traps have you set lately?"

The deputy's face hardened. "You'd better watch your step around here, Chance. Get smart with me and I'll see you wind up in the County Jail."

Sid's knuckles turned white as he gripped the table.

"Don't worry about it, Deputy Tracy," Jaz said, looking up at the officer. "We're on our way to see Bronson Fradkin. I'm sure he'll take care of everything."

Tracy spun on his heel and stalked off.

Sid exhaled a long sigh. "Thanks for saving me. Another couple of exchanges and I would have done something rash."

"That's what I was afraid of," she said, reaching over to squeeze his hand. "It would've been deserved, but not wise."

26

SID MOVED THE car to a different two-hour parking spot. They walked around the block to The Executive Building, where Fradkin's office was located. Jaz looked about at the old storefronts as they passed. Most had weathered looks, some the appearance of relics from an era long past. It made the newness of the lawyer's brick office building seem out of place. A small coffee shop, sort of a Starbucks knockoff, occupied a narrow space next door.

"I'll wait for you in there," Sid told her when they stopped out front. "Call on the cell phone if you need me."

Jaz suspected he had been worrying about her. She gave him a stern look. "Face it, Sid. I'm a big girl. I can take care of myself."

"I know. But like Jeff said, that man is pure evil."

"My strength is as the strength of ten, because my heart is pure."

He broke out laughing. "Now you're stealing my stuff."

Jaz grinned. "I remembered the line, but I don't know who said it."

"Sir Galahad in Tennyson's *Idylls of the King*."

She waved and turned to the building's heavy wood door, which looked as solid as that of an English manor house. Inside she found an elevator and a directory of second floor tenants. To the left, ornate script lettering on the windows of a glassed-in reception area spelled out "Law Offices of Bronson Q. Fradkin." Jaz walked in and approached a prim, white-haired woman whose desk sat beyond a cluster of empty chairs.

"Jasmine LeMieux to see Mr. Fradkin," she said in a pleasant voice.

The woman looked up. "Do you have an appointment?"

"No, but I came down from Nashville to see him. I hope he isn't too busy."

"Let me check." She went to a nearby door, knocked, opened it, and spoke to someone out of sight. A moment later, she was back, smiling. "Mr. Fradkin will see you."

She ushered Jaz into the inner sanctum.

Bronson Fradkin's office was rather large for what she would have expected of a country lawyer. From the looks of things, however, he didn't think of himself as a country lawyer. The oversize desk, cushioned chairs, stately cabinets and tables, all were fashioned of lustrous cherry wood that shined as though a polishing cloth had just been applied. Scenes from fox hunts and polo matches decorated the walls. Everything about the place showed a plan to portray its occupant as a man of refinement, a sporting gentleman. He came around the desk dressed in an expensive suit, gold cufflinks, and diamond-studded tie pin flashing in the light from a shiny brass banker's lamp.

He reached out a soft, smooth hand. "Miss LeMieux, what a pleasure to meet you. Please have a seat."

Jaz shook his hand, which she guessed had never held a horse's reins, at least not since he was a kid. She sat in the chair across from his desk. It was like walking into a masquerade ball. Everything hinted at pretense. "It's nice meeting you, Mr. Fradkin. You have a beautiful office."

A slim man with precisely parted brown hair she doubted was his own and a cultivated look of distinction, Fradkin appeared pleased at the compliment. He took his seat behind the desk and smiled at her.

"To what do I owe the pleasure of this visit from such a distinguished lady?"

She raised an eyebrow. "Maybe you have me confused with somebody else."

The Surest Poison

"You're being modest, Miss LeMieux. I've read about your fascinating career. Champion boxer, outstanding police officer, corporate executive. I also understand you've been playing a new role as a private investigator. You're quite a talented young lady."

"And you're quite a flatterer, Mr. Fradkin."

"So which Jasmine LeMieux am I talking with today?"

She gave him a teasing smile. "Which would you prefer?"

"As an attorney who has had a rather successful career in dealing with corporate matters, I hope you're exploring the possibility of my being of service to your company."

"Let's say that could depend on how you impress me with your knowledge of other matters."

"Ah, now we're getting to the real purpose of your visit."

"Back in the mid-nineties, you were listed as the registered agent for a company named Auto Parts Rehabbers in Ashland City. What kind of business was it?"

He leaned forward on his desk as if giving the question serious thought. "It's been a long time, but as I recall, the company did just what the name implies. They took used auto parts and reconditioned them. What's your interest in this bit of ancient history?"

"History has a way of coming back to life sometimes with a new relevance, don't you think? We're trying to locate the manager, a Mr. Tony Decker. Can you tell me where we might find him?"

His face took on an exaggerated look of disappointment. He shrugged. "Gosh. I wish I could help, but that was, what, twelve or so years ago? I hadn't thought about that operation in years. I have no idea where the man could be now."

How thick could he lay it on, she wondered? She suspected he had been thinking about Auto Parts Rehabbers ever since he first read the story regarding the TCE spill in Ashland City. "I'm told you represent his twin brother, Trent Decker, in a lawsuit," she said.

Fradkin's eyes lit up like he'd just discovered gravity. "Oh, you're thinking that it was Tony who referred his brother to my law firm. No, no, that wasn't the case at all."

"Then how did he happen to hire a lawyer so far away from Nashville?"

"It was a referral, all right, but from another of my former clients. Sorry, as I said before, I haven't seen or heard of Tony Decker in at least a dozen years."

"The Auto Parts Rehabbers' property was sold to them by Hank Keglar of Lewisville. Isn't he one of your clients?"

"Yes, I have represented Mr. Keglar in the past."

"Did you handle the sale?"

"I don't remember. I did more real estate deals back then than I do now."

"You must have set up the limited liability partnership. How did First Improvement Corp come into the picture?"

The warm, friendly look he had cultivated at first began to fade, his eyes turning cool. "It was a privately held corporation that chose to keep its business private. I'm afraid I can't tell you any more about them."

"You're aware that First Improvement was owned by First Patriots, Limited, which was chartered in Anguilla."

Fradkin folded his hands on the desk. "You've been doing quite a bit of digging, Miss LeMieux. What's the purpose of this exercise?"

"The owners and management of Auto Parts Rehabbers are responsible for a massive environmental pollution incident at the plant site. They're going to have to answer to the state for the enormous cost of the cleanup."

The warm glow returned. "I've read the stories. The state is after Wade Harrington and HarrCo Shipping to take care of that."

My, how his memory had suddenly returned. Jaz stood and smiled back at him. "Well, Mr. Fradkin, I think you'd better prepare your clients for a major change in the landscape. Nice talking with you."

27

SID SAT NURSING his coffee, wondering what could be happening in Bronson Fradkin's office. He knew Jaz was right. She could handle herself as well as anyone he knew. Fradkin, however, was a skilled and ruthless lawyer. He had seen the man at work too many times.

She came through the doorway as he was about to head back for a refill. He got up and pulled out a chair for her.

"How did it go?" he asked, noting her smile. "I don't see any bruises."

"He was a perfect gentleman. Well, almost. He didn't look all that happy when I left."

She went over the high points of her discussion with Fradkin.

"What was your overall impression?" Sid asked.

"He knew what I was there for from the start. And he knows everything that's going on with the pollution case. I'd say Trent Decker came to him by way of Tony, and I've no doubt he knows where brother Tony is hiding."

"There's one other call we should make here, though I doubt it will bring any more positive results."

"Hank Keglar?"

"Right. He's not as sophisticated as Fradkin, and he doesn't hesitate to operate on the dark side of the law."

"Where is his office?"

"At a bar he owns on the highway going out of town. It was a real headache for the police. Fights, drunks, prostitutes, drugs, you name it. If there's anything illegal going on around here, you can bet he's involved in it. But with the help of Fradkin and the sheriff, he lives a charmed life."

Jaz let her gaze sweep around the counter behind them. "Do they have cappuccino here?"

"Sure. It may not be the kind you prefer, but keep your seat. I'll get it for you."

He walked over to the counter and placed the order with an effeminate young man who wore gold earrings and a gold stud on one nostril. He knew the people you encountered in small towns these days could be little different from those in the big cities. The cappuccino machine soon droned away like a concrete mixer in high gear. When the drink was ready, Sid carried it to the table, where Jaz sat talking on her cell phone. She had a satisfied look as she shut if off.

"That was my phone company source. Our friend Rackard kept the line quite busy after my visit to the garage Friday night," she said. "He called Bronson Fradkin and another number in this area that we haven't been able to track down yet. I wish I'd known that before I talked to Fradkin. Rackard also called Dixie Seals."

"Wait a minute. Dixie Seals?"

"The business run by Trent Decker."

"Who claims not to have heard of his brother in years."

"Sounds like Tony may have been around there Friday night, doesn't it?"

"I need to look into that for sure."

"Okay. Now, how about Mr. Keglar?"

Sid toyed with his cup for a moment. "I'd say it was time to pay him a courtesy call."

"And hope he's courteous in return?"

"That would be novel."

Jaz took a tentative sip of the cappuccino. "I'll go with you. It might give you a little easier entree."

"Don't count on it. Mr. Keglar is not your ordinary adversary."

* * *

The Surest Poison

The Long Branch Saloon had a rustic wooden front that fit the name like cowboys fit saddles. Inside were black walls, round tables and booths, and a long bar made of dark wood that could have come right out of some Old West ghost town. Lamps made to look like oil lanterns cast a pale glow over the room. Two men sat at the bar, workmen dressed in jeans and ball caps, beers shedding trickles of foam on the counter. A woman with streaks of gray in her hair and a man in a tweed sports jacket leaned toward each other at a table just beyond the bar. The man's shirt collar gapped open to bare a gold medallion on a heavy necklace and the hint of a hairy chest.

Sid walked ahead of Jaz to the bartender. "We'd like to see Hank Keglar," he said.

The tall, thin man picked up a phone from a shelf behind the bar and punched a number. He looked back at Sid. "Who wants to see him?"

"Sidney Chance and Jasmine LeMieux. Tell him we only need a few minutes."

The bartender spoke into the phone, listened, then pointed to the far end of the bar. "Go through that door, down the hall, last room on the right."

The two men at the bar put down their beers and let their eyes track Jaz as she walked past. Sid figured Fradkin had already tipped Keglar about their presence in Lewisville. He followed the bartender's directions and entered a narrow passageway. It had been years since he was in this place, and he'd forgotten how desolate it looked. With one small bulb in the ceiling, the area gave the dusky appearance of a cave entrance. Dark brown walls emphasized the perception. Even the floor had a rough feel, covered by a frayed carpet of indistinct color. Sid and Jaz walked along in silence, stopping at the last door. Sid knocked.

"Come in," a deep voice called.

Sid opened the door and stepped inside, Jaz just behind him. The room had the look of a primitive office. Its furnishings were sparse. There was a metal desk like something out of a salvage store, a few well-worn wooden chairs, a felt-topped table that might have been liberated from a casino. The most prominent feature was the huge, grotesque man seated behind the desk. He had a neck like a tree trunk, arms like a bear. The hair below his rolled-up sleeves looked almost as thick as a grizzly's. He weighed four hundred pounds at a minimum. What passed for a smile was more like a sneer.

"The famous shamus and his moll," Hank Keglar said in a low, rumbling voice. "A handsome pair. Right, Dirk?"

He turned to the ominous figure perched on a barstool in the corner of the room. At least three inches taller than Sid, the man wore gray sweat pants and a white tee shirt that showed bulging muscles below massive shoulders. His bald head and gold earring called up images of Mr. Clean, except for the lack of a smile and the presence of a jagged scar on one cheek.

Sid glanced at Dirk, then turned his icy gaze back to Keglar. "This is my business associate, Miss Jazmine LeMieux," he said, gesturing at Jaz. "We're interested in your connection to Auto Parts Rehabbers, a company in Ashland City that went under some dozen years ago."

"And what makes you think I had any connection?"

"You sold the property where the plant was located to the company run by Tony Decker. Then you took it back in a foreclosure three years later."

Keglar settled back in his massive chair. "So it was a real estate transaction. I've sold lots of properties to people or businesses I had no interest in."

"How did you meet Decker?"

"I don't remember. I think he heard about the property and came to see if I was interested in selling. I gave him a mortgage. He defaulted on the loan and I took the property back. End of story."

Sid and Jaz remained standing in front of the desk, where they would have stayed if Keglar had invited them to sit. Which he didn't.

The Surest Poison

"You're a tough businessman," Sid said. "If Decker owed you money, I'm sure you kept him in your sights. Where could we find him?"

"I got no idea. I suspect he's dead by now."

"Why would you think he's dead?"

"Because he was like you, Chance. A nosy nobody."

Sid ignored the remark and thought about the way the HarrCo sale was handled. "Why was Auto Parts Rehabbers different from the way you sold the property to Wade Harrington? He said he never saw you. The deal was all arranged through a real estate agent."

The big man's look had turned surly. "Every deal's different. Even you oughta know that."

"So you talked to Decker. He was only a part-owner. Who did you to talk to with First Improvement Corporation?"

"I don't remember no First Improvement Corporation. Who I talked to about a business deal years ago is ancient history. What do you care?"

Jaz smiled. "Ancient history is what Bronson Fradkin called it. Did he handle the deal for you, Mr. Keglar?"

"Why don't you private dicks go back to Nashville where you belong? You got no authority in Lewisville, Chance. You're a has-been."

Sid gave him a hard look. "My guys almost nailed you once. You can bet the next time I'll make sure it sticks."

Keglar turned to his enforcer and growled. "Show these phony cops the way out, Dirk."

Sid dismissed the bald giant with a wave of his hand. "We can find our way. Don't think you've heard the last of us, Keglar."

As Sid ushered Jaz out the door, Keglar took a parting shot.

"You'd just better hope to hell you've heard the last of me, Chance."

28

THE CITY CAFÉ was quiet, with only a few afternoon coffee drinkers and one late luncher. Jeff Lewis came over to join Sid and Jaz, bringing coffee and tea.

"How did it go?"

Sid chuckled. "We may need to sneak out of town. Jaz ruffled Fradkin's feathers and I did my best to provoke Hank Keglar."

Lewis took the seat next to him. "You always did like to live on the edge."

"Sometimes, if you shake them up, they get a little anxious and make a careless move. The guy we're looking for is named Tony Decker. You know anything about him, Jeff?"

He looked thoughtful. "I don't think so. Is he from Lewisville?"

"Memphis. We're pretty sure he has connections to Fradkin and Keglar, both of whom claim they have no idea where he is now. In my opinion, they're both lying."

"You need to get them under oath."

Jaz grunted. "I'd wager they have no more respect for the perjury laws than for any others."

"So what do you do now?" Lewis asked.

Sid sipped at his coffee. "We keep digging." He turned to Jaz. "When are you going to hear from your man in Anguilla?"

"If he's going to find anything, he should have some answers by now. I'll contact him as soon as we get back."

"Where's Anguilla?" Lewis asked.

Sid told him about First Improvement Corporation and

The Surest Poison

its oddly-named corporate parent, First Patriots Ltd.

"I seem to recall talk around town some years ago," Lewis said. "People saying they had heard about these off-shore corporations. They were supposed to get great tax breaks. I don't remember who it was, but I'll ask around and see if I can find out. It may be useful, maybe not."

"We'll take all the help we can get," Jaz said.

ON THE WAY BACK to Nashville, Jaz asked Sid if he had made contact with Reggie, the Clarksville friend of Larry Irwin, the Auto Parts Rehabber employee whose body was found beside Little Marrabone Road.

"Not yet. Why don't you give him a call? Maybe we can catch him before he leaves work."

Slipping out his pocket notebook, he showed her the number for the Automotive Maintenance Shop at the university in Clarksville. She soon had Reggie on the phone and identified herself.

"Herschel Owens, Larry Irwin's cousin, told us you were disturbed by a phone call Larry made to you on the night he died," Jaz said. "What did he tell you?"

"He was scared. You could tell by the way he talked. He said this guy had called him about a place where he worked several years ago. I didn't understand what the situation was, but it sounded like the place was run by a bunch of crooks. The guy apparently threatened him. I'm not sure why."

"Did he mention the name of the company?"

"It was an auto parts place in Ashland City. He worked there before we met."

"Auto Parts Rehabbers?"

"Yeah, that sounds like it."

"What do you mean it was run by a bunch of crooks?"

"Guys who'd been in prison. Larry had been in trouble, too, but his was juvenile detention. He didn't work at the place too long. He said he had a hunch those guys might have been dealing with stolen property."

"Did he give you any details, why he thought that?"

"No."

"And the man who called threatened him?"

"He didn't spell it out, but I'm sure that's what he meant."

"Do you recall anything else he said that might shed some light on what happened to him?"

He was silent for a moment. "You know, I think he had a feeling something like this might happen. I wish he'd told me more, but that's it."

Jaz closed her cell phone and repeated what the young man told her.

A traffic light up ahead shifted to red, and Sid slowed for an intersection in Columbia. "We knew Decker and Rackard were ex-cons," he said. "I wonder what the stolen property angle could involve?"

"Good question. More worrisome is who called Larry Irwin? Was it the killer?"

"We need to contact Bart and let him check out Irwin's phone calls."

She found the detective at his cubbyhole in the East Precinct office and gave him the information.

"Are you guys trying to steal my job?" he asked in a whimsical voice.

"Not me," Jaz said. "I'm what's known as the famous shamus's moll." She told him about their interview with Hank Keglar. She had to pull the phone away from her ear to mute the laughter.

"I'd like to have seen Sid's face," Bart said. "But getting back to Irwin, I wonder why his cousin, this Owens guy down in Rutherford County, didn't call me? He have something against cops?"

"Sid didn't treat him as roughly. PIs have to be nice to people. You don't."

"Me not nice? Come on, Jaz, you know I'm a pushover."

"Depends on who's doing the pushing."

He laughed again. "I'd better get off this telephone and try to get in touch with your Mr. Reggie in Clarksville."

"Any chance your Shelby Park victim once worked for Auto Parts Rehabbers?" Jaz asked.

"Gillie Younger? Not that I know of. That name hasn't showed up so far. Guess I need to dig a little deeper. If you come across anything else interesting, let me know."

"We'd appreciate the same on this Auto Parts Rehabbers angle."

They made it back to Nashville in time for rush hour, pulling into the LeMieux driveway as the sun disappeared behind the hills that ringed the city. Jaz suggested Sid come inside to see if anything new had showed up on her computer. They encountered John and Bobby on the way to her office.

"Get much work done today?" Jaz asked.

The older man smiled. "This boy's a pretty good worker if you can get him to quit talking so much."

Bobby relaxed his face into something close enough to be a grin. "You didn't have a lot to say, either, Grandpa."

"Yep, it's been kind of quiet around here. How was your day, Miss Jasmine?"

"Busy. Did you check your house to be sure everything's okay out there?"

"Yes'm. It was sort of cool in there, so I turned the heat on and let the furnace warm up the place. I used some hot water to clean the bathroom. Funny how it can get so dirty with nobody living in it. You know my feelings, though. I like living in this nice house, but I was happy out there with our four rooms and a bath."

"I know," Jaz said. "But I feel better with you and Marie living in the big house with me."

When she and Sid were in her office, she checked her computer and looked around.

"Anguilla wants me to call."

She punched a few buttons and soon got through to the man in the Leeward Islands.

"This is Jazmine LeMieux. I hope you bear good tidings."

He had a soft voice and a slight accent. "These records are not available for public scrutiny, Miss LeMieux. Completing this assignment was like being midwife to an angry female tiger. Very touchy."

"What were you able to find?"

"First Patriots was set up by a clever barrister who is very good at obscuring details. Since no one checks the names on accounts to make sure they are bona fide, he changes them into aliases. The names associated with First Patriots, Limited, for instance, are quite familiar to Americans. They are Benjamin Franklin and Helen Keller."

Jaz let her shoulders slump. "That's not much help."

"I'm sorry. Perhaps the address would be of some help. It is a post office box in Nashville, Tennessee, USA. Of course, you realize the corporation was set up more than fifteen years ago. I cannot say if the address is still current."

"That's something we'll have to check out," she said.

He gave her the box number and zipcode. It was located at the downtown branch post office.

29

A LAYER OF LOW clouds moved across Nashville after dark, obscuring the moon. By two AM, the Franklin Road area, except for the lighted, four-lane thoroughfare itself, lay in darkness. All that glowed in the LeMieux household were digital clocks and lights on the electronic console in Jaz's office. Quiet prevailed except for a gentle snore in one of the bedrooms.

A narrow lane ran along one side and around the rear of the LeMieux estate. Houses across the road sat back in the trees, out of sight of the street. A brown van pulled off the pavement and parked near a rear corner of Jaz's property. Two men dressed in black got out. One wore a backpack. They heaved themselves over the sturdy white wooden fence and started up the hill.

The men trudged in the darkness without speaking until they spotted the outline of the small house behind the mansion. A one-story frame structure, it had a partial basement, half below ground level. First, the intruders made sure Bobby Wallace's car was still parked in front. For a full two minutes, they stood like statues, listening for any unusual sounds. Hearing none, they walked down the four steps to the basement door.

The lock proved but a momentary delay. Inside was a small, dirt-floored room. The man with the backpack held a flashlight while his partner placed a radio-activated detonator in the center. A few feet away stood a gas water heater on a concrete base. Swapping places, the second man held the flashlight while the other took off his pack and pulled out a few tools. He squatted beside the water heater, removed a small panel and checked he pilot light. The flame burned a steady blue. He turned the control knob to "off." The flame disappeared.

Using a wrench, he loosened a connection in the gas line. He pulled the pipes apart until he could hear the hiss of gas escaping. Both men flinched as the odor of rotten eggs filled their nostrils. The man with the flashlight pressed a button on his wristwatch, starting the timer. The other one stuffed the tools in his backpack. They headed for the door, locked it, and started down the hill.

The operation had been planned with precision, though on short notice. One of the men had a friend who worked for the gas company. Considering the size of the basement and the flow from the gas line, it would take around six minutes for the concentration to reach the critical point, where a flame would ignite it. The night before, they had timed the walk from the house to their vehicle. It took three minutes.

Reaching the fence, they climbed over and returned to the van. The driver swung into his seat. He tossed his pack into the rear and started the engine. He put the vehicle in gear and waited.

Eyes fixed to the timer display on his digital watch, his partner called out:

"Six minutes. Go!"

He toggled a control on the remote.

A loud explosion came from up the hill as they raced away.

30

JAZ AWOKE TO an ungodly roar. In her large bedroom on the back of the second floor, she felt a rumble like an earthquake. She jumped up, ran to the window, pushed the curtains aside. What she saw turned her blood to ice. Flames leaped above the small house in back, which appeared to be in shambles. In the bright, flickering light, she saw Bobby's car blown onto its side. Flaming bits of debris had landed next to a large oak tree behind the mansion.

She hurried to the bedside table and grabbed the phone. There wasn't time to think, just react. Thank God there was a dial tone. She punched in 911. When the operator answered, she gave the address and said there'd been an explosion, a fire was raging. She jammed her feet into a pair of slippers, grabbed a robe, and ran out to the railing that circled a large area open to the great room below. Lights had come on in the room after the emergency generator kicked in, providing power to essential areas.

She heard shouts downstairs, where the Wallaces lived, then the sound of running feet. Bobby appeared in the light of the big room.

"Is everybody okay?" Jaz called, her voice tense.

"We're all right. You?"

"I'm fine, but we need to get everybody out of the house. The flames look awfully close. I've called the Fire Department. I'll go down to my office and make sure they can get through the gate."

"I'll round up my folks," Bobby said and hurried off.

Jaz bounded down the stairs and into her office. She was breathing hard but still under control. She hadn't paused long enough to consider what might have happened. The backup power supply had the Welcome Traveler Stores logo bouncing about the computer screen. She glanced at the small monitor beside the front gate controls, a duplicate of what John used in a pantry off the kitchen. As soon as she opened the gate, she saw flashing lights approach.

Back in the foyer, she found Little Bob choking back tears and hanging onto his mother's pajamas. John and Bobby helped Marie toward the door.

"The firemen are here," Jaz said. "Let's get outside until we can see how bad it is."

The sound of sirens and billows of acrid smoke filled the cool night air. Jaz and John Wallace hurried toward the side of the mansion as the fire truck approached. The firemen played out snake-like hoses that writhed along the driveway. A District Chief's car followed not far behind.

Now that she had a moment to sort out her thoughts, Jaz realized the possible source of the explosion. The little house had a gas water heater, as well as a gas furnace. As soon as the firemen jumped out of the truck, she hailed one of them.

"There was an explosion at the house in back and there's a gas line running to it," she shouted.

"Was anyone inside?" the fireman asked.

"No," Jaz said. "We were all in the main house."

"I'll radio word to have the gas company shut off the line."

The District Chief ran up, decked out in his white fire hat. He moved around to get a better look at the rear of the mansion. "Let's get some water on that big tree and along the back of this house before it gets involved, too," he yelled. "It's hot as hell back there."

SID GROPED FOR the telephone on the nightstand. The red numbers on the clock showed 2:28 a.m. He pressed the phone to his ear.

The Surest Poison

"Hello."

"Sid, it's Wick. There's been an explosion and fire at Jaz's house. I just got the call on the radio."

He came awake in an instant. "An explosion?"

"Right. It's her address on Franklin Road. I'm headed that way. I thought you'd want to know."

Sid's heart pounded, his thoughts racing. Jaz's house? Was she hurt? He recalled the confrontations in Lewisville with Hank Keglar and Bronson Fradkin, the veiled threat from Keglar as they were leaving. What had he gotten her into?

"Thanks for calling, Wick," he said. "I'm on my way as soon as I can get dressed."

He threw on his clothes, locked the house, dashed out to the garage. In less than five minutes, he pulled out of the driveway. From Neelys Bend Road, he took a shortcut to Old Hickory Boulevard, and sped over to I-65. Traffic was light this time of morning. With five lanes funneling toward town, he drove like a cop on an emergency call. He flipped open his phone and punched the speed dial number for Jaz. After a few rings, it went to voice mail. He thought about calling Wick's cell phone but realized he didn't have the number in his contact list. He concentrated on keeping a sharp lookout for blue lights. This was no time to get pulled over. Particularly by some rookie who wouldn't know Sidney Chance from Sydney Greenstreet. Come to think of it, the guy wouldn't know who Sydney Greenstreet was, either.

Images of destruction flitted across his mind, becoming more horrific the closer he got to Franklin Road. If this was some of Hank Keglar's doings....

AS THE FIREMEN poured water in back of the big house and onto the remains of the smaller one, flashing blue lights raced up the driveway. A Metro officer with sergeant's stripes climbed out and rushed over to where Jaz and the others stood watching the firefighters.

"Jaz, what happened?" he called.

She turned her head. "Wick!" She threw her arms around him. "This is awful. The little house in back blew up."

He hugged her, then looked around at the elderly couple and the younger trio. "Is everybody okay?"

"Yes, thank God." She gazed off at the flames and sighed.

Then she saw Marie with her head bowed, John's arm around her shoulders. Jaz moved over to where they stood and reached out to take the older woman's hand.

"It's all right, Marie," she said.

Marie shook her head as she looked around. "That was our home for the better part of thirty years. A lot of memories just went up in smoke."

Jaz sympathized with her. She felt the same way. Her father had been proud of that little house. He made sure it was built well and furnished it with the best appliances and furniture he could find.

She turned back to Wick and introduced him to the Wallaces.

"You must be the young fellow from Ashland City," Wick said as he shook Bobby's hand.

Bobby darted a nervous glance at Jaz.

"Yes," she said, "he's John and Marie's grandson. His family is staying here for a while."

Wick gave a knowing nod. "Nobody was living in the house back there?"

"No. Not since John and Marie moved in with me several years ago. They keep things going while I'm in and out. I don't know why I bothered to spend money maintaining that place. I guess so I'll have somewhere to live if the business goes bust and I lose the family home."

"Miss Jasmine," Marie said in a scolding voice.

"Get after her, ma'am," Sergeant Stanley said with a chuckle.

"To tell the truth," Jaz said, "that house had a lot of sentimental value. I've used it as a guest house on several occasions the past few years. We got it ready for Bobby in case he wanted to stay out there. We're lucky Marie talked him out of it."

The Surest Poison

"That ought to teach you to listen to your grandma," Marie said.

Bobby hung his head and shrugged.

"I heard on the radio that the Fire Department called for a gas line shutoff," Wick said. "Do they think the explosion was caused by a gas leak?"

"That's a possibility," Jaz said. "There was a gas water heater in the basement. I remember reading about a case once where a basement filled with gas until the pilot light of the water heater touched off an explosion."

Wick rubbed his cheek, which showed a hint of whiskers in the light from the vehicles and the still-glowing fire. "I haven't had any experience with that sort of thing, but I'd say that should do it."

She looked back at the flames with a growing sense of uneasiness. Recalling Sid's concern yesterday over the threats to Bobby, she wondered if the explosion might not have been accidental. There was also the menace in Hank Keglar's voice as they left the Long Branch Saloon. She realized this was something she should have considered earlier. Evidently she'd been away from the job too long to have regained all of her cop mentality.

WHEN SID RACED through the open gate, he spotted Wick's blue lights and the flashing red of the fire engine. He saw flames dancing around the remains of the shattered structure in back as he approached the house. The heavy smell of smoke almost made his eyes water. He ran to the cluster of people watching from the edge of the driveway.

When he was only a few feet away, Jaz turned and saw him. Her eyes opened wide with surprise. She wore a white cotton robe, her hair tousled, but she appeared unhurt. It was a beautiful sight.

Sid reached his arm around her shoulder, and she hugged him. "I imagined all sorts of things on the way over here," he said. "Are you okay?"

She looked up with moist eyes. "Yes. Thank God Bobby and his family were staying in my house."

"Wick told me there was an explosion."

"It could have been a gas leak."

"You didn't hear anyone around?"

She looked up at him. "I know what you're thinking."

"I thought about Hank Keglar and Bronson Fradkin all the way over here."

Before she could reply, Wick shouted, "Here comes the TV trash."

Sid let go of Jaz as they turned and saw a white truck with a dish antenna on top speeding up the driveway.

"If you don't want the Wallaces bombarded with questions, you'd better get them back in the house," he said.

Bobby had already bolted toward the front door. Jaz told the others to go inside with him. It was safe now. She darted a glance at Sid.

"I must look like the wrath of God. Not my best outfit for appearing on television."

"Want me to throw 'em out?" Wick asked.

"No. I don't think that would improve my image."

"I'll be glad to fend them off until you can change," Sid said.

She gave him a tired grin. "Forget it. I'm not that vain."

While the TV crew was making their way up from the truck, Sid walked over to where the white-hatted fireman stood. He watched his men move their hoses to cover the areas with the most remaining flames. Sid introduced himself.

The fireman had a sharp nose, bushy brows, and a determined chin. His dark eyes followed his men like a mother hen watching her chicks. "It shouldn't take long to get the fire out. The investigators will have to let it cool for a while before they can start looking for the cause."

"Do you think it was a gas leak?" Sid asked.

"Sounds like it, but you're never sure until you can get in and sift through the debris. They'll have to determine where the leak was located, if that's what it was."

Sid looked around as a TV light illuminated the area. He saw a reporter in a turtleneck sweater pushing a microphone into Jaz's face. He listened as she explained how she had been wakened by the sound of an explosion. After that the cameraman moved around to get shots of the fire. When the reporter came over to interview the District Chief, Sid walked back to Jaz's side.

"Good performance," he said.

"Yeah, Emmy Award stuff."

Wick Stanley wandered up after nosing around. "Whose car was parked back there by the house?"

"Bobby Wallace's," Jaz said. "I saw it on its side when I first looked out the window."

"Yeah," Wick said, "it's pretty beat up. That was a powerful blast."

"The case I mentioned earlier involved a lot bigger house and a full-size basement. The explosion not only destroyed that house, it took out the one next door, too." She repeated for Sid the report she had read.

He looked back toward the flames. Though beaten down to a manageable level, they still weaved about in a macabre dance. "I want to be convinced that this was an accident. I intend to be here when the fire investigators come."

31

THE SOFT GLOW of dawn tinted the horizon as Sid arrived at his driveway. It had been a difficult night, but he couldn't decide whether to hit the bed or give up, shower, eat breakfast, and go to the office. The alarm system indicated nothing was amiss. Finding himself too keyed up to get back to sleep, he headed for the shower. He took his time, soaking away the stress. The newspaper arrived as he sat down to eat. When he finished his cinnamon roll, he lingered over the sports section and a final cup of coffee. The phone rang as he was reading a story about the Titan's quarterback.

"I just saw you on TV," Jack Post said. "They only identified Jaz, but I recognized you. That was terrible about the fire at her place. They said nobody was hurt."

"That's right. It involved the small house out in back where the Wallaces used to live."

"What caused the explosion?"

"They believe it was a gas leak. I plan to go over there when the fire investigators come out."

"Do you think it was something other than an accident?"

"I have my suspicions."

"Do you have someone in mind?"

"I do."

"Who?"

Sid grimaced. "Are you planning to write a story on this, Jack?"

The old reporter laughed. "No, but asking questions is in my blood."

The Surest Poison

"Well, if you talk around too much, you may spill some of mine."

"From what I've heard, you do pretty well on your own."

"Thanks, buddy. You're a real pal."

Jack laughed again and said, "See you around. I was just about to head out of town."

Sid hung up the phone. He wasn't ready for Jack's brand of amusement.

It was too early for businesses to be open when he got to the office. He booted his computer and checked his email. Nothing earth shattering there. When the phone rang, he looked at the caller ID. Bailey, Riddle and Smith. He lifted the phone.

"Arnie?"

"Good morning, Sid. That hearing for Wade Harrington is only about a week off. I hope you have something for me."

He must not have seen the morning news, Sid thought. He decided to leave that alone and just give the lawyer a rundown on what he and Jaz had turned up. That included information on the two corporations involved in the ownership of Auto Parts Rehabbers.

"And they have a Nashville post office box?" Arnie asked.

"Right. I'll dig into it as soon as I can find my source."

"Well, you'd better come up with something soon or we'll be facing more trouble than a sack full of rattlers."

And I'll be the first one to get bitten, Sid thought.

At eight o'clock, he began sifting through his contacts with post office connections. When he found the right man, he explained the problem.

"Unless it's still an active account, it could take a lot of digging," the contact said. "I'm not sure how far back the records go. I'll let you know what I find."

A little later in the morning, as Sid poured his third cup of coffee, Bart Masterson called.

"Wick told me about the fire and explosion at Jaz's house last night," Bart said. "How's she doing?"

Sid set his cup on the desk. "She's okay. I think she's a little shaken by the possibilities, though."

"What possibilities?"

He reminded Bart of their visit to Lewisville. "I wouldn't put it past Hank Keglar to pull a trick like this."

"Have the fire investigators taken a look at the scene yet?"

"No. They'll come out a little later, when things have cooled off. I intend to be there when they arrive."

"Good idea."

"Have you gotten the results from your check of Larry Irwin's phone calls?" Sid asked.

"Yeah, but it didn't provide anything to get excited about. There was a message on the answering machine where you left your number. He got one call from the guy in Clarksville and another one from a card-loaded cell phone. I tracked it down to the store where it was sold. Nobody remembered anything about the man who bought it. He used a bogus ID."

"No doubt that was the call that disturbed Irwin. Maybe it was the killer."

"Could be. So far, he's getting away with murder."

Not long after he finished talking with Bart, Jaz called.

"I just heard from the fire investigator," she said. "He's going to be here around noon."

Sid looked at the clock. Eleven-fifteen.

"I'm headed that way."

"I've also received another interesting piece of information," she said. "A neighbor who lives behind me said he recalled something from last night that I might like to know. He's an older man. He said he gets up a couple of times each night to use the bathroom. He was up right before the explosion. He heard a vehicle accelerate out on the street about the same time as the blast."

"Could be coincidence." Sid glanced at the holstered Sig on his belt, where it had remained since the case heated up. "Or it could be the smoking gun."

32

SID ARRIVED AT Jaz's house a short time before the investigator. She led him out a rear door to survey the destruction. Except for the areas blackened by flame, it resembled the aftermath of a tornado. Seeing it in the daylight, he could imagine how the blast had taken place. The walls appeared to have been pushed away from the small basement area. With fire following the explosion, little remained intact.

"Let's take a look behind there," Sid said. "See if we can find any evidence of someone prowling around."

Jaz stared out across the debris. "There hasn't been any rain for the past day or so. Might rule out any visible tracks."

"Maybe there's some tall grass mashed down."

She smiled. "John doesn't believe in leaving tall grass around."

As they walked about the area, he had to agree. The grass looked as short as a Marine's haircut. The high pressure from the fire hoses had taken a toll, though. The water likely erased any visible tracks, except for what the firemen left.

They heard a car approaching as they headed toward the front. A Metro Fire Department vehicle drove up, manned by a uniformed fireman who appeared to be in his early forties. Small and compact, like a featherweight boxer, he had short, sandy hair and looked about with sharp, inquisitive eyes. He had a holstered weapon strapped at his waist and carried something like a large toolbox.

"Cran Quincy," he said, holding out his hand to Sid. "Real name's Cranford, but that sounds too intimidating."

Sid shook his hand. "Sid Chance." He motioned toward Jaz. "This is Miss Jasmine LeMieux. It's her property."

Jaz accepted the handshake. "Nice meeting you, Cran. Just call me Jaz. I'd better warn you in advance that Sid and I are both former cops, and current private investigators. We'll try to stay out of your way, but we have a lot of questions about what happened."

"How's that?"

She told him how the explosion had awakened her that morning and about their suspicions as to the cause, bolstered by the call from her neighbor.

"So you think somebody blew up the water heater?"

Sid looked around at the pile of rubble. "Something like that. But you can tell a lot more than is obvious to us."

"Let's go take a look," he said and started toward the debris.

Like a cat sniffing out mouse holes, he wandered about in silence, observing the jumble of broken and charred wood, the remains of doors and windows, shattered pieces of furniture. He took a digital camera out of his case and snapped a series of pictures. After several minutes, he turned toward the back of the house.

"I think you're probably right about the ignition point," he said. "Let's see what we can find around the basement."

Sid and Jaz followed him.

"Watch your step back here," Quincy said. "Right now it's an accident scene. I presume I don't need to tell you if you're right, it'll be a crime scene."

Quincy moved slowly, photographing the area before entering. He stopped to jot his observations in a notebook. He put down his case and donned a pair of gloves, pushing debris aside to get to the water heater. It had been thrown against a dirt wall, which cushioned the blow enough to keep it somewhat intact.

"If gas leaked into the basement, the pilot light could have touched off the explosion," Quincy said.

Sid stared at the battered heater. "Take a look at this. The

The Surest Poison

pipe appears to have come apart at a connection."

The investigator bent down and shined his light at the pipe. "You're right. A joint would be the weakest spot."

Standing behind him, Sid let his gaze sweep over the smashed appliance. He'd had a problem with a gas heater at home and knew how they worked. As he looked down at the controls, something caught his eye.

"Look, Cran," he said, "the pilot light is turned off."

"It shouldn't be," Jaz said. "John used some hot water yesterday to clean the bathroom."

Quincy straightened up. "So what set off the explosion?"

He walked over to where the heater had been torn loose from the gas line. He reached down and felt around the bare end of the pipe.

"There's no damage at all to the threads where this was connected. The nut must have been loosened. That would allow the gas to escape and collect in the room. But if somebody did this, how did they set it off without blowing themselves to bits?"

"A detonator?" Jaz asked.

Sid looked around. "Radio controlled?"

Quincy tapped his pen on the notebook, looking thoughtful. "Could be. They're pretty easy to make. If you've never looked, the Internet is full of instructional material. Diagrams and everything."

He gave them a short course on radio-controlled detonators. He said the simplest ignition source for a gas explosion would be a model rocket igniter. It would be connected to the guts of a remote-controlled toy, like a car or a model airplane, which would provide a long-range signal. Armed with that knowledge, they began to sift through the debris in search of any pieces that might be left of a make-shift detonator.

Marie came out to inquire if they didn't want to stop for lunch. They didn't. After an hour of burrowing through the rubbish, shifting bits of wood and metal and glass to see under, between, and around, Cran Quincy brought things to a halt with a low whistle. As Sid and Jaz watched, he dug out the remains of a small circuit board, two wires still attached, half-buried in the dirt wall at the high side of the basement.

He held it out with his gloved hand. "This looks like it could be the guilty party. See the remains of electrical tape here? That secured the battery to the board. The two wires would have set off the rocket igniter, sending up a flame to ignite the gas."

Sid studied the gadget. "Cheap and effective."

"Very. You don't have to be rich to be a terrorist."

"You just need to be ruthless," Jaz said.

"Like the guys in Lewisville." Sid gazed about at the wreckage.

"Has somebody been threatening you?" Quincy asked.

"Yes," Jaz said. "But I don't know how serious it was."

The investigator's eyes narrowed. "Why would they blow up this place instead of the big house where you live?"

Jaz just shrugged.

"That Ford out front that was blown over. Who does it belong to?"

"Bobby Wallace," Jaz said. "He and his family are here for a few days. But they're staying in the main house."

"To an outsider, it might appear that he was staying in here. Does he have any enemies?"

33

MARIE INSISTED on feeding them in the dining room. She had the table set with two places when Sid and Jaz came in. After washing off dirt accumulated during the search, they sat down to sandwiches and a rich potato soup with a seasoning that had a tantalizing aroma. The venerable chef put Sid at one end of the table, which he took to be the seat of honor Jaques LeMieux had occupied before his death.

He tasted the soup, licked his lips, and looked around at Jaz. "Delicious. I'd like to borrow Marie for about a month."

"Not a good idea. She'd have you as fat as Arnie Bailey."

"Okay, I don't need that. My morning run would turn into a morning roll."

"Speaking of things rolling, what's your assessment of Cran Quincy's reasoning about the position of Bobby's car before the explosion rolled it over?"

"You mean the idea that the blast was aimed at Bobby, not you?"

"Yes."

He munched on the sandwich. "It makes sense. We've already agreed the people who threatened Bobby likely know about your bringing him over here. When the bomber saw his car parked in front of the little house, they could have assumed he was inside."

"If it was Keglar or Fradkin after me, you'd think they would have bombed the mansion."

"Or set it on fire, at least."

"And if that's the case, and it certainly sounds reasonable, we may be misreading the role of the guys in Lewisville."

"True. Last night could have been the work of somebody else, somebody with no ties at all to the Auto Parts Rehabbers case."

"Quincy taped off the area around the little house and said he was starting a criminal investigation. If that thing he found turns out to be part of a detonator, he's going to have lots of questions."

Sid lifted his napkin, dabbed it against his lips. "I suspect Bobby's going to find himself in an interrogation room."

"Something like that may be what he needs."

After thinking about that for a moment, Sid lowered his voice. "Bobby hasn't heard anything about this, has he?"

"No. We talked this morning about the possibility that a gas leak caused the explosion. There was no hint that anything might be amiss."

"If he suspects something, he may want to find some other place to stay. Has anything been done about filing an insurance claim on his car?"

"He said he would do it this morning, but I haven't talked to him since."

When they finished eating, Sid suggested they walk the rear of the property and look for clues pointing to an intruder. They started behind the mansion, where large old growth trees flourished on the gentle slope of the hillside.

"John's been cleaning up back here," Jaz said. "Bobby helped him yesterday. They gathered a big pile of limbs and sticks that blew off during that strong wind we had last week. I'm sure he picked up any stray trash that might have blown in. If we find anything, I'd say it was dropped last night."

They criss-crossed the area a couple of times, chasing off a flock of blackbirds that made a fluttering roar during their departure. As they walked along, Sid told her about the call that morning from Arnie Bailey.

"He's feeling the pressure of a deadline," Jaz said. "When we get through here, we'd better get back onto your case."

"The newspaper in Ashland City will be out tomorrow with our story. I'm not too encouraged about how much good it'll do."

"Where do we need to concentrate?"

"We have to find a way to put pressure on the guys who can lead us to Tony Decker. I don't know that another trip to Lewisville would help, but we certainly need to work on twin brother Trent.'

They dropped the subject after reaching the back of the property with no sign of trespassers. Sid turned to the fence that bordered the road.

"Let's try along here."

They walked slowly, examining the ground all the way across. Near the far corner, Sid found a small spot where the grass had been trampled, as if someone had landed there after climbing over the fence.

"Let's check beside the road," he said.

They swung over the fence and glanced about.

"Look." Jaz pointed to a nearby area. "Faint tire tracks. Somebody drove in here."

Sid leaned over, stared at the stretch of bent grass. Two trails, spaced wheel-width apart. At the far end, dirt had been dug out over a short stretch.

"Looks like they pulled in, then spun the tires when they started off in a hurry," he said. "That matches your neighbor's report of a vehicle roaring away."

Jaz moved her head back and forth as she walked along the tracks. At one point, she stopped and bent down. "Give me one of your evidence bags, Sid."

He had brought along several small paper bags from Marie's kitchen. "What do you have?" He held the container open for her.

She took a pen from her jacket, scooped up a small creased piece of ruled paper, and dropped it in. Sid borrowed the pen and wrote the date, time, and location on the fold. He stuck it in his jacket pocket.

Jaz had a troubled look on her face. "What if it's blank?"

He replied in a somber voice. "I suppose we'd have to commit hara kiri."

She broke out laughing. "And I thought you were the serious one."

"My mama taught me not to be too predictable."

Jaz patted him on the back. "She taught you well."

They climbed over the fence and walked toward the house. A breeze blew the remaining fire odor away from them, leaving the cool November air invigorating. A rabbit popped out from behind a tree and scurried off, its white ball of a tail bobbing in the sunlight. The day seemed too idyllic to have followed such a night.

Back in Jaz's office, she took a pair of tweezers and removed the scrap of paper from the evidence bag. Using a couple of letter openers, she spread it out on her desk as Sid watched over her shoulder.

"Cancel the hara kiri," he said as soon as he saw the writing.

It read:

Rogers
D 637 Van 120

"What do you make of it?" Jaz asked.

"Handwriting isn't bad. Probably notes taken by phone. Somebody named Rogers, something designated D 637, a guy named Van, and twelve or a hundred and twenty who knows whats?"

"In other words, it could mean anything."

"Right. We might try the names on Bobby, see if they get any reaction."

"Okay, let's do it."

They found him at the kitchen table with his grandfather, drinking iced tea.

"I saw you two snooping around out back," John Wallace said when they walked in. "What were you looking for?"

Jaz smiled. "I was just showing Sid around the south forty.

The Surest Poison

You did a great job cleaning up the place. Has Bobby been a good helper?"

"The boy's not afraid of work. I'll give him that."

"I need to get back to my job," Bobby said, frowning. "I hope the insurance company will hurry up and get me money to buy another car."

"I'll loan you the money until they come through," Jaz said.

His face began to relax. "I'd sure appreciate it."

"Bobby, do you know somebody named Rogers?" Sid asked.

The young man's eyes narrowed. "Who?"

"Rogers. Or somebody named Van?"

Bobby looked puzzled. "No, sir. I've never heard of either one of them. Who are they?"

"Just a couple of names we came across and thought you might know," Jaz said.

Marie walked in and looked at Sid and Jaz. "Do you all need something else to eat?"

"I'm still full," Jaz said.

Sid patted his stomach. "Likewise."

"How about something to drink? I'll bet Mr. Sidney would like a cup of coffee."

"Strong and black," he said. "You're spoiling me."

"That's what I'm here for. If you're going to the office, I'll bring it in there."

When they got back to Jaz's desk, Sid gave her a stern look.

"I want you to call a security service and have them send over a couple of guys to patrol around your house tonight."

She smiled. "You still think I can't take care of myself?"

"I know you can take care of yourself, Wonder Woman. But if you're going to get any sleep, you can't be out there watching your flanks."

"I've been thinking about that. I wouldn't want anything to happen to the Wallaces."

When the phone rang, Jaz answered it, then turned to Sid with a questioning look. "It's for you."

Sid took the phone. "Hello."

"Mr. Chance, you've been expending a lot of effort searching for a man by the name of Tony Decker."

"That's right, who is this?"

"Get your pen ready, I have an address for you."

Sid found a pad on Jaz's desk and wrote down what the man read off. It wasn't a street address, however. It was a web address, starting with http://www.commercialappeal.com. When he finished, the man hung up.

"That looks like a news story from the Memphis newspaper's archives," Jaz said.

She sat at the computer and typed the web address into her Internet browser. When she hit Enter, a file appeared on the screen beneath the newspaper's logo and the heading Obituaries.

DECKER, TONY—Formerly of Ashland City, TN. March 9, 1999 at a Memphis hospital. Graveside services Friday at 2 p.m. at Memorial Cemetery. KELLY & COPES FUNERAL HOME.

34

LATER THAT AFTERNOON, after Sid had left, Fire Investigator Cran Quincy called.

"Miss LeMieux, I thought I would let you know my hunch was correct," he said.

"About the detonator?"

"Yes. I showed the piece of circuit board to a friend who flies radio-controlled planes. He confirmed that it came from a model airplane."

"Since nobody around my house knows anything about those expensive toys," Jaz said, "that makes it virtually certain someone left it here to set off a gas explosion."

"That's what I've concluded. I'll need to come back out and look for evidence of an intruder."

"Sid and I did that this afternoon, Mr. Quincy." She told him about the scrap of paper they found beside the tire tracks.

He sounded a bit miffed. "I'll come out and pick up that paper. I also need to ask you about those threats you mentioned, and I want to know more about the young man whose car was destroyed."

"Fine," she said. "I'll be here the rest of the day."

Jaz sat at her desk and debated the best way to handle Bobby. Should she tell him the explosion might be linked to his problem? Cran Quincy was already considering the likelihood that Bobby could have been the target of the blast, not her. When the investigator learned about the abduction and threat, he would demand some answers. Bobby could save everyone a lot of trouble by coming clean now.

She found Marie and Connie in the kitchen preparing dinner. Fresh vegetables bubbled in pots on the stove, while the aroma of banana pudding drifted out of the oven. Connie stood at the counter chopping cabbage for slaw.

"Where's Bobby?" Jaz asked.

"John took him into town to buy a car," Marie said.

Connie looked around. "He appreciated your letting him have the money. He needs to get back to work."

"I think he's going to have to answer some questions before anything else," Jaz said.

"About what?"

"About who's after him. The fire investigator is coming over. He says someone set off that explosion, and he suspects they may have been after Bobby because his car was parked outside the house."

Both women gave her startled looks, their eyes large black marbles.

"Do you think that's what happened?" Marie asked in a hushed voice.

"It's a good possibility. And Bobby needs to explain why. When he gets back, tell him I want to see him in my office."

AFTER SID RETURNED to Madison, he called Trent Decker at Dixie Seals.

"We received a tip today to check an on-line story from the Memphis *Commercial Appeal*," he said. "It was an obituary that showed your brother Tony died in a Memphis hospital on March ninth, 1999."

"That's news to me, Mr. Chance. As I told you Sunday, I hadn't heard anything of my brother in years. I guess now I know why."

"That leads to an interesting question," Sid said. "If Tony wasn't around Dixie Seals last Friday night, why did Pete Rackard call your phone number after Jaz LeMieux questioned him about Tony?"

"Who is Pete Rackard?"

"Your brother didn't tell you about his cohort at Auto Parts Rehabbers?"

"I don't know what you're talking about."

"I assure you, Mr. Decker, telephone records don't lie. Rackard called Dixie Seals Friday night."

"What time was the call made?"

"It was around six o'clock."

"We were closed, Mr. Chance. Rackard must have dialed a wrong number."

Like hell he did, Sid thought. That would be one coincidence that definitely defied belief, but he had no basis to question it. After that fruitless exchange, he called Jaz and gave her a replay of Trent Decker's comments.

"If so, that was the busiest wrong number I've ever come across," she said. "According to the log, it lasted seven minutes."

"I wish I'd known that. I agree with your assessment on Sunday. Trent Decker knows a whole lot more about this than he's admitting. I'm going to call him back."

"Before you do, let me tell you about the conversation I had with Cran Quincy," Jaz said.

She recounted the investigator's findings regarding the use of radio-controlled model airplane parts to trigger the explosion.

"That guy impressed me," Sid said. "Do you think he can get anything out of Bobby?"

"I don't know. That's the most stubborn young man I've ever encountered." She gave a soft laugh. "I guess I could threaten to call in his loan."

"Might be worth a try. After Quincy comes by, let me know what he makes of that note we found."

"Okay. Have you heard anything on that P.O. box from your post office contact?"

"No. I have a call in for him. He should be getting back to me soon."

When he got off the phone to Jaz, he called Trent Decker

again. The woman who answered said he had left for the day.

FIRE INVESTIGATOR Cran Quincy arrived shortly after Jaz talked to Sid. She met him at the door and escorted him to her office. After inviting him to have a seat, she handed him the evidence bag containing the slip of paper.

"This is what it looks like." She held out a blow-up of a photograph made while the paper was spread out on her desk.

He studied the picture for a moment, then looked up, his eyes wide. "Rogers. That's where my friend bought his model airplane, Rogers Toy Mart."

35

SID SHUT DOWN his computer and started tidying up his office. It was well past the normal time to close shop, though he had never worked by the clock. When the phone rang, he checked the caller ID. It showed his post office contact.

"What did you find?" Sid asked.

"This has been one more day," the man said, sounding exhausted. "Sorry I'm so late. The record shows the box changed hands a few times in recent years, but I tracked it back to First Patriots. It was rented in 1990 by a lawyer named Percy Pickslay, who listed an address in the J. C. Bradford Building on Fourth Avenue."

"That was back in the days when there was a J. C. Bradford Building." It was now a hotel.

"Right. I couldn't find him in the current phone book."

"I'll find him. Thanks for checking it out."

Sid knew the simplest way to learn something about a Nashville lawyer was to call Judge Gabriel Thackston.

"Hi, Judge, it's Sid," he said when he got Thackston on the line. "I need a little information."

"Sure, I'm full of it. How about the intricacies of four-card monte. It was popular with the troops during the Civil War, you know."

"Thanks, but I'll leave the cards for the Five Felons."

"Very well, what else can I help you with?"

"I'm trying to track down information on a corporation named First Patriots, Limited. It was chartered in Anguilla, but I've learned a lawyer named Pickslay provided the company's Nashville post office box. Had an office in the J. C. Bradford Building some years back."

"Percy Pickslay. As I recall, he was disbarred some ten years ago. I believe he defrauded investors in a stock deal."

"Is he still around town?"

"I haven't heard anything of him in a good while. I can ask around, if you'd like."

"Please do," Sid said. "And while you're at it, see if anyone knows anything about First Patriots, Limited, or who Pickslay might have been involved with in setting up the company."

"Be happy to. What can you tell me about this business at Jazmine LeMieux's house last night?"

Considering how much the Judge liked to talk, Sid was afraid to get specific in case it should complicate the investigation. "Looks like a gas leak from a water heater caused an explosion. Demolished the small house behind Jaz's place. I've been over there. It left a monstrous mess."

"The news people indicated nobody was hurt."

"That's correct. The couple who used to occupy the house now live with Jaz."

"The next time you talk to her, tell her I said to be careful."

Sid chuckled to himself. And she'd say mind your own business, I can take care of myself. But the question of whether the gas explosion had been aimed at Bobby or Jaz provided a lingering concern. He decided to call and see what she had learned from the fire investigator, if he had managed to crack Bobby's resolve to remain silent.

"Quincy was here," she said. "He wanted to know about our problems in Lewisville. He didn't get to talk with Bobby, but I told him what had happened. Bobby was off with his grandfather, looking for another car."

"Did Quincy pick up the note?"

"He took it. He also solved one of its riddles."

"What riddle?"

"The Rogers you thought was somebody's name? Looks like it could be Rogers Toy Mart. Quincy said that's where his

The Surest Poison

friend bought a radio-controlled model airplane."

"That's out Nolensville Pike, isn't it?" Sid asked.

"Right. I'm sure he'll check it out."

"I'm not waiting for him. If they're open tonight, I'll head over there and see if anyone remembers a recent purchase."

"What if there were several?"

"I'd say our man isn't a real model plane enthusiast. He'd be asking questions to make sure he got the right thing."

He told her about the call from his post office contact and Judge Thackston's offer to look into Percy Pickslay.

"I'll back up the judge and search the Internet for him," Jaz said.

"Did Quincy mention any plan to question Bobby?"

"He wants Bobby to call him. I plan to stay after Bobby until he does."

Sid looked up the Rogers Toy Mart number and found they closed at eight o'clock. He locked the office, hurried out to his car, and headed for Briley Parkway, which would take him past the sprawling Opryland Hotel complex. Briley ended at Thompson Lane a short distance from Nolensville Pike where Rogers was located.

The big toy store occupied a brick building adjacent to a strip center. Sid nosed into a parking slot and walked to the entrance, eyeing the conglomeration of toys that crowded the windows. One featured wagons, scooters, trikes, all manner of wheeled toys. Stuffed animals of every variety filled another window.

A few customers wandered about, but the store didn't appear busy with closing time near. Sid found a clerk and asked about model airplanes with radio controls.

"Sure. We've got several in that display over there," he said, pointing. He was a sloe-eyed young man in khaki pants and a blue knit shirt, likely had at least one Korean parent.

Sid showed his P.I. license. "I need to know if you've sold any in the past week."

"I'm pretty sure we have. I know we sell a lot of them, but

you'd need to talk to Mr. B. He's the manager. I'll get him for you."

He returned with an older man whose pinched face seemed to reflect the fallout of a difficult day drawing to a close. "You're a private detective?" he asked Sid.

"That's right." He showed his PI credentials. "I need to know if you've sold a radio-controlled airplane in, say, the last week."

"What happened? Did a model plane go through somebody's picture window?"

"No. Nothing like that. I'm looking for a person who bought one and may have used parts from it in the commission of a crime."

"My, my. That sounds ominous." Mr. B.'s frown deepened.

Sid persisted. "Did you sell one of these recently?"

"Yes, we sold one Sunday afternoon. The fellow must not have known much about electronics, though. He asked a lot of questions, wanted to know how the radio controls worked."

"Did the plane have a circuit board about this size?" Sid held his fingers to indicate what Cran Quincy had described.

"Yeah, it would be somewhere close to that."

"Did the guy pay by credit card, so you could look up the name?"

"No. I remember he paid cash."

"Could you describe him?"

The manager looked off to the front of the store as if something there might spark a memory. "I'm not very good at describing people. The only thing that stands out, his face resembled that loud-mouthed professional wrestler. You know... what's his name, Hulk Hogan? This man wasn't that big, of course, but he had that wild-looking mustache that hung down on both sides."

"Was he tall, short?"

"Maybe a few inches shorter than you. A little on the stocky side."

"Color of hair?"

"A light brown, best I can remember."

"Eyes?"

"I don't recall."

"Did he also buy a model rocket?"

"No. He looked at some but didn't buy anything."

"Okay," Sid said. "Thanks a lot. You've been very helpful."

He strolled out to his car, climbed in, and checked his watch. Almost eight o'clock and he hadn't eaten yet. He had a description of the suspected bomber, but no idea where to start looking for him. He headed for his favorite barbeque restaurant as troubling questions rumbled about in his mind.

36

THE CLOCK BUZZED Wednesday at six a.m. Sid rolled out of bed, pulled on his sweats, and headed out for his morning run. The cool air cleared the mental cobwebs accumulated during the night, shifting his mind into gear for the tasks that lay ahead. By the time he stepped from the shower, he was ready to tackle the world.

Then the day started to chip apart.

First came Jaz. The ringing phone caught him half-dressed. When he answered, her anxious voice hit him with the bad news.

"Bobby took off during the night," she said, "with Connie and Little Bob. He bought a car similar to the one that was wrecked by the explosion. This morning it was gone. I guess I was too hard on him."

"How so?"

"I browbeat him last night until he called Cran Quincy."

"What did Quincy say?"

"He told Bobby to be downtown this morning at nine, prepared to explain what was going on."

"Bobby didn't give any indication that he planned to run?"

"No, but he left a note on the table in the foyer."

"What did he say?"

"He thanked me for letting them stay at the mansion. But he said that for the protection of his family, he had no choice but to take them where nobody could find them. I should have seen something like this coming. He was upset last night after learning the explosion might have been targeted at him. I tried to reason with him. I told him the best way to end it would be to help us go after the people causing the problem."

"They must have put major pressure on him. He's young and vulnerable. I don't suppose he gave any hint where he might be going?"

"None."

Sid sat on the side of the bed, cradled the phone on his shoulder, and pulled on his socks. "Did you ask his grandmother about any close friends, any familiar places he might hide?"

"I will as soon as I can. Right now Marie's in no shape to talk."

"Did you have a chance to look into Percy Pickslay?"

"It appears he's been involved in things like witness profiling. In the outlying counties most of the time, but he has a few lawyers in Nashville as clients."

"You have an address for him?"

"He lives in Centerville."

This was a small town southwest of Nashville, birthplace of the late Sarah Cannon, better known as country comedienne Minnie Pearl.

"I'll try to track him down," Sid said. "Call me after you talk to Marie."

He checked an on-line directory, got a phone number in Centerville for Percy Pickslay and called it. An answering machine picked up. He listened to a low-pitched drawling voice explain that Pickslay was out of town "on a case" but could be reached by cell phone. When Sid tried the cell number, he got a voice mail instructing him to "leave your number and I'll get back to you as soon as possible."

The second crack in the day's facade. After leaving his phone number, he ate breakfast and headed for the office.

Switching on the computer, he found nothing more interesting than a pitch from a supposed former African leader's wife to help liberate twenty million bucks from her impoverished country. He switched out of email and turned to the telephone. Perhaps the Judge had come up with something.

"Good morning, Sidney. Looks like a beautiful day. I trust things are going well for you?"

Sid wasn't sure he was ready for the Judge's switch to an upbeat outlook. "Things would be going a lot better if I could make some progress on this case."

"Are you still looking for Percy Pickslay?"

"Jaz found him in Centerville, but I haven't been able to reach him. Have you heard anything?"

"I talked to a colleague last night who knows him. He hadn't heard of First Patriots, but he said Pickslay set up all kinds of corporations. He liked to make his deals sound great by putting First in the name."

"Did he mention any partners?"

"No names, but he said Pickslay dealt with small town lawyers. They were able to sucker in the more gullible types."

"I'd sure like to tie Bronson Fradkin into his stable of dealers."

Thackston chuckled. "I'd be surprised if Fradkin wasn't a co-conspirator. Pickslay came from Centerville, and it isn't far from Lewisville."

"Thanks, Judge. Let me know if you hear anything else."

"I will. Has our girl recovered from her experience with the fiery inferno?"

"She's doing fine, except for her problems with the house staff's grandson."

"The young man you went to check on Friday night?"

"Right."

"What has he done now"

"Flew the coop. Disappeared."

"Ahh, that should be no problem. Jasmine told us you're the quintessential missing person locator."

"We'll see about that. My batting average at the moment would get me sent back to the minor leagues."

Judge Thackson laughed. "Keep swinging, my friend."

Sid hung up the phone, reached in a file drawer, and

The Surest Poison

pulled out the folder labeled "HarrCo Shipping." He opened it and spread out some of the more significant items on his desk. Notes on the interviews in Ashland City and Lewisville, phone calls to Larry Irwin's cousin near Murfreesboro and his friend in Clarksville, the interview with Gordon Gracey, copies of Jaz's backgrounder on Trent Decker, and the Tony Decker obit from the *Commercial Appeal* archives. He was browsing through the material when he heard the outside door open. The image on his TV monitor showed Jack Post, hat cocked at a jaunty angle.

Sid walked to the office door. "Come in, Jack. What are you doing around here this early in the day? I thought you were out of town."

He returned to his desk as Post headed for the chair across from him.

"Got back last night," the old newsman said. "I had to see a real estate agent down the hall."

"You selling your condo?"

"Nah. My ex put her house, what used to be my house, on the market. I had to bring some signed papers."

Sid grinned. "You must spend more time with her now than you did when you were married."

"Maybe. I just took her to Memphis. That's where I met her, you know. Back when I worked for the *Commercial Appeal*."

Sid shuffled through the papers and pulled out the copy of Tony Decker's obituary. "This guy we're looking for, Tony Decker, came from Memphis. We got an anonymous tip to check out the paper's web site and found his obit on it."

Post got up and walked over to read the sheet Sid held out. He twisted his face into a disparaging look.

"This came off the newspaper's web site?"

"Jaz printed it out from the computer."

"Something's screwy. There's no Memorial Cemetery in Memphis, and I never heard of any Funeral Home named Kelly and Copes."

Sid stared at him. "You're sure?"

"I know the town, man. I used to work there. I drive down there every whipstitch, especially when DeeDee's got problems."

Which was most of the time, Sid thought. "How could this get on their web site?"

"A hacker, maybe? Somebody paid off somebody at the paper?"

"I find that hard to believe."

Post appeared to take that as an affront. He glared across at Sid. "If you don't believe me, go downtown to the library. They have the *Commercial Appeal* on microfilm. Look it up for yourself. I guarantee you won't find that obit in the newspaper."

37

As SOON AS Post left, Sid called Jaz.

"Somebody's giving us a bum steer," he said. "Tony Decker isn't dead."

She gasped. "What?"

He told her about Post's visit.

"That's unbelievable," she said.

"Don't tell Jack. I think I insulted him when I said that."

"Somebody we've contacted is trying to throw us off the trail."

"Here's another thing. The Judge's friend says First Patriots is the type of name Pickslay used for his deals. And he worked with small town lawyers like Bronson Fradkin."

"Did you talk to Pickslay?"

"No. I left a message for him to call me. What's the latest on Bobby?"

"I got Marie calmed down after a bit," she said. "She overheard Bobby talking on the phone last night to an old high school buddy. He lives on a farm down toward The Narrows. Marie thinks that's where they went. If it is, we'll have to sneak up on him or he'll run again."

"It might be better to let him cool down a bit before we do anything. Did you call Quincy?"

"Yes. That was before I talked to Marie. He wasn't too happy about Bobby leaving, but I said we'd do our best to track him down. Quincy plans to go by Rogers Toy Mart this morning."

Sid realized he had forgotten to mention his trip to the toy store last night. He told her what he had learned from the manager.

"Give me that description of the customer again," Jaz said.

"A few inches shorter than me, light brown hair, a wild-looking mustache that hung down on both sides like Hulk Hogan's."

Her voice ticked up a notch. "I saw a mechanic who looked like that at Pete Rackard's repair shop Friday night."

Sid paused a moment, weighing the impact. "You realize what it would mean if this is the same guy?"

"Yeah. It would mean we've just turned our apple cart upside down again."

"We'd be in limbo as to whether the target was you or Bobby."

"But we don't know for sure if that mechanic is our man. Have you had any more ideas on the meaning of that note we found?"

Sid pulled out his copy. "We need to think outside the box. We know Rogers was not someone's name. How about Van?"

"Try van with a small V."

"Hmm. Could be what he drove out to your house."

After a moment, Jaz said, "Let's suppose the notes were written during a phone call. Somebody says you can get the radio controls at Rogers Toy Mart. Use the van. What's the rest of it?"

"Sorry, but I make no claim to being clairvoyant."

"You're great at deductive reasoning, though. Work on it a bit and see what you come up with."

"I'll try." He took his pencil and underlined the items that still stumped them. Then a sudden thought hit him. "I know something I can do about your mechanic sighting."

"What?"

"I'll take my little spy camera down to Franklin and get a picture of him. I'll show it to Mr. B. at Rogers Toy Mart and see if we can get an ID."

"Be careful. Better not let the Rackard folks find out who

you are. They'd throw you out in a heartbeat."

"Don't worry, I can handle that," he said. "I'll head on out there and stop by your place on the way back."

NASHVILLE TV forecasters earned their pay attempting to cope with the way conditions changed from day to day, rain or sleet or snow, heat or cold, clouds or sun. Sid didn't remember it in the forecast, but a bright ball in the sky spread its golden glow over Franklin, boosting the temperature to an almost summery sixty-nine as he arrived at Rack's Auto Repair. The overhead doors on the side stood open, giving access to slots where cars and trucks sat with hoods up, one on a jack minus its wheels. He parked his pickup near the open doors and walked toward the shop area.

A large man with a beer belly and a limp came from between two cars. His shirt had a patch with "Pete" embroidered on it. From Jaz's description, it had to be Rackard.

"What kind of problem you got?" he asked.

"I'd like somebody to check my battery," Sid said. "It's been acting a little strange."

Rackard pointed to an open space. "Pull it in there. Somebody will be with you in a minute."

Sid drove his truck inside and set the brake. Before stepping down to the shop floor, he checked the small flat camera mounted in a pocket inside his shirt, utilizing a design that left a small hole for the lens to shoot through. He stood beside his truck and looked around until he spotted the wild-looking mustache. The mechanic was working on a sleek yellow Porsche.

Sid walked over to him. "That's a sharp looking car. What model is it?"

The mechanic turned, providing a full face view. It also showed the name on his coveralls, Shak. Sid pressed the small activator in his pocket. Since the camera's shutter made no sound, Shak was none the wiser.

"That little baby's a 911," the man said. "It's only a few

months old. It'll set you back around ninety-thou."

Sid thought about asking what it would take to blow it up. He smiled. "Nice car, but I think I'll keep my truck."

He triggered another exposure before strolling back across to his pickup. He found another mechanic hooking the truck battery to a large tester. After making a few adjustments, the grease-smudged man looked up.

"This yours?"

Sid nodded.

"Ain't nothing wrong with the battery. What's it been doing?"

"I've had some problems with the lights. I guess it's in the electrical system."

"You'll have to leave it with us."

"Some other time." He glanced at his watch. "I need to get moving. What do I owe you?"

"No charge. You'd better call for an appointment, though, before you bring it in for electrical work."

Sid thanked him and climbed into the truck. He backed out and headed for Jaz's. Fifteen minutes later, she met him at the front door looking relaxed in cutoff jeans.

"You're getting with this unseasonable weather," he said, pointing at the shorts.

"I wear what's comfortable. Marie doesn't think it's ladylike."

"Reminds me of Daisy May."

She made a little curtsy. "Did you get a picture?"

"Here's our man," he said, pulling out the small digital camera and an adapter cord.

"Let's go see what you have."

She led him into her office, plugged the adapter into her computer, and downloaded the photo. She zoomed to full screen.

"He's the one I saw," she said. "Doesn't that match Mr. B.'s description?"

"It does to me. Print it out, and I'll see what he says."

The Surest Poison

Before the sheet rolled out of the printer, a knock sounded at the open door.

"Don't you folks know when it's time to eat lunch?" Marie asked. It was said more in disbelief than disapproval.

Sid glanced at his watch. "I guess you're right."

"I have a nice fruit salad and some bran muffins, if that would do."

Jaz gave him a questioning glance. "Okay for you?"

"I don't want to impose, but it sounds fine."

"Impose? I never heard such talk." Marie shook her head.

Jaz took him by the arm. "He'll eat. Come on, Sid."

Jaz insisted they eat in the kitchen and not mess up the dining room. Marie objected but went on about her business. She appeared accustomed to Jaz being adamant about her decisions. While they were eating, Jaz asked him if he had heard anything new regarding Bart Masterson's homicide cases.

"When he called yesterday to ask about you, he said he had checked out Larry Irwin's phone calls the night of the murder. One, which could have been the killer, was made from an el cheapo phone."

"Untraceable."

"Bart tracked it down to the store where it was bought but reached a dead end there."

When they finished lunch, Jaz went back to her office and put the photo in an envelope. "Let me change into something a little more decent, and I'll go with you," she said.

She was back a few minutes later dressed in designer jeans and a white shirt with JLM embroidered above one breast. Catching a hint of perfume that conjured up images of Arabian Nights, Sid marveled at how she could make any outfit seem exotic.

Jaz patted the side of Sid's well-worn truck before climbing in. "Did you equate Rack's with those poor folks around Ashland City?" she asked.

He shrugged. "I thought it would make me look more like

a harmless old country boy. For sure Rack's isn't for poor folks. This guy Shak was working on a fancy Porsche." He slid in under the steering wheel and looked around. "You're not going to let me live that down, are you?"

She gave him a sultry look. "One of these days, maybe. We'll see."

On their way to Nolensville Pike, Sid ticked off what they had uncovered thus far and what they still needed to find. Although confident all the major players had been identified, they weren't sure where each of them fitted in. They had nothing on the owners of First Patriots, Ltd, and Tony Decker remained as elusive as ever, presuming he was still alive.

"If it turns out that the mad bomber works for Pete Rackard," Jaz said, "do you think that means Rackard was more than just an employee of Auto Parts Rehabbers?"

"He was into it in a big way. I still don't understand how these ex-cons got involved in the business."

"Remember, Larry Irwin's friend Reggie said he thought it was run by a bunch of crooks, who may have been involved with stolen property."

"Yeah. We need more evidence of that."

"Has Percy Pickslay returned your call?"

"No, and I'm beginning to wonder if he will."

"Would it be worth a trip to Centerville to look for him?"

"That may be our only hope."

When they arrived at Rogers Toy Mart, they found Mr. B. helping a woman whose shopping basket was stacked with toddler toys.

"She must have triplets," Jaz said.

"If that's the case, I don't envy her husband."

They waited beside a row of shelves laden with dolls, dollhouses, doll clothes. The make-believe moppets had more accessories than a well-heeled teenager.

When the woman pushed her basket on past them, Sid opened the envelope and approached the manager. He introduced Jaz.

The Surest Poison

"Nice meeting you, Miss LeMieux. A fire investigator, had a funny name, came by here this morning asking about sales of radio-controlled airplanes. Same as you, Mr. Chance."

"We worked with him on the case yesterday," Sid said. He pulled out the photo. "See if this looks like the man you told me about."

Mr. B. frowned as he studied the picture. "If that's not him, it's his twin brother."

38

IN THE PARKING lot, Sid called Investigator Quincy and told him the toy store manager's reaction to the photo.

"I was out at Rogers this morning," Quincy said. "I figured it was you when he told me somebody had already been there asking the same questions. And Miss LeMieux recognized this Shak fellow?"

"As soon as I mentioned the mustache description, she remembered him."

"You realize it's still no more than circumstantial. For all we know, Shak could be out flying his model airplane right now. But it's enough to warrant questioning him. I'll need to check his alibi for early yesterday morning."

"We wondered if the Van on that piece of paper could refer to a vehicle. You might see if he owns or has access to a van."

"I think I'd better talk to the two of you first and get all the details on this threat Miss LeMieux mentioned."

"We're at your disposal."

"I have a case I'm finishing up. Can we make it in the morning?"

"Where and when?"

"Why don't we meet at her house at ten. I can head out to Williamson County after that."

Sid flipped the phone shut and turned to Jaz. "Your house at ten in the morning. Okay by you?"

"It had better be. Looks like you've already made the arrangements."

He knew it ran counter to her principle of stay in control,

but as long as she was playing in his league, she'd have to play by his rules.

As they headed toward Franklin Road, Arnie Bailey called. He sounded fired up. "I just heard from Wade Harrington," he snapped.

Sid held his breath. He hoped it was not another demonstration. "What's happened?"

"He had a copy of the Ashland City paper with a long story about the trichloroethylene situation. He said there was a side article asking anyone with information about Auto Parts Rehabbers to call you. Have you heard anything yet?"

"You're the first caller. I'm glad the story's out, but I'm not too encouraged about the prospects of learning anything new as a result of it."

"What were you able to track down from that post office box?"

"We got the name of a disbarred lawyer who opened it."

"Who's that?"

"Percy Pickslay."

"Might have known. Deals like that are what got him into trouble. He's a moneygrubber. He's out chasing jurors rather than ambulances these days."

"So I heard, but I haven't been able to get in touch with him yet."

"He was at the courthouse when I left a short time ago. I think he's working on a trial for one of my former law partners, Lew Jonas. You may know Lew. Chances are he could tell us if Percy is still around."

"Do you think Pickslay would still have records regarding a company he helped set up fifteen or twenty years ago?"

"The man saves anything that might have a monetary value in the future."

"Could you contact Jonas and find out if he's still around? If you can locate the guy, I'll go corner him right now."

"Give me a few minutes," Bailey said. "I'll get back to you."

They were almost to Jaz's house. She reached into her

handbag for the remote to open the gate. "I hope you can find Pickslay in Nashville," she said.

"Yeah. It would save a trip to Centerville tomorrow."

"Which would give us a chance to go looking for Bobby."

Sid swung his truck into the entrance. "Let's see where things stand after we talk with Cran Quincy in the morning."

They drove through the gate and up to the parking area in front of the house. John Wallace sat on the veranda with an ancient-looking tool box repairing a white rocking chair.

"You had a call a little while ago, Miss Jasmine," he said. "I think it was that fellow who arranged to bring Bobby's family over here. I left the number on your desk."

"The local Welcome Traveler Stores manager," she said to Sid. "Thanks, John."

As they walked into her office, Sid's phone rang. It was Arnie Bailey.

"There's a coffee shop down Second Avenue called The Bottomless Cup," Bailey said. "It's near Lew Jonas's office."

"Yeah, I've seen it," Sid said.

"Get down there as fast as you can. Lew will be sitting with Pickslay. He said he'd try to keep him occupied until you got there."

"Thanks, Arnie. I know Jonas when I see him. I'm on my way."

He shut off the phone and looked at Jaz. "I have to get downtown to catch Percy Pickslay. I'll let you know if I have any luck."

AFTER SID LEFT, Jaz called her manager friend. Their special relationship stemmed from the fact she had helped him get his position a few years earlier. He was assistant manager at a store where she participated in the grand opening. He planned and directed the activities almost single-handed. She was so impressed by his ability to organize things, plus his dedication to the job, that she recommended him for promotion.

"Hello, Nick," she said. "Is there something I can help you with?"

"On the contrary, I have some information I think you should know."

"What's that?"

"I happened to overhear a conversation by one of the boys who drove that family out to your house last Saturday. He was telling another employee what a neat place you had. I got after him. I reminded him my instructions were to keep that trip in confidence. He said he was sorry, but other people already knew about it anyway."

"What other people?"

"Sunday morning a guy came into the store and buttonholed him, asked if he was the one who drove the people to the big house on Franklin Road the night before. He admitted he was. The fellow wanted to know was the family staying in the mansion. He said he let them out in front of the little house in back and figured they were staying there. After what happened the other night, I thought you ought to know."

39

Located on the first floor of one of the Victorian Era commercial structures on Second Avenue that had been renovated into a popular shopping district, the The Bottomless Cup attracted a wide array of customers from professionals to construction workers. Two young women stood at the counter ordering lattes as Sid looked around the room. He spotted Lew Jonas at a table in back. The lawyer was an Arnie Bailey clone except for a full head of hair where Arnie had almost none. A skinny, weasel-faced man sat across from him, his arms too long for the sleeves of his pin-striped coat.

Sid walked back and stopped beside the table. "Mr. Pickslay?" he said.

The man looked up with questioning eyes. "Yes?"

Lew Jonas smiled. "Hello, Sid. I recognize you from Arnie's description. Percy, this is Sidney Chance. Have a seat, Sid. I'll get you a cup of coffee. How do you like it?"

"Black. Thanks." He settled into a chair beside Pickslay as Jonas got up and moved to the counter.

"You a friend of Lew's?" Pickslay asked.

"A friend of a friend. All in the line of duty."

"What kind of duty?"

"I'm a PI."

"Oh?"

"I've been on the lookout for you, Mr. Pickslay."

"What for?"

"A number of years ago, you were involved in the organization of a corporation called First Patriots, Limited. The compa-

The Surest Poison

ny was chartered in Anguilla in the British West Indies."

Pickslay shrugged. "I was involved in a lot of companies, chartered in Anguilla and a dozen or so other places."

"Do you remember First Patriots? You used a downtown post office box for the address."

He laughed. "Do you know how many post office boxes I had at one time? I used the same address for lots of different entities."

"Would you still have records that show who was involved in First Patriots?"

"I don't throw anything away."

"So I was told."

"By who?"

"As my dear mother would say, by whom?"

"What are you, some kind of teacher?"

"No, but she was. I need to know who the stockholders were for First Patriots, Limited. I'd be willing to pay a reasonable fee for the information."

Pickslay grinned. "Now you're talking my language. I'm in the information business these days, you know."

"Can you have it for me by tomorrow?" Sid asked.

"Five hundred bucks."

Sid gave a grunt of exasperation. "Five hundred? For a few names? That's exhorbitant."

"Supply and demand, Mr. Chance. You must have gone to a lot of trouble to track me down here. That tells me your client wants those names with a passion. My advice is to take the offer before the price goes up."

Lew Jonas walked up with a coffee for Sid and something foamy for himself.

"Thanks." Sid took the cup and set it on the table. "Excuse me for a moment while I make a phone call."

He moved over beside the wall and punched in Arnie Bailey's number. The secretary put him through.

"I just wanted an okay on a proposition," Sid said.

He outlined what Percy Pickslay had proposed for divulging the identity of the First Patriots, Ltd. owners.

"That's the crux of our case, isn't it?" Arnie said. "We need those names to prove who was responsible for that chemical dump. Tell him we'll pay five hundred for documentary evidence."

"Good enough. If Pickslay comes through, we should be able to wrap up this thing tomorrow."

"Have you found Decker?"

"No, but when we get these names, it should lead us to his door."

That wasn't a given, but it satisfied Arnie for the moment. Sid walked back to the table and took his seat. He looked across at the disbarred lawyer. "It's a go, Mr. Pickslay. But my client wants documentary evidence. It could be an original or a copy certified as true by you and a notary."

Jonas chuckled. "Sounds like you two have been doing some business."

Sid held up his cup. "How about a toast to the successful conclusion of our little commercial endeavor." He took a sip of coffee. "When and where can I pick up the document?"

Pickslay glanced around the room. "I need to be back in Nashville tomorrow morning. Why don't we meet right here at eight-thirty?"

"Deal." He reached out to shake Pickslay's hand.

40

BACK AT HIS OFFICE in Madison, Sid found three calls on his answering machine from people in Ashland City. The news story had produced results after all. He started returning the calls. The first was a woman who had once rented a room to a man employed by Auto Parts Rehabbers. His name—John Smith. Sid tossed his pencil on the desk and made a face. She couldn't remember where he came from or where he went after he moved out.

The second caller had once dated a man who worked for the company. He went by the name Slick Lawhorn.

"He was slick, all right," she said. "When I got home that night, my billfold was missing, along with about seventy dollars."

"Do you remember where he lived, or what happened to him?" Sid asked.

"If I did, I'd have gone after him with a baseball bat."

He recognized the voice of the third caller before she gave her name, Vickie Thomas. When he got her on the phone, she began to apologize.

"I intended to call you back after we heard about Larry Irwin. That was such a shock. I didn't know it when we talked, but he worked under my husband at American Universal. I'm sorry. I got so busy with other things that I forgot to call you."

"I'm sure the police talked to your husband."

"A couple of times. He didn't have any idea who could have done it, though. They asked about Auto Parts Rehabbers. Do they think his death could have been related to his job there?"

"That's a possibility, but they're more concerned that somebody had been threatening him."

After a moment, she said, "Come to think of it, at the funeral home I talked to a neighbor of his. She told me a man asked about Larry's house the day before he was killed. I wonder if it could have had something to do with this?"

"Did she say what happened?"

"She had gone to the mailbox when this car stopped beside her. The driver wanted to know which house was Larry's. She said he didn't have a number on his house or on his mailbox. When she pointed it out, the man just drove on."

"Do you remember the woman's name?"

"No, but she lived next door to Larry."

Sid thanked her and put in a call to Bart Masterson. He told Bart about Vickie Thomas's funeral home chat.

"I think there was a neighbor we never managed to interview," the detective said. "We'll check her out."

"Anything new on the case?"

"We haven't had much luck tracking back into Gillie Younger's past. He did a lot of odd jobs before going to work for Metro. We haven't found any permanent employment. How are you doing with the chemical spill folks?"

"We're making some headway. An ex-lawyer named Percy Pickslay is giving us the names of the First Patriots, Limited stockholders. The corporation was one of the owners of Auto Parts Rehabbers."

"I'm familiar with Pickslay. I didn't know he ever gave anything away."

"Matter of fact, he's doing it for a finder's fee."

Next he called Jaz to give her the good news about the deal with Pickslay. She gave him the bad news regarding what happened Sunday morning at the Welcome Traveler Store, where the employee was asked about Bobby's trip to her house.

Sid's grip tightened on the phone "You mean—"

"It sounds like they were gunning for Bobby after all," she said.

"First it was you, then Bobby, then you, now Bobby . . . this is one convoluted mess."

"Yes, and we need to find Bobby before whoever it is gets to him."

"Why don't we make a run to Cheatham County tonight and see if he's at the friend's?"

"I was going to suggest that, but I didn't want to interfere with your plans."

"Plans? The way things are going right now, I'm just reacting. I don't have time for plans."

"Okay. I'll get Marie to find somebody who can give us directions. What time do you want to go?"

"How about I pick you up around seven?"

Sid turned to his computer and began assembling all the information they had gleaned on Auto Parts Rehabbers. He wanted to have a full report ready for Arnie Bailey after the meeting with Percy Pickslay in the morning. As he put it together, he concentrated on the holes in the case.

The murder of young Larry Irwin was one troubling aspect. Could it have been related to Auto Parts Rehabbers? The shooting took place Wednesday night a week ago. That was the day Arnie Bailey gave him the case, the day he started his investigation. But how could it tie in? Had Larry known something he shouldn't?

Another major concern was the uncertainty over what provoked the explosion on Jaz's property. Was it really aimed at Bobby? If one of Pete Rackard's men set it up, that also pointed toward a link to Auto Parts Rehabbers. After Jaz's visit to Rack's Auto Repair, Rackard had called Bronson Fradkin and another number in Lewisville. Was it to Hank Keglar? Blowing up the little house could have been meant as a warning to Jaz.

He searched his desk for the text of the note they found behind Jaz's fence. He began doodling with the "D 637" and the number "12o." Was the latter a scrawled version of 120 or 12 "o"? Could it mean twelve o'clock? Maybe they were to have everything ready by midnight. The explosion took place sometime after 2 a.m. The other letter and numbers remained meaningless.

The main missing piece was Tony Decker. Sid still believed twin brother Trent held the key. Trent had lied from the start. Rackard's phone call Friday night that showed Dixie Seals' number must have been about Tony. One part Trent may not have lied about was the idea of bringing his brother into the business. He thought it possible that Tony worked for the company under an assumed name.

He picked up the phone, called Dixie Seals, and asked for Trent Decker.

"Mr. Decker is in conference and left instructions not to be disturbed," he was told.

When I get him, he'll be disturbed, Sid thought. "Ask him to call Sidney Chance as soon as he's available. Tell him it's very important."

He left both office and cell numbers.

41

WHEN SID PARKED his pickup at the mansion around seven, Jaz brought out maps and aerial photos from MapQuest, marked to show the approximate location of the farm where Bobby might be hiding. Marie had found another of Bobby's friends who was familiar with the area and provided some landmarks.

"I hope you don't object to taking my truck," he said as he opened the door for her.

She didn't hesitate. "In this case, I think it's quite appropriate. We should look like we belong on a farm."

They headed west out of Nashville on U.S. 70, also known as State Route 1. This was the original Memphis-to-Bristol highway hewed out of the wilderness a century ago. It spanned the state from southwest to northeast, a distance of well over 500 miles.

The road ran through one of the more rural sections of Metropolitan Nashville, along the Harpeth River, before crossing into Cheatham County. Jaz kept watch on the traffic to make sure no one followed. There was no moon, leaving the area dark except for the occasional sprinkling of light from an isolated house. They passed through a few communities not large enough for a post office. Just past one called Shacklett, they turned onto Butterworth Road. Jaz confirmed there were no vehicles in sight when they made the turn. Butterworth meandered northward through farmland and forests toward the scenic area known as The Narrows of the Harpeth River. Sid recalled the photo in the reception area at HarrCo Shipping. After a few miles, they rounded a sharp curve and encountered a narrow lane that matched the aerial view Jaz held.

"Turn here," she said. "Now we watch for a silvery metal gate and a dirt trail going back into the woods."

Sid eased along until they spotted the gate on the left.

"Want me to get it?" Jaz asked.

"Keep your seat." Despite years of working with women as equals, he couldn't get away from the gentlemanly ways his mother had taught him.

He pulled up, got out, and opened the gate. After moving through, he closed it and followed the pair of tire tracks into the dark mass of trees. About fifty yards in, they saw a clearing with a two-story farmhouse in the middle. From what they could make out in the headlights, the house appeared old but well kept.

"There's Bobby's car," Jaz said, pointing to a dark-colored Ford parked beside a large white diesel pickup.

As they drove into the clearing, two large German shepherds raced out of the darkness, barking like hounds after a fox. Outside lights flashed on at the corners of the house. Pretty effective burglar alarm, Sid thought as he pulled onto the graveled parking area and switched off the engine. The dogs continued to bark and pace around the truck.

A large man in overalls, built like an NFL lineman, came out the front door, yelling at the dogs. Sid lowered his window.

"These fellas don't sound like they're playing," he said.

"If they don't know you, they can be downright nasty." The man spoke in a deep baritone. He walked to the truck in his bare feet. He appeared to be about the same age as Bobby, with short bristly hair and an uncertain look on his face. The dogs calmed down but continued to pace like sentries on guard duty, uttering an occasional growl.

"You must be Ned," Sid said. That was the name Marie had given them.

"That's me. Something I can do for you?"

"My name is Sidney Chance, and my partner here is Miss

The Surest Poison

Jasmine LeMieux. We need to talk to Bobby urgently."

"I sort of figured that."

"Is it safe to get out and mingle with your friends there?" Sid smiled at the dogs.

"Not till I give 'em strict orders to behave. The problem I got is, Bobby, he don't want to talk to you."

"He needs to, for his own good as well as Connie and Little Bob. I'm sure you know Bobby's grandparents live with Jaz. They asked her to help him, and I'm backing her up."

"How you gonna help him?"

"Did Bobby tell you about his problem?"

"Sort of. He didn't tell me who it was or what all's involved. He's afraid it could hurt his family."

Sid stuck his head out the window. "Look, Ned, if we can track him down here, so can somebody else. And they won't hesitate to shoot those dogs. Did Bobby tell you about the explosion at Jaz's place?"

"Yeah, sounded like a real bad scene."

Sid related the evidence that pointed to Bobby as being the target of the explosion. "If he'll tell us what's going on, I guarantee we'll find the people responsible and see that they're prosecuted."

"Mr. Chance, I've been close to that boy since we played football in high school. I've never known him to be as uptight as he is right now. When he called me about coming out here, I swore I wouldn't let anybody get close to him."

Jaz leaned across Sid. "Both of us are former police officers, Ned. We've been in a lot of tough situations. I can assure you the people Bobby's up against aren't the kind to give up until they get what they want, or get caught. If you're his friend, the best thing you can do for him is convince him to tell us what he knows. That way he can get back to leading a normal life. He can't go on hiding much longer."

The young man rubbed his broad forehead and shook his head. "Gimmie your phone number and I'll see what I can do. Maybe he'll let me bring him back in the morning."

Jaz handed him her card. "If he's concerned about coming to my house, we'll meet him back here."

"See what I can do," he repeated. He turned to the dogs and gave a stern command. "Stay!"

Sid backed the truck around and headed down the trail toward the road.

He glanced at Jaz. "What do you think?"

"If anybody can convince Bobby to change his mind, I'd say Mr. Ned is the man."

As they drove back to Jaz's place, Sid told her about his speculations on the evidence relating to Auto Parts Rehabbers. He reminded her of Pete Rackard's call to Dixie Seals.

"Do you plan to confront Trent Decker tomorrow?"

"Yes. I don't expect him to return my calls. As soon as I pick up those papers from Percy Pickslay, I'll head out to Dixie Seals."

Back at the LeMieux mansion, Jaz invited him in for a nightcap. Marie met them in the foyer.

"Did you find Bobby?" she asked, her face pinched from worry.

"They were with his friend Ned." Jaz told her what happened.

"I hope that boy will come to his senses," his grandmother said. She looked at Sid. "Can I get you anything?"

"I'm fine," Sid said.

"Let me see if I can talk him into a little glass of wine," Jaz said. "Then you can bring us some of that delicious-looking chocolate cake you made this afternoon. We'll be in the rec room. It's about time to get the news on the Fox channel."

Jaques LeMieux had furnished the room with several casino card tables, a reading corner with plush chairs, a TV set and a wet bar. Photographs from his hunting trips decorated the walls. Jaz had rearranged things a bit, keeping one card table, the wet bar, and a few chairs. She added a large flat screen TV and exercise equipment. Paneled in walnut, the room had soft recessed lighting.

The Surest Poison

Sid looked around. "Nice layout," he said.

"Not quite as fancy as Dad had it." She moved to the bar and poured two glasses of cabernet and offered one to him.

He took it reluctantly. He knew too many alcoholic ex-cops. Since his flirtation with booze after the Lewisville fiasco, he normally avoided nightcaps.

"We should have Miss Demeanor and Five Felons Poker Club meetings here," he said. "That's a cool table."

She looked around. "I'm afraid they'd think me ostentatious. Anyway, the guys are too steeped in tradition. Wick would swear only bad luck could come from such a change."

Grabbing a remote, she switched on the local Fox channel. She sat on a cushioned love seat and set her glass on the low coffee table. "Care to join me, Mr. Chance?"

He sat beside her as the picture of a smashed car on the side of the road filled the screen. Savoring the aroma and taste of the wine, Sid paid little attention to the news anchor until he heard Percy Pickslay's name.

"Pickslay?" he said, leaning forward.

"He's dead."

The car had swerved off I-40 on the west side of Nashville, crashing into a bridge abutment. The accident occurred within the past hour. A newsman at the scene reported an eyewitness traveling some distance back saw someone turn into Pickslay's path, forcing him onto the shoulder of the highway. The car had just passed the witness at a high rate of speed.

"He identified it as a late model black Chrysler," said the newsman. "The driver didn't stop to see what had happened. The witness reported there was a Nashville Predators sticker on the back bumper."

Sid and Jaz looked at each other.

"Sounds like the car that passed us on Ashland City Highway Friday night," she said.

42

As THE ANCHOR moved to a story about dozens of cats and dogs crowded into a small house that smelled like a barnyard, Marie came in with two slices of chocolate cake on a tray and a cup of coffee for Sid. She frowned at the looks on their faces.

"Is something wrong?"

"Our case just flew out the window," Sid said.

Jaz told her how Percy Pickslay's death complicated the outcome of Sid's investigation. The gray-haired housekeeper shook her head. "I am so sorry. What will you do now?"

"Pickslay is from Centerville," Jaz said. She looked around at Sid. "That's Hickman County. Do you know anybody in the sheriff's office down there? With my experience the other night, I wouldn't put it past these people to torch his house, or wherever he keeps his records."

"Good point," Sid said. "The sheriff used to be a tough old boy named Alex Emmons. I don't know if he's still the man in charge. I need a phone number."

"Let's go to my office." She turned to Marie. "Just leave things in here. We'll be back."

Sid finished his wine as Jaz tapped a few commands on her computer keyboard. She wrote a number on a pad.

"Try this." She handed him the phone and held out the slip of paper.

Sid punched in the number. After a couple of rings, the Hickman County Sheriff's Office answered.

"This is Sidney Chance in Nashville," he said. "I need to get

The Surest Poison

in touch with Sheriff Emmons right away." He hoped to God Emmons was still the man.

"Chief Chance?"

That caught him off guard. "Former Chief Chance. Who's this?"

"Deputy Ross. You helped us out with a drug investigation a few years back. You gave me some advice I'll never forget. Don't overlook the obvious. Sounds funny, but oh so true. Is this an emergency situation?"

"Did you hear about Percy Pickslay's death in a car accident?"

"Yeah. THP contacted us."

The Highway Patrol would have been involved, Sid thought. "It may be pure speculation, but there's a possibility he was run off the road by somebody involved in a case I'm investigating."

"Are you back in Lewisville?"

"No, I'm doing private work in Nashville. But if my hunch is right, these people could try to destroy some of Pickslay's records that I'm after. I talked to him this afternoon, and he agreed to bring the information to me in the morning. The wrong people could have found out about it. Do you have any idea where he might keep his old case files?"

"At his house, I'd guess. He works out of there."

"Could you have somebody check out the place, keep an eye on it tonight?"

"Not much going on around here. I think we could do that. I'll have the sheriff call you. What's your number?"

Sid gave the deputy his cell number and handed the phone to Jaz. "Let's go eat our cake and wait for Emmons to call."

Back in the rec room, he picked up a plate and dug into the cake with its thick layer of chocolate icing. Though not a chocoholic, he could do serious damage to a much larger portion. He stood in front of the TV, which both ignored.

"I've been thinking about what it would mean if that car on

I-40 was the one we saw Friday night," Jaz said.

"That deputy reminded me of some advice I once gave him, advice I should have taken myself."

"What's that?"

"Don't overlook the obvious." Sid put down his fork. "That car sighting reinforces the link between Bobby's problem and Auto Parts Rehabbers."

She nodded. "We were coming from Bobby's house when it passed us." Her blue eyes snapped open wide. "The explosion . . . Pete Rackard's man. Of course. The fellow asking about Bobby at the Welcome Traveler Store must have been working with them."

"Bobby told Connie the man who called him was somebody he knew from the past, but he's refused to say where."

Jaz picked up the remote and muted the TV. "It could have been Auto Parts Rehabbers. He would have been out of high school for only a short time back then."

Marie came in with a coffee pot and offered Sid a refill.

"Just half a cup." He set his plate on the tray. "This cake is delicious."

"Glad you like it. Anything else for you, Miss Jasmine?"

"Does Auto Parts Rehabbers sound familiar to you? Could that have been a place Bobby worked just out of high school?"

She held her hands to her cheeks, concentrating. "Maybe. I don't know. I'm sorry. I just can't remember. John says he thinks I'm getting Alzheimer's."

"He's just teasing," Jaz said. "Don't worry about it. Isn't it about your bedtime? If we need anything else, I can get it."

Sid held up his hand. "Nothing else for me, thanks."

The elderly woman had a pained look. "I know you said Bobby and Connie and Little Bob are safe now. But what happens next?"

"They'll be okay," Jaz said. "I'm hopeful Bobby will be here in the morning."

"If he isn't, we'll go get him," Sid promised.

After Marie left, Sid finished his cake and coffee and

checked his watch. "I thought I'd have heard from the sheriff by now."

"Maybe he's on another call."

"I doubt he gets involved this time of night, unless it's something major."

Sid's cell phone rang.

He flipped up the cover and answered it.

"Chief Chance, this is Sheriff Emmons."

"Hi, Sheriff. Appreciate your calling. How are things in Centerville?"

"It's pretty hot right now."

"Hot?"

"Yeah. And I need some answers."

"Did Deputy Ross explain what I was after?"

"He did. And when my men got to Pickslay's house, somebody had just torched it."

Sid bolted upright. "A fire? How bad?"

"Thanks to my deputies, not all that bad. They got busy with a couple of fire extinguishers and had it pretty well beaten down before the firemen arrived. There's some exterior damage, but the fire didn't get inside. A dark-colored car went racing off right after they got there. They thought it was the firebug, but they had the choice of giving chase or trying to save the house."

"Good decision."

"Yeah, I doubt they'd have caught the car. By the time they could've gotten started, it would have been too far ahead."

"Could they identify it?"

"One of the guys thought it was a Chrysler, black."

"According to the TV, a witness to that wreck on I-40 said a black Chrysler forced Pickslay off the road into a bridge abutment. Did they by chance see a Predators sticker on the back bumper?"

After Sheriff Emmons uttered a growl like a snarling dog, he barked into the phone, "Damn right. You'd better tell me what you know about all this, Chance."

Sid filled him in on the chemical spill investigation, including the explosion and fire at Jaz LeMieux's. He told about his meeting with Pickslay during the afternoon and the ex-lawyer's deal to bring him the information on First Patriots, Ltd.

"Sounds like you saved yourself five hundred bucks," Emmons said.

"But I don't have the names. They're needed for a hearing in a few days. How about giving me a look at that file?"

"No telling where it would be. That man has box after box of files in his basement."

"I'll come down and go through them."

The sheriff hesitated. "I'd say you need permission from the owner."

"Who's his next of kin?"

"That would be his brother, Dave. He runs a gas station down here."

The actual owner would depend on Percy's will, Sid thought. He hoped Emmons wouldn't be that much of a stickler. "If you could give me a phone number, I'll call Dave and get his permission."

"I think I saw a phone book around here. Let me look . . . here it is."

The sheriff read off the number.

"Does Dave know about his brother's death?" Sid asked.

"Yeah. I broke the news to him a little while ago."

"Do you plan to leave somebody there, in case whoever set the fire should come back to finish the job?"

"Yeah. Maybe we'll get lucky."

Sid broke the connection, then called Dave Pickslay. He explained who he was and what he needed.

"Have you been down in that basement?" Pickslay asked.

"No."

"Then lots of luck. I'll have to decide what to do with all that mess. Back up a truck, I reckon, haul it off, and bury it somewhere. I loved my brother, but I didn't approve of a lot of the things he did. All that stuff is best buried with him."

"I take it you're saying it's okay for me to come down and look for that file?"

"If you've got nothing better to do than dig around that basement, you're welcome to it. I'll call Sheriff Emmons and tell him."

Sid shut off the phone and turned to Jaz.

"It's a go?" she asked.

He checked his watch. It would soon be ten o'clock. "Yeah, it's a go. And I'd better get moving."

"To where?"

"Centerville. Where else?"

"It's what, seventy or eighty miles?"

"Yeah. An hour and a half drive down through the boonies. Too bad your company doesn't have a helicopter."

"We have one on call. It's tied down at John Tune. The pilot's a nice young guy named Agee, who used to be with the 101st Airborne at Fort Campbell. You want a helicopter, I'll call him."

"I'm not sure Arnie Bailey would go for a chopper bill."

"Forget Arnie. You've been going at it all day long. You don't need another three-hour drive." She grinned. "That might be too taxing on your pickup."

"Don't worry about my truck. A chopper would save some time, though."

"How long has it been since you took a moonlight helicopter ride?" she asked.

"As I recall, it was on the Cambodian border at a place called Duc Co. That'll tell you how long it's been."

"And I'll wager it wasn't in the comfort of a Bell Jetranger III. Come on in the office. I'm calling Agee."

When they arrived at John Tune Airport, the general aviation facility near I-40 on the west side of town, the pilot was waiting in the cockpit. The sleek helicopter, painted silver with red trim, perched on its long skids, the rotor revolving slowly overhead. Sid followed Jaz up the single step into the cabin, ducking his head as was always advisable around choppers. The burgundy interior had two seats up front and a three-seat bench in back.

Jaz introduced Sid as she slid onto the right section of the rear seat. Agee was short and broad-shouldered, dressed in a military-style flight suit. He had a boyish face that reminded Sid of a character in a Disney movie.

"Either of you want to ride up here with me?" Agee asked, raising his voice to compete with the engine's roar.

Sid folded into the left seat and reached for his belt. "I'll stay back here with the Queen Bee."

"Queen Bee?" Jaz frowned.

"It's your hive, ma'am." He turned to the pilot. "What does it cost to operate this gadget?"

Agee adjusted his headphones before replying. "About two-fifty an hour." He looked at Jaz. "I've made all the arrangements. I talked to the sheriff's office. They'll meet us at the hospital parking lot. That's where we're landing."

"Have you been there before?" Sid asked. This was far from combat, but he had never liked flying into strange places in the middle of the night.

"Yeah. I flew down there with a Life Flight crew. They'll have a patrol car with the headlights pointing to the LZ."

It had been eons since Sid encountered that term for Landing Zone. In his imagination he could almost hear the sound of AK-47 fire. He dismissed the unpleasant memory as Agee glanced at him and spoke as if having read his mind.

"Miss LeMieux said you were with Special Forces in Nam."

Sid nodded. "Were you in Iraq?"

"At the start of the war. I got out right after we took Baghdad."

"Good timing."

He grinned.

"How long is the flight?" Jaz asked.

"About thirty minutes. Everybody ready?"

Sid gave him a thumbs up.

43

THE CHOPPER lifted off the ramp, then headed southwest through the murky night sky. Below them lights scattered about like incandescent blobs floating on a black sea. As the rotor clattered above, the terrain soon darkened to an occasional glow or a streaking arrow formed by a car's headlights.

Sid and Jaz soon gave up conversation attempts and settled back to enjoy the flight. As he thought about the job ahead, Sid was happy she had insisted on coming along. Finding that file could turn into a daunting task, even with the two of them digging for it. One thing for sure, this chopper beat the devil out of driving. He'd try to pay for the flight, but he knew she'd refuse his offer. It's a simple business expense, she'd say. No problem.

Sid considered how to handle tomorrow morning's multiple agenda—Bobby's return, the meeting with Fire Investigator Quincy, the confrontation with Trent Decker—hopefully aided by the identity of the Auto Parts Rehabbers' ownership. As he ticked off the possibilities, the pilot looked over his shoulder.

"Get ready for landing, folks. We're about three minutes out."

Sid craned his neck to get a better view and saw the glow of lights from the town ahead. As the chopper flew lower, he spotted the parking area at the hospital. Two pairs of headlights crossed at the spot they had picked for touchdown. With his landing lights on, Agee made a turn around the area and settled toward the tarmac. After touching down, he shut off the engine. Sid and Jaz unbuckled their seat belts as the rotor slowed its sweep.

"We could be here an hour, or maybe several hours," Jaz said as the pilot turned to face them. "Do you want to stay here, go with us, or would you rather head back and let us call when we're finished?"

Agee shrugged. "I don't have anything better to do. I'll stay with the chopper. I may check in at the hospital, see what kind of coffee they have."

"I'll call you on the cell phone as soon as we see how it's going," Jaz said.

They found Deputy Ross waiting beside one of the patrol cars. A heavyset man with bushy black hair and an infectious smile, he shook hands with everybody and agreed with the pilot's plan to stay at the hospital.

"They got good coffee," he said, grinning. "I may stop by a little later myself."

With Sid and Jaz in the back seat, he drove through the darkened streets to a three-bedroom frame house on a wooded, corner lot. He parked in front and they got out.

"One of our guys is inside, in case the people who started the fire should come back," Ross said.

"Where was the fire set?" Sid asked.

"In the back. Lucky for us, they used kerosene instead of gasoline. I guess they wanted something they could light up close without burning themselves to a crisp."

"Kerosene would burn slower, for sure."

"They started it on the back porch, figuring it would soon move inside, where they'd poured a lot more on he floor. But it gave our guys time to put the damper on before the flames got to the main part. Messed the porch up pretty good."

Ross knocked at the front door. It was opened by another uniformed deputy. A strong odor of kerosene greeted them as they stepped inside. Ross introduced Sid and Jaz and explained what they would be doing.

"How're you managing this stink?" Ross asked the deputy.

The Surest Poison

A thin young man who wore his hat pushed back like a World War II fighter pilot, he pulled out a handkerchief and blew his nose. "Not too bad," he said. "With this cold, I'm not smelling a whole lot of anything."

Ross accompanied them to the basement. The lights had been left off upstairs, but down here a couple of 100-watt bulbs provided plenty of illumination for searching the files.

Ross stared at the stacks of cardboard boxes and shook his head. "That pilot's gonna have coffee running out his ears by the time you get through this stuff. The deputy upstairs will call me when you're ready to leave. Good luck."

Jaz walked over to one of the stacks as he headed up the stairs. She studied the top carton and turned to Sid. "Our man may have saved us a lot of time. The end of the box has a list of files. Should be what's inside."

Sid opened the box. It was stuffed to capacity with regular manila folders and larger ones with accordion pleats. Rubber bands helped contain their bulging contents. When Sid pulled one out to check it, the rotted bands popped off like flying red worms. He read the name on the folder and compared it to the list on the box.

"You're right. Now we need to look for First Patriots."

Each took a stack of boxes and began going down the file lists. Some of the writing was faded, and Percy Pickslay's penmanship often mimicked the style doctors used for writing prescriptions. As Judge Thackston had advised, the lists were filled with "Firsts." Sid thought he had found what they were searching for until he pulled the box out of the stack and opened it. He fished around until he came across the folder and discovered the actual name on the file was "First Patriarchs."

After encountering a similar disheartening experience, Jaz let out a shout:

"Found it!"

"Where?"

He turned and saw her down on her knees.

"On the bottom of this stack, where else?" she said.

He helped her move boxes out of the way until they reached the one that rested on the concrete floor. Dampness had rotted a hole in the bottom, and the box fell apart when Jaz tried to lift it. They sorted through the folders until she picked up one with First Patriots scrawled on the front.

"Take it over there under the light," Sid said.

She set the expandable file on a rickety table and pulled out its contents. She began to sift through the papers.

"Here are letters from the lawyer in Anguilla," she said.

Sid watched over her shoulder as she moved to the back of the file. He spotted the names at about the same time Jaz did. "Remember what your contact said about aliases?" he asked.

"Benjamin Franklin and Helen Keller."

The letter from Pickslay with the stockholders' names showed "Bronson Fradkin and Henry Keglar."

44

HANK KEGLAR'S voice echoed his anger. "They left Pickslay's place carrying a big fat package. A sheriff's car drove them to the hospital, where they took off in a chopper."

"For where?"

"Nashville."

"Are you sure they had that file?" Fradkin asked.

"What else would it be? Didn't that bitch tell you they knew about First Patriots?"

"Yes. And the folks in Nashville were sure Chance had made a deal with Pickslay to get the file."

Keglar snorted. "Well, we're certain Percy didn't follow through with his end of that deal. My contact in the Hickman County Sheriff's Office says his brother gave Chance permission to look through Pickslay's files."

"If your people had just followed through with burning—"

"Don't blame my people. They didn't screw up. A damned sheriff's car came by just as they got the fire started. Excuses don't cut it in my book, but I'll see if our business partners around Nashville can take care of Chance. I don't want to hear about any more interference from that sorry shit."

"You're calling—?"

"Yeah. Both of them have a lot to lose besides money."

"Like getting charged with arson?"

"And murder."

AGEE BROUGHT THE chopper in for a graceful landing at John Tune Airport shortly after midnight. Sid followed Jaz down to the ramp, carrying the First Patriots file wrapped in a brown paper grocery bag. He had showed the file to Deputy Ross in Centerville and called Arnie Bailey with the news. The lawyer had been ecstatic.

"Bring in Tony Decker now and we'll have it complete," he said.

"I'm going after his brother in the morning," Sid said. "If Tony is still alive, I'll get him."

He and Jaz walked at a brisk pace through the chilled night air to his truck in the airport parking area.

"Are you taking that file home?" she asked.

"I think I'll drop it by the office and lock it in the safe."

He held the truck door open for her.

"Not a bad idea," she said, "considering everything that's happened."

On the way to her house, they talked about what to do in the morning. Sid's first priority was to take the First Patriots file to Bailey, Riddle and Smith by eight o'clock. Jaz would call him as soon as she heard from Bobby. If there was time, he intended to head over to Dixie Seals before meeting with Fire Investigator Cran Quincy.

Back at the LeMieux spread, Sid stopped in front of the spotlighted house.

"You don't need to get out," Jaz said, reaching for the door handle. "Go get some rest before we start this rat race all over again."

"Thanks for all your help," he said. "The helicopter ride was great. I owe you for that one."

She waved a hand. "With what you've done for Bobby, I'd say we're even."

"We'll talk about it in the morning."

Sid drove back to Madison thinking about his pending confrontation with Trent Decker. The man was a smooth liar, but he had tangled with plenty of those in the past. He would copy a few of the papers from Percy Pickslay's First Patriot's file to use as leverage. Preoccupied with his thoughts as he

The Surest Poison

pulled into the parking lot at his building, he failed to notice the light out over the entrance until he switched off his headlights. He stepped out of the truck and looked around as he tucked the thick folder under his arm. Except for the darkness around the door, everything looked normal. A slight sparkle caught his eye. Something lay on the concrete walkway. He bent over and saw shards of broken glass. It looked like the globe that covered a light above the building's doorway. He saw a large rock on the concrete nearby. As he swung his head around to check the parking lot, a soft scuffle sounded behind him where large shrubs stood beside the entrance. Too late he realized it was the sound of sneakers.

He started to turn in that direction, reaching for the Sig.

He caught a glimpse of a billy club and threw up his arm. The action deflected the nightstick no more than an inch. It struck him a sharp blow on the side of the head. He crumpled to the pavement.

45

SID FELT SOMETHING slip from under his arm. He tried to move but his arms wouldn't cooperate. He forced his eyes open, though they refused to focus. Slowly, he reached his hands behind him, pushed into a sitting position. He rubbed his head as his vision returned to normal. Hearing a noise, he looked around but saw no one. As he began to gather his wits, he realized what he had heard was a vehicle driving off.

His head ached. Moving his fingers gingerly, he touched a tender lump above his right ear. Slowly, the pieces started falling into place. Where he was. What he had been doing.

He looked around, the confusion fading away.

His heart nearly stopped.

The First Patriots folder was gone.

He stumbled back to his truck. Climbing into the seat, he pulled out his cell phone. For a moment, he sat staring at it. He knew he should call someone, but who? Jaz . . . Arnie Bailey . . . Sgt. Wick Stanley?

He punched in Jaz's number and waited.

"Hello," she answered after a few rings, sounding about as groggy as he felt.

"Sorry to wake you," he said, "but I'm a bit addled."

He told her what had happened.

"Oh, God. What are you going to do?"

"I don't know. I need to go home and get my thoughts together."

"Shouldn't you go by the Emergency Room and let them check you out?"

"Take two aspirin and call me in the morning," he said. "I never lost consciousness. All I'm suffering from is a dandy headache and a sore spot. I just felt I needed to tell someone what happened, and you were elected."

"Thanks for thinking of me first."

He wasn't sure how to take that. "Go on back to sleep, Jaz. I'll talk to you in the morning."

"Are you going to call Metro?"

"I doubt it would help. There was nobody around to see anything. I can't imagine finding any clues to who did it. And I don't feel like sitting around for another hour or so answering questions from some cop high on caffeine."

"But you could have been killed."

"Since I wasn't, I suppose all he wanted was the file. Let's just hope we can get something out of Bobby in the morning."

Before leaving, he looked around the parking area to be sure his assailant had left nothing behind. Drawing a blank, he drove home, swallowed a couple of painkillers, and fell into bed. He knew it wasn't what the medical folks recommended, but at the moment he couldn't care less.

46

THURSDAY DAWNED as gloomy as Sid felt when he rolled over to silence the alarm. The headache no longer felt like a bass drum pounding, only a small snare. When he touched the lump on his head, however, it hurt worse than a stubbed toe. He thought about skipping his run and napping another thirty minutes. That would amount to letting whoever whacked him win the round, he decided. He struggled out of bed, pulled on his sweats, and lumbered out the door.

Despite his best intentions, he ended up cutting it short. He persuaded himself that he needed to call Arnie and be ready for Jaz's summons. After a hot shower and breakfast, his perseverance quotient jumped several notches. He read the newspaper account of Percy Pickslay's fatal accident and discovered that it took place in Cheatham County, just outside Metropolitan Nashville.

At 7:30, he called his client, Arnie Bailey.

"I have some not so good news," he said when Arnie answered.

"I'm not sure I want to know."

Sid told him about losing the First Patriots' file.

"The whole damn file is gone?" Arnie groaned in disbelief.

"Every trace of it."

After a moment of heavy breathing, Arnie asked, "How's your head?"

"Sore, but intact."

"Did you and Jaz both read the file, the part about Fradkin and Keglar?"

The Surest Poison

"Not only us but Hickman County Deputy Ross as well."

"We'll need all three of you to testify at the hearing. That piece of paper would have been the whipped cream on the sundae. When do you plan to talk to Tony Decker's brother?"

"As soon as I find out about Bobby Wallace."

"Who's Bobby Wallace?"

"He's the grandson of John and Marie Wallace, who work for Jaz." Sid explained the situation, including their suspicions that Bobby may have worked for Auto Parts Rehabbers.

"This case is becoming more confusing than a Supreme Court decision," Arnie said. "Let me know something as soon as you work it out."

Sid was ready to leave for the office when Mike Rich called.

"Remember that new case you told me about the other day?" he asked.

"The pollution deal in Ashland City?"

"Yeah. I heard something odd last night I thought might be of interest to you."

"What's that?"

"I was with my wife doing her weekly grocery shopping when we ran into one of my clients. She's an elderly woman who lives not far from us. She moved here from Ashland City a few years ago."

"I hope she wasn't affected by the trichloroethylene."

"No," Mike said, "but she mentioned reading about it in the Ashland City newspaper, which she still gets. It had a story saying you were looking for former employees of Auto Parts Rehabbers."

"Did she know someone?"

"That's the odd part. She told us she had read something in the newspaper here last week about a man found shot to death in Shelby Park."

"His name was Gillie Younger."

"I know."

"So what's the connection?"

"She says Mr. Younger worked on the garbage truck that

picked up her trash. He helped her with some boxes back during the summer, and she repaid the favor with cold drinks when the weather was so hot. At some point she mentioned having lived in Ashland City. Younger told her he had worked there for a company that reconditioned auto parts. He didn't give the name, but she thought it might be Auto Parts Rehabbers."

That brought the morning's first grin.

"Mike, you get today's Avenging Angel award."

He laughed. "Did my little old lady hit the jackpot?"

"She sure did. Give me her name and address. I need to get it to my homicide detective friend right away. She has probably helped pin the tail on a very nasty donkey."

He wasn't positive of the donkey's identity yet, but he had a pretty good idea. When he called Bart Masterson, the detective's voice mail answered. He left word that he had an important new development on the Gillie Younger murder.

It was after eight by the time he reached his office. The phone was ringing when he opened the door.

"I was about to hang up and try your cell," Jaz said. "Do you still have the headache?"

"Not like last night, but I have a sore lump that feels as big as a barn door. I just walked in here. I've been on the phone at home."

"I know. I tried to get you a couple of times."

He told her about Mike Rich's tip and the chat with an unhappy Arnie Bailey.

"Tell Arnie not to wet his pants," Jaz said. "We can all testify that Fradkin and Keglar were listed as owners of First Patriots, and I have the link to First Improvement Corp. But if Younger and Larry Irwin were killed by the same gun, and both worked for Auto Parts Rehabbers, that puts a whole new slant on things."

"Right. I have a call in for Bart."

"It should also give us more ammunition to go after Bobby. I just heard from his friend, Ned. They plan to be here in about forty-five minutes. Can you head over this way now?"

"I'll have to delay my trip to Dixie Seals, but that's okay. There's one point we need to nail down before I confront Mr. Decker."

"What?"

"We're told Tony Decker is dead, then we find out the obituary is a fake. Everybody denies having seen him or talked to him in years, but they all appear to be lying. Your source confirms Trent Decker's story, but what if he or she picked up on something as fake as that *Commercial Appeal* obit? Somebody is an accomplished scammer here. We need to confirm if Trent is really a twin, or is he Tony?"

"I have an idea," Jaz said. "Maybe I can find the answer by the time you get here."

THE SKY WAS an edgy gray that resembled the underside of a pewter lid. Sid wondered if this could be what it looked like to unlucky turkeys on Thanksgiving morning, which was only a couple of weeks away. He didn't feel in a lot better shape. When he reached the gate on Franklin Pike, Jaz buzzed him in. All the bare trees along the driveway added to the somber look of the day.

John Wallace met him at the front door and directed him to Jaz's office. An eerie quiet filled the house as he walked across to *ma cachette*.

"Anybody home?" he asked, knocking on the open door.

Jaz looked around. "Come on in. I just got off the phone with one of my good contacts."

"Checking what?" He strolled over to the chair beside her desk.

"You said you wanted confirmation about Trent and Tony."

"So what have you come up with?"

"A way to determine whether Tony has a twin brother named Trent."

A smile began to tug at his lips. "You have a contact in the state Office of Vital Records."

"Doesn't everybody?"

"I don't recall what's included on birth certificates. I presume it has information on multiple births?"

Jaz turned to the computer screen, which showed a sample birth certificate. "There's a line here that says 'This Birth—Single, Twin, Triple, etc.' I just asked her to take a peek for me when she has a chance. It shouldn't take long. I'll—"

"Front gate warning," blared a computer-generated voice, interrupting her.

They glanced at the gate monitor. The large white pickup that sat beside the farmhouse in Cheatham County last night idled outside the barrier. Jaz pressed buttons on the security console.

"Come on up to the house," she said into the microphone as the gate opened.

She and Sid met the two young men at the porch steps. Bobby walked with his head half-bowed, eyes turned up as though staring over a pair of glasses. Ned, about the same height but bulkier, wore an animated smile beneath a Tennessee Titans cap.

"Good morning," he greeted them. "You have a real cool place here, Miss LeMieux."

"Thank you," she said. "And thanks for bringing Bobby in. Let's go back to the rec room. I think we'll be more comfortable in there."

As they walked into the foyer, the elder Wallaces stood waiting, faces as solemn as an honor guard, though they didn't appear in a mood to bestow any honors. Bobby looked from one to the other.

"Good morning, Granny," he said.

"Where's Connie and Little Bob?" she asked, irritation showing in her dismal look.

"They're still at Ned's."

"He's all yours after we have a little talk," Jaz said and led the way to the rec room.

Inside, Sid glanced around. "Why don't we gather around

the card table? That will put us all eyeball-to-eyeball."

Jaz had suggested he take over the inquisitor role, since it had worked well at the first confrontation with Bobby. As soon as they were seated, he stared across at the young man.

"We know what's going on, Bobby," he said. That was a bit of an exaggeration, but they would soon know for sure. "Let me lay it out for you:

"Early on Halloween morning, a man named Gillie Younger was shot to death in Shelby Park. You were abducted that night and threatened. That same night, a young man named Larry Irwin died from a gunshot fired from the same weapon that killed Younger. Thursday, Jaz and I spent most of the day asking questions and being very visible around Ashland City. Somebody must have reported what we were doing. Friday afternoon, they held Little Bob for an hour, then turned him loose. When we went to your house that night, you told us you had been threatened again by phone, that they knew Jaz had been there. Somebody followed us to Ashland City Highway after we left. On Saturday, Jaz and your grandparents had you brought to this house."

Sid watched Bobby's reaction as the story unfolded. His eyes got bigger and bigger, his mouth dropping open.

"Sunday, a man approached one of the Welcome Traveler Stores employees who drove you over here. The guy asked if you were staying in the mansion. He was told you got out at the little house in back, where they left your car. Monday night, someone broke into the basement and rigged a device to cause a gas explosion. We traced one of the men involved to Pete Rackard's garage in Franklin. The car that followed us from your house Friday caused a wreck last night that killed a man. All of these incidents are tied into a company named Auto Parts Rehabbers, the company you used to work for in Ashland City. Was Tony Decker the man who threatened you?"

Bobby sat there stunned, blinking his eyes, as they all stared at him.

For a long moment, the silence was as thick as Marie's

cake batter. Sid would have sworn he could hear Bobby's heart beating. When the young man spoke, his voice was little more than a whisper.

"I couldn't see him for the blindfold, but that voice wasn't something you'd forget. He said somebody was dead, and I would be next if I didn't keep quiet. Then he said they would get my family, too. I didn't know about all this other stuff you say was going on."

His hands shook as he spread them out in a gesture of futility.

"What did he not want you to talk about?" Sid asked.

Bobby breathed a deep sigh. "About pouring out a lot of TCE, a chemical they used in the plant. It was a few months before they closed it down. I did janitorial work, Gillie Younger and me. After they used the TCE to clean parts, they stored it in big drums at the back. That's what it came in. Once before they shipped off a bunch of drums. To be recycled, I guess. But Mr. Decker said that cost too much money, just dump the stuff out behind the plant. There was more than twenty drums. It was quite a job. I got Gillie to help with the last bunch of 'em. It smelled awful. Made me sick as a dog that night."

47

NED HAD AN ODD look on his face. "Is that what all this fuss has been about on TV?"

"That's it," Jaz said.

He slapped Bobby on the back, grinning. "Man, you gonna be a celebrity."

"I don't know what you're talking about," Bobby said, looking confused.

Jaz cut her eyes toward him. "When Marie and I were at your house Thursday night, Connie said all you read in the paper or watch on TV is football, basketball, and hockey. You'd better start paying a little more attention to the world around you."

"Did you know people near the old Auto Rehabbers plant have been getting sick because of the TCE pollution?" Sid asked.

Bobby gave him a wide-eyed, blank look, and slowly shook his head.

"What did Larry Irwin have to do with all the TCE dumping?" Jaz asked.

"He showed me how to load the drums on the towmotor."

"They must have thought they couldn't trust him to keep quiet," Sid said. "Unlike you, he didn't have a family to threaten."

Bobby was still frowning. "What happens now?"

Sid sat back and rubbed his chin. "We have one more thing to establish. Did you ever hear Decker say anything about having a twin brother?"

"No."

"We haven't been able to find Tony Decker, but there's a man named Trent Decker who claims to be his twin brother. He runs a company called Dixie Seals out off I-24 near the county line. We have a hunch that Trent and Tony are the same person. I'm going out there to talk to him this morning."

Bobby rumpled his brow. "What if you don't find Tony? What's going to happen to me and my family?"

"Don't worry," Jaz said. "We have enough evidence to prove their responsibility without you. They won't see you as a major threat any longer."

Sid checked his watch. "Fire Investigator Cran Quincy will be here soon. You need to tell him what you've told us, Bobby. He'll be looking into Pete Rackard's involvement in that explosion and fire. Metro Homicide will also be interested in your story. I expect to hear from Detective Masterson at any time now."

"All this sounds like one of them TV cop shows," Ned said, tipping his cap back. "I think I'll stick around a while. When things settle down, Bobby, I'll take you back to my place, and you can get your wife and kid."

Sid and Jaz went back to her office, while Bobby and his friend headed to the great room where his grandparents waited. Sid picked up a phone book off a small bookshelf beside her desk and began flipping through it.

"What are you looking for?" Jaz asked.

"Dixie Seals. I need an address."

"You'd better get a phone number, too, and see if he's there. He may be making sales calls on Nissan in Smyrna or the General Motors plant at Spring Hill."

Sid found the listing and started to write down the address. "Whoa . . . where's your copy of that paper we found out beyond the fence in back? What's the number on it?"

She punched a few keys. "The one-twenty?"

"No. The D—"

"Six-three-seven."

His face brightened. "D six-three-seven. D for Dixie.

The Surest Poison

That's Dixie Seals' street address. My guess is the driver picked up the van at Dixie Seals at twelve o'clock, maybe drove somewhere to get his buddy with the explosive apparatus, then set off on what they thought would be a mission of murder."

"Thank God they misjudged that outcome," Jaz said. "But if Bobby's car hadn't been parked there . . . ." She sighed. "My house would be a pile of cinders now."

Sid's cell phone rang. He checked the caller ID. "It's Jeff Lewis from Lewisville."

When he spoke, Lewis sounded unsure. "I came up with something, Sid, but I don't know if it'll be of any help."

"What do you have, Jeff?"

"I asked around and learned Fradkin was involved in promoting offshore corporations ten or fifteen years ago. You were here around that time. I'm surprised you didn't hear about it."

"If you'll remember, I wasn't very high on Mr. Fradkin's list of people to do business with. His cronies weren't clamoring to have me join their club, either."

"I suppose you're right. Anyway, it appears the deals were set up by a lawyer named Percy Pickslay."

"He was killed in an accident last night."

"I heard about it on the news."

"Did anyone mention Hank Keglar's involvement in the corporations?"

"Yes, I think he liked to stay in the background, though. Except when some deals went sour and people started complaining. Keglar put the quietus on them."

"They say Pickslay lost his law license from ripping off people."

"Fradkin claimed to know nothing about it," Lewis said, adding, "He put on a show of innocence. He's a good actor."

"Was anyone invited to invest in First Patriots?"

"I haven't found anybody who knew about the company."

"We learned last night there were only two investors."

"Really?"

"Fradkin and Keglar."

Sid told him about the fire and finding the files on First Patriots, Ltd. "The fire appears to have been set by the people who ran Pickslay off the road," he said. "We think it was the same car that followed Jaz and me last Friday night."

"That's scary. Did they get a license number?"

"No. But they got a description. It was a late model black Chrysler with a Nashville Predators sticker on the back bumper."

Lewis made a gasping sound. "You know who owns a car like that?"

"Who?"

"Hank Keglar."

"You're sure?"

"I've seen his gorilla Dirk driving it around town."

"Thanks, Jeff. I appreciate the info. Now I have some work to do. Give Maribeth my love."

Sid shut off the phone and gave Jaz a dire look. "Hank Keglar is in the thick of it." He told her what Jeff Lewis had said. "When Bart calls, I'll have an earful for him."

"Do you think it was Dirk who hit you last night?"

"I don't know. I'd sure like to know how they knew I'd have that file, though. I suppose our foray into Centerville by chopper created quite a buzz around town." He glanced at his watch. "Hand me that phone. I'd better check on Mr. Decker."

"Whether or not he's Tony, that note makes it plain he was right in the middle of the plot."

Sid listened while the phone rang several times. He was about to hang up when a male voice answered, "Dixie Seals."

"I had about decided nobody was home," Sid said.

"Sorry. We're closed this morning. I was getting ready to set up the voice mail gizmo to let callers know. One of our employees was killed in an automobile accident, and his funeral is at eleven."

"Is this Trent Decker?"

The Surest Poison

"Yes, who's this?"

"Sidney Chance, the private investigator who came by your house and called you about the obit on Tony Decker." He decided not to mention the seven-minute phone call from Pete Rackard until they met in person.

"Oh, yes. I remember."

"I had a few more questions for you and wanted to drop by. How much longer will you be there?"

"I don't know what else I can tell you since you say my brother's dead."

"We've turned up information refuting that report."

"You mean he's still alive?"

"That's the way it looks."

"Well, I haven't heard from him. But if you want to come over now, I'll wait for you. I'm the only one left around here. The funeral home isn't far, and I don't need to be there until time for the service."

Sid handed the phone to Jaz. "I'm going out there." He told her about the funeral and Dixie Seals being closed.

"What about Cran Quincy?" she asked.

"You and Bobby can tell him all he needs to know. I want to catch Decker while he's available. Call me on the cell phone if you hear from your vital statistics friend."

Jaz stared at him. "Be careful, Sid. Don't forget those murders."

He reached up to pat the swollen place on his head. "I haven't forgotten last night, either. I'd be happy to return the favor. And I have this."

He lifted his jacket to show the Sig holstered at his belt.

Jaz shook her head. "I know you, Sid. That weapon won't move from its accustomed place unless there's no other way."

"You do what you have to do."

"Don't wait too long."

48

JAZ PROVIDED chairs for her three guests and took her seat behind the desk. Marie slipped in like a cat on the prowl, dispensed soft drinks, then disappeared. Cran Quincy wasn't sure about Ned sitting in on the interview, but the jovial young man said he was Bobby's bodyguard and he'd like to stay. While they were going through the preliminaries, Jaz's phone rang.

"Excuse me a minute," she said and answered it.

"This is Marcy," said a pleasant female voice. "I found your record."

"What does it say?"

"One male, white baby boy named Tony Virgil Decker was born in Memphis, Tennessee, at four thirty-six a.m. on March 14, 1965."

"That's our boy. Did he have a twin?"

Marcy paused. "Nope. Single birth."

"Thanks."

Jaz held the phone in her hand and pressed the button to break the connection. "It appears Mr. Tony Decker has been masquerading as a twin brother who doesn't exist. Let me call Sid and tell him."

She lifted her finger and punched in his cell number. He answered on the second ring.

"What's up?"

"You can call him Tony, if you'd like," she said.

"No twin?"

"No twin. No clone. Just Tony."

The Surest Poison

"Thanks. I'm pulling onto the interstate. I'll let you know when I have something."

As she put the phone down, Quincy stared at her with those penetrating eyes. "I think you had better clue me in, Miss LeMieux. What's going on here?"

"A lot," she said. "In the past twenty-four hours we've been busier than a convoy of eighteen-wheelers on a two-lane detour."

She sketched out the situation with Percy Pickslay's death and house fire, the stranger who had inquired about Bobby at the Welcome Traveler Store, and their conclusions regarding the cryptic note found where the firebugs had parked. She had Bobby relate the story of Tony Decker's threats.

"So all of this is related to the chemical pollution case in Ashland City?" Quincy asked when they finished.

"That's our take on it. Sid called Homicide Detective Masterson to give him the latest, but he must be at home playing zombie after an overdose of overtime."

Quincy grinned. "He can have the murders with my compliments. I'm only concerned with the arson here. I'll head on out to Franklin. I need to get one of the locals to go with me when I question Rackard and the mechanic named Shak. If there's a connection to Dixie Seals, the cops may have to give me a hand with Decker."

Quincy got up and started for the door. Before Jaz could join him, her phone rang again.

"Bobby, would you show Mr. Quincy out?" she asked and picked up the phone.

"What's Sid talking about with this new info on the Gillie Younger murder?" Bart Masterson asked.

"He called you two or three hours ago."

"I know. After an all-nighter, I had to crash for a bit."

"You haven't talked to Sid?"

"He doesn't answer his cell phone. I thought he always kept that thing turned on."

"He does, except when he's in the woods. I talked to him

not long after he left here on his way to see Tony Decker."

"The pollution case guy?"

"Right. He ran Auto Parts Rehabbers."

"Where'd you find him?"

"We discovered he's pretending to be a twin brother. We also learned Gillie Younger and Larry Irwin both worked for him at the Rehabbers plant. Bobby Wallace confessed they were all involved in the chemical dump. He says Decker threatened him and his family if he talked about it."

"Damn, Jaz," Bart said. "That means he could be our killer. And Sid goes off to confront him? Wasn't he the one who told you a good cop doesn't go in without backup?"

As Sid's failure to answer his cell phone hit home, Jaz sat up with a start. "I'm going out there."

"Where is it?"

She gave him the address.

"I'll meet you."

49

SID WORE A GRIN as wide as the five lanes of I-24. After the call from Jaz, he had something worth shouting about. He had Tony Decker cornered. It never failed. Sooner or later, they all screwed up. Decker got a little too clever with his obituary scam. Sid thought about buzzing Arnie Bailey but decided to wait until after the confrontation. He also considered trying Bart again. Decker had to qualify as a major suspect in the murder of his former employees. The homicide detective would have plenty of questions for him, but if Bart was awake, he would have returned the call. Sid had spent way too much time running on idle with this case, waiting around for something to happen. He was in no mood to delay things any longer. If he got the answers he expected, he would hand Decker over, gift wrapped, and tied with a big red bow.

Though the sun still lurked behind the clouds, the sky seemed a bit brighter as he sped down the interstate toward the exit for Dixie Seals.

He found the number 637 on a sign designating a gray prefab building that was not just a twin, but one of triplets that lined the street. Two brown vans sat behind a security fence at the side of the building. Sid pulled into the parking lot in front. A black Lincoln and a small pickup were the only vehicles in view. The Lincoln occupied a slot with "Mr. Decker" painted on the concrete. The truck, parked some distance away, must have been left by an employee who rode with a friend to the funeral home. Decker had said he was the last to leave.

A computer-generated notice on the building entrance

advised that the firm would re-open at three o'clock. The door was unlocked, however, and Sid stepped inside. The entrance hall didn't seem big enough to qualify as a lobby. Maybe a vestibule. He faced an open window behind a counter, closed doors on either side. Two straight chairs sat along one wall. A small display of gaskets stood against the other. The window opened onto an unoccupied office with several desks, filing cabinets, the usual paraphernalia of a small business.

Sid walked up to the window. He called out in his bad cop voice, "Decker!"

A few moments later, the door on the left opened. The man they had met as Trent Decker four days earlier smiled at him. He wore a blue business suit, the thick ponytail dangling in back of his collar. "Come on in, Mr. Chance. Let's go back to my office."

He took a few steps along the hallway and turned through an open door on the left. Sid followed him into a modest-sized office with dark wood furnishings that looked stylish but not expensive. Colorful photos of concept cars decorated pale brown walls. Pastel green drapes covered the windows.

Decker moved behind his desk and waved to a chair in front. "Have a seat and tell me what I can do to help."

Sid eased into the chair and looked Decker in the eye. This was not a social call. Chit-chat did not appear on his agenda.

"Let's start with this," he said. "Since I talked to you on Tuesday, we learned the Tony Decker obituary was a hoax."

"You told me on the phone my brother was still alive."

"Yes, Tony Decker is still alive, and I'm certain he was here last Friday when Pete Rackard called. The call lasted seven minutes."

"How could that be? We were closed."

Sid ignored his protest and continued. "Monday we asked Bronson Fradkin and Hank Keglar in Lewisville about Tony and Auto Parts Rehabbers. That night someone placed a device under the small house behind Jaz LeMieux's mansion, setting off an explosion and fire that destroyed the place."

Decker stiffened. "Why are you telling me all this?"

"Because we found evidence indicating the people who touched off the explosion came here for a van before going to Jaz's place."

"That's preposterous."

"Is it? Somebody thought Bobby Wallace would be in the house that was destroyed. They were afraid he might talk. Well, this morning he did. He said he recognized Tony Decker's voice when he was threatened last week. He told us how he had dumped more than twenty drums of TCE behind the plant on Tony's instructions."

Decker bolted up from his chair. "I'm going to have to ask you to leave, Mr. Chance. This has nothing to do with me, and I don't have to listen to any more of it."

Sid rose as well. "I think it does have to do with you. You've been masquerading as Trent Decker the past ten years, but the party's over. We checked your birth certificate, Tony. You have no twin brother."

Decker looked down and reached for his desk drawer.

Sid drew the Sig, pushed back the slide with an ominous clack.

"Keep your hands out of the drawer," he ordered. "Up where I can see them."

He held the gun in his right hand, keeping an eye on Decker. With his left hand, he reached for his cell phone.

Decker's face softened into a smile. His hands relaxed. Sid tightened his grip on the gun. What was the man up to?

"Vince, why don't you relieve Mr. Chance of that weapon he likes to threaten people with?" Decker said.

Sid was ready to call the bluff when he felt something round and hard press against his back.

"I guess this three-fifty-seven Magnum trumps that nine millimeter." The man behind him reached around for the Sig.

50

SID HELD THE gun until he heard the unmistakable snap of a trigger being cocked.

"Easy does it," Vince said, grasping the weapon.

He moved around to where Sid could see a shiny revolver held by the thick, muscular man he had kicked off the porch Friday night. The one he had dubbed "Scarface." Judging by the grin on his jowly face, he enjoyed the switch in roles.

The carpet was a soft plush. The man had moved like a ghost. It made Sid feel a little better about being taken by surprise last night. He wasn't losing his touch.

"I believe you've met before," Decker said.

Scarface waved the gun. "He ain't so cocky now."

Sid gave him a look icy enough to freeze steam. "I should have hauled you off to jail right then."

"You ain't no cop now, Chance."

"You obviously didn't follow my instructions last night, Vince," Decker said. "We wouldn't be in this mess now if you'd done the job right."

"I swung that club hard as I could. He went down like a flat tire. I thought he'd had it."

Sid stiffened. He reached up to touch the sore spot on his head. "You're the guy who did this, huh? It's a good thing I got my arm up in time."

Sid's cell phone rang and Decker motioned to Vince. "Get that thing."

The man with the scar continued to grip the revolver but shoved the Sig into his pocket. He eased behind Sid and

The Surest Poison

slipped the phone out of its scabbard. It soon fell silent.

Sid considered making a move for the gun but thought better of it. Decker likely had one in his desk drawer. Anyway, this didn't appear to be an opportunity with acceptable risks. What they had in mind for him wasn't clear, either.

Decker moved from behind his desk. "Let's get him tied up before he causes any more problems."

"Then what?" Vince asked.

"I need to call Lewisville and give them a heads up. We'll stash him in an office down the hall until we find out what they want to do." He glared at Vince. "If he got his arm up last night, you should have known you didn't put him out of commission."

"I didn't see no arm. That whack woulda dropped an elephant. He must have a head like a rock. Anyway, I got your damn file."

Sid gripped his fists and took a deep breath. He'd love to deck the guy with a quick right cross, but a .357 Magnum round wasn't worth it.

"Not my file," Decker said. "That was for Hank and Bronson."

They force-marched him into a smaller office with a desk, a roll-around secretarial chair, a computer, a printer, a two-drawer file, and a metal straight chair. They sat him in the straight chair and Vince held the gun on him while Decker went back to the shipping department. He returned with a large coil of twine. Wrapping it around and around, he tied Sid's arms and legs. They went out and closed the door. Sid heard the lock click.

Except for the computer's soft hum, silence filled the room. Cars in various colors and shapes scrolled about the flat monitor on the desk. Though the lights were off, the window provided ample illumination, despite the morning's dusky skies. Sid spent a few moments surveying the small office, looking for anything that might be a help in freeing himself. He saw no sharp edges to saw against. A letter opener stuck out of a cup on the desk. There was no way he could get his hands on it.

Because of his long legs, they had tied his ankles to the outside of the chair. He found he could push with his feet and maneuver the chair over the tight weave of the carpet. Turning to face the window, he saw the street lay too far away to attract any attention, even if he had some way to wave. He tugged at his hands and flexed his wrists. The twine didn't allow enough movement to work anything loose.

Inch by inch, he walked the chair over to the desk. In and out boxes accommodated a stack of papers. Besides the cup with the letter opener, a few pens and pencils, there was a photo of a plump young woman and a stout, smiling man. A box of tissues sat at one side, a single tissue on top bearing the imprint of a lipstick blot. A woman's desk. He eased the chair around until he could get a hand on a drawer and pull it open. Then he turned until he could see inside.

It contained a folded red and yellow scarf, a half-eaten chocolate bar, judging by its turned-back wrapper, a box of Christmas cards, a few small unidentified objects, and a zippered plastic case with a floral motif. It looked like one of those reward gifts from a department store make-up counter. Since the chair had a solid back, his arms weren't tied to it, giving his hands the ability to maneuver up and down. He scooted around until he could reach into the drawer and feel for the cool of the smooth plastic.

Pulling out the case, he felt around until he found the zipper. Then began the tedious task of pulling while holding it steady. Long fingers helped. When he got it open, he reached inside. He held his breath as he almost dropped it. He felt a small bottle, maybe fingernail polish, and a round container that could be powder. When his finger hit a sharp point, he checked further, moving until he traced the outline of a long metal fingernail file. Feeling the rough edge, he knew it would cut through the twine if he could work it like a saw.

Grasping the handle between his thumb and two fingers,

The Surest Poison

he slipped the file out of the case, which fell to the carpet. He rotated the file, turning the sharp end to point toward his wrist. He pushed until he felt it contact the twine that bound him. He began to work the slim metal shaft back and forth, back and forth, back and forth.

How long had it been since they left him, he wondered? There was no clock on the wall. He couldn't see his watch. He knew they could return at any moment. He prayed for a busy phone line in Lewisville.

His fingers soon tired, but he kept sawing.

Then it happened.

He felt his bonds loosen. Still holding the file, he twisted his wrists as hard as he could. The strands began to pull apart. He worked one hand free and swung both arms in front. His wrists burned from rubbing against the twine, but he quickly shucked off the rest of it. Bending down, he sawed away at the strands binding his ankles.

As soon as he was able to move, Sid bounded over to the casement window and started cranking it open. At the rattle of a key in the door lock, he realized he was too late.

51

JAZ RACED down Franklin Pike to Old Hickory Boulevard, which cut across the southern end of the county, changing names to Bell Road before it reached I-24. She had checked the map before leaving and found Dixie Seals almost to the Rutherford County line, off a reincarnation of Old Hickory Boulevard several miles down the interstate. Under the best of driving conditions, it was a twenty-to-thirty-minute drive. Today was not the best of conditions. She got tangled in slow-moving traffic around a major intersection. A few minutes later, she found herself behind a long funeral procession. She thought of trying to pass the line of cars with their headlights on but knew she'd be butting heads with the aggressive funeral escorts. She had witnessed them dash back and forth from front to back, lights flashing, loudspeaker blaring to force people out of the way.

She put on her headset and punched the number for Bart.

"Masterson," he answered.

"Where are you?"

"Dodging idiots. I had to stop for gas. I should have done it on the way home this morning, but I was bushed."

"I'm stuck behind a funeral procession on Old Hickory Boulevard."

"I should be coming out I-24 by the time you get there. If I blow by you, just kick it in afterburner and ride my draft."

She clicked off the phone. By now she had begun to fight off unwanted images of Sid lying in a pool of his own blood. Her impulse was to jam her foot on the accelerator, but she cooled it until the funeral turned off at an intersection.

WHEN THE KEY rattled in the lock, Sid dashed across the office. He barely made it behind the door before it opened. He heard a gasp as Vince stepped in, revolver in hand, and faced the empty chair. The stocky man's scarred face reddened as he rushed toward the open window. Sid came up behind him and delivered a hard chop to his wrist. The gun bounced out. Following through with all his weight, Sid flung the startled man against the wall. The .357 hit the floor and fired.

The shot made a deafening roar in the small room. The bullet ricocheted off the metal desk and tore through the end wall. Sid shook off the shock of the discharge, though he could hear nothing above the ringing in his ears. He glanced down at Vince. The man lay motionless on the floor. Blood trickled from a scalp wound where his head had hit a metal stud in the wall. Sid grabbed the revolver off the carpet. He knew the shot would bring Decker on the run.

Sid hid behind the door again. Moments later, Decker burst through, waving a .38 revolver. He froze when he saw the body on the floor.

"Put the gun on the desk," Sid commanded.

Decker's head jerked around to see the weapon aimed at his chest and Sid's grim look.

"Now!"

Sid could barely hear his shout over the deafness resulting from the .357 Magnum blast, but he sensed that his facial expression would leave no doubts about his intentions.

With a grudging move, Decker placed his snub-nosed revolver on the desk.

Sid gestured with Vince's gun. "Hands over your head and face the wall." A pair of handcuffs would come in handy now, he thought.

Through the open window, he heard the screech of tires in the parking area. Who had Decker called? It was too soon for anybody to come from Lewisville. Could it be Pete Rackard, maybe the mechanic called Shak? Had Decker left the front door unlocked?

That question was answered by a loud crash at the front of the building, a sound he had heard on a number of occasions during his police days. A door being kicked in.

A booming voice followed. "Police! Come out with your hands up, Decker."

Sid backed into the hallway, keeping the gun on his prisoner. "Bart! Come on back."

He returned to the office, glanced at the .38 on the desk, and found what he expected.

Moments later, the detective hustled in, followed by Jaz. Both had weapons drawn.

"Meet Tony Decker," Sid said when they came to a sudden stop. "He's a candidate for a pair of cuffs, Bart. If you test fire that S&W 642 on the desk, I suspect you'll find the weapon that killed Gillie Younger and Larry Irwin."

The mustachioed man on the floor sat up, groaning, lifting a hand to his head.

Bart looked around. "Who's he? You shoot him?"

"No. I just banged his head against the wall. He got what he deserved. He's the one who clobbered me with a nightstick outside my office last night. He stole the First Patriots file."

"He have a name?"

"Decker called him Vince. I'd guess he works here."

Bart cuffed Decker and turned to Jaz. "Keep you eye on this one."

Sid laid the .357 on the desk. He bent down and reached into Vince's pocket, pulling out his Sig.

"What's your full name, Vince?" Bart asked the man on the floor.

"Vincent Askew," he said. He leaned back against the wall.

"Don't move," Bart growled when he reached for his pocket.

"I need a handkerchief," he said with a whimper.

"Get him a handkerchief, Sid."

Sid found one in the man's pocket, handed it to him, and

The Surest Poison

he wiped it against his head. He looked at the blood and frowned.

"You'll live," Bart said.

He'd already called for police backup. Now he radioed for an ambulance.

Patrol cars soon swarmed the parking lot. The paramedics bandaged Vince's head and pronounced him fit for jail. As Sid's hearing began to improve, he gave a brief account of what happened after his questioning of Tony, alias Trent, Decker.

He turned to the handcuffed prisoner. "Who did you talk to in Lewisville?"

"I want a lawyer," Decker said.

"Bronson Fradkin?"

Decker clamped his mouth shut and turned away.

When they headed out of the building, the Dixie Seals owner stared at the battered doorway. He flashed his eyes at the detective.

"Look at the mess you made of my building."

"I'll have it fixed and send you the bill," Bart said. "Right now I'd say that was the least of your worries."

Sid walked out to the car with Jaz. She stopped beside the Lexus and glared at him, hands jammed against her hips.

"You didn't want me going to Bobby's by myself Friday night, remember? Why didn't you wait for me to come out here with you?"

He couldn't think of a reasonable-sounding answer, so he shrugged. "I didn't want to get both of us shot."

She gave him a short jab to the ribs. Sid dodged backward. It wasn't just a token tap. "I don't care how big you are," she said. "If you pull that again, I'll put you on the canvas."

52

Back at the Franklin Road mansion, Sid called Arnie Bailey and told him Tony Decker had been unmasked and lodged in the Metro Jail.

"A little good news for a change," the lawyer said. "I trust you'll have me a full report. This should take care of Wade Harrington's problem."

"Will our testimony about First Patriots be enough to get the state to go after Fradkin and Keglar?"

"They could go after the corporation, but if it was dissolved or has no assets, there would be no point in it."

"Would they have any personal liability?"

"Not unless you can prove they were involved in the decision to dump the TCE."

Fat chance, he thought. "I have your report about ready. With all that's gone on, you've run up a pretty good tab."

"Send it along with your report," he said. "I'm sure Harrington will be happy to pay it."

After Sid and Jaz told Bobby about Decker's arrest, and convinced him he was no longer a threat to anyone, he left with his friend Ned to retrieve his car from the Cheatham County farm. A short time later, Investigator Quincy called. He had drawn a blank. Pete Rackard denied knowing anything about anything. The mechanic with the mustache was off today, but he had a name. Nate Shackleford. So far, he hadn't turned up.

Sid, on an extension, briefed Quincy on what happened at Dixie Seals.

The Surest Poison

"So you got your head-basher," Quincy said.

"Right. I returned the favor."

"Do you think Rackard was in on all of this?"

"I'm sure he was. We know from some phone calls that he got in touch with Decker and Branson Fradkin as soon as Jaz left his garage last Friday. If we could get somebody to rat on him, that would help."

"How about Shackleford?"

"When you get him, give it a try," Jaz said. "Tell him blowing up a house thinking someone was inside is attempted murder. Maybe that will shake something loose."

"Where does he live?" Sid asked.

"In an apartment off Granny White Pike. I checked it out. He lives with a guy named Vincent Askew."

"Vince?" Jaz blurted.

"That's the guy who clobbered me in the head," Sid explained. "Check with Homicide Detective Masterson. Maybe the two of you can play them off against each other."

After they got off the phone, Sid returned to the visitor's chair in Jaz's office. He leaned on the arm, resting his chin on one hand.

"You look like The Thinker with a headache. Why the glum look?" she asked. "You've closed your case and left Bart in the position of owing you a big one. That's a real plus."

"I don't like loose ends."

"Oh? Whose end is loose?"

"Fradkin and Keglar are two very guilty loose ends."

"Did you give Bart the information you got from Jeff Lewis about the black Chrysler?"

"Percy Pickslay's accident isn't a Metro case. I read in the paper that it took place across the line in Cheatham County. How about looking up the sheriff's number in Ashland City? Put it on the speaker if you want to listen in."

They soon had Sgt. Meyer on the speaker. After reminding him of their meeting the previous week, Sid told him about Pickslay's tie-in to the TCE pollution behind the HarrCo plant.

"A friend of mine in Lewisville says a car identical to the one that ran Pickslay off the road belongs to Hank Keglar," Sid said. "He runs a bar down there and was a part-owner of that corporation Pickslay set up to help start Auto Parts Rehabbers. He also owned the building. It looks like one of his thugs in the same car tried to burn the lawyer's house in Centerville last night."

"Damn, Chance, we'd better get that car impounded before anything's done to it. We found traces of black paint on Pickslay's left front fender after the accident."

"One piece of advice, Sergeant. Get the Highway Patrol or the TBI to do it. If you contact Sheriff Zachary's office in Lewisville, Keglar will know about it before you can hang up the phone."

There was a peck at the door, and Marie Wallace stuck her head in. "I just took a pan of brownies out of the oven. I'm brewing a pot of coffee. Would y'all like something?"

Sid looked around. "Since I haven't had any lunch, it sounds like a great idea."

"You didn't eat lunch?"

Jaz shrugged. "It's been a busy day, Marie. I'll settle for a brownie, too, and something to drink."

After Marie left, shaking her head, Sid asked Jaz to get Sheriff Emmons in Centerville on the phone. He briefed Emmons on what he had learned from reviewing the First Patriots' file they found in Percy Pickslay's basement.

"I'm familiar with both Fradkin and Keglar," the sheriff said. "I'm currently working with the district attorney on a case that has some ties to Keglar."

"What does it involve?" Sid asked.

"Since it's an ongoing investigation, I can't give you any details, but your name came up in the discussions."

"My name? How?"

"We picked up a small-time punk who's been dealing drugs around Centerville. We found out he moved here a couple of years ago from Lewisville. The DA identified him as the guy

Sheriff Zachary used to set you up on that bribery charge."

Sid gripped the arms of his chair. "What's he doing running loose? Zach should have prosecuted him for dealing and making false accusations against me."

"Obviously, he didn't."

"How is Keglar involved?"

"Sorry, Chance, I've probably said too much already. I'd suggest you talk to Sam Grizzard."

Grizzard was the DA in Franklin who threw out the bribery charge against him. "Thanks," Sid said. "Meanwhile, you need to know something else I've just learned.

He told Emmons what Jeff Lewis said about the black Chrysler with the Predators' bumper sticker. He added he had already alerted Sgt. Meyer in Ashland City.

"Let me get onto that and see what's been done," Emmons said and hung up.

Marie came in with brownies, coffee for Sid and tea for Jaz. She set them on a small table next to the desk. "Anything else?"

Jaz shook her head. Sid said, "No, thanks."

He pulled out his cell when Marie left.

"Who are you calling now?" Jaz asked.

"Grizzard. I still have him in my contact list."

He found the number and punched Talk. He'd likely have better luck meeting with the the DA in person, he thought, and arranged to be there in forty-five minutes.

"I'll go along," Jaz said. She gave him that determined look he had learned to be wary of, the one that said cross me and I'll reduce you to a eunuch.

Sid eyed her with equal wickedness. "This is my fight, not yours."

"Who said anything about fighting? I thought you were looking for some answers."

"I may need to go back to Lewisville for the final answer."

"Then you'll need someone for backup."

"This is something I have to do myself."

"It's a guy thing, isn't it? You have to protect your macho image. The hero must vanquish the demon."

Sid took a deep breath. He knew what he wanted to say, just not quite how to frame it. He started with, "You don't understand . . . " when Bobby Wallace walked in.

Bobby looked a bit sheepish. "Ned reminded me that I need to thank you folks big time for what you did," he said. "I know I must have seemed pretty dumb, but when it involved Connie and Little Bob—"

"Don't worry about it." Jaz dismissed it with a wave of her hand. "We realize you were under a lot of pressure." She turned to Sid. "Remember when Larry Irwin's friend in Clarksville told me he had the impression that Auto Parts Rehabbers might have been dealing in stolen property? You said your police investigation in Lewisville indicated that's what Hank Keglar was involved in."

"Right. We didn't find enough evidence to charge Keglar, but our informant said he had connections to a gang of car thieves." He finished his coffee and glanced back at Jaz. "If you wanted a ready source of cheap used auto parts to recondition, where would be a good place to look?"

"Car thieves."

"It was around 1995 when we honed in on Keglar. That was the year Auto Parts Rehabbers closed their doors. It's possible Keglar felt the heat and decided we were getting too close, that it was time for him to get out of the business. Bobby, do you remember hearing anything about where the used parts came from that Pete Rackard's crew worked on at the Rehabbers plant?"

Bobby shoved his hands into his pockets and hunched his shoulders. "I helped unload 'em sometimes. They were usually just piled in cardboard boxes."

"What kind of boxes?"

He pondered that for a moment, then grinned. "Some were whiskey boxes. Like Jack Daniel's or Jim Beam."

Cartons that whiskey bottles came in could mean only one

The Surest Poison

thing in Sid's mind. "Do you remember seeing any company names on the boxes?"

"No, I don't think so," Bobby said. Then his face crinkled into a smile. "Take that back, I do remember something Gillie and I thought was a real hoot."

"What was that?" Jaz asked.

"The Long Branch Saloon."

Sid grinned. "Thanks, Bobby, that's exactly what we were looking for."

His eyes widened. "It was?"

"You just confirmed our suspicions," Jaz said. "And now that everything's under control, you can take Connie and Little Bob home whenever you're ready."

His face brightened. "I appreciate your letting us stay with you, but as soon as that boy gets home from school, we're out of here."

Sid turned to Jaz. "We'd better head for Franklin. This should get Sam Grizzard's attention."

53

The DA's office for Tennessee's 21st District was in the Williamson County Courthouse in Franklin. A modestly plump man with glasses that sat far down on his nose, his tweed jacket giving him more the look of a law professor than a district attorney general, Samuel Grizzard stood behind his paper-strewn desk as Sid and Jaz walked in. He stuck out a hand as wrinkled as his white shirt.

"Chief Chance, good to see you again."

Sid shook his hand and smiled. "You're looking great, General. I don't know if you're acquainted with my associate, Miss Jasmine LeMieux?"

Grizzard came around his desk and clasped both hands around hers. Sid remembered him as a good lawyer and prosecutor and just as good a politician.

"Nice to meet you," he said. "I'm familiar with who you are, though our paths haven't crossed before. Please have a seat."

"Nice meeting you, Mr. Grizzard," Jaz said and sat in a chair across from his desk.

When both men were seated, the lawyer leaned back in his high-backed leather chair. "Would this visit relate to the calls I've been getting from sheriffs around the area?"

"Yes, sir," Sid said. "I provided some information to Sheriff Emmons and a sergeant in Cheatham County."

"Which is out of my district. Emmons had him call me, though."

Sid was glad to hear both men had followed through. "So what's the situation in Lewisville?"

The Surest Poison

Grizzard smiled. "Interesting place, as you know. A state trooper went looking for the Chrysler with the Predators sticker but reported it was nowhere to be found. Fortunately, Sheriff Emmons' investigator located it at a body shop over in Perry County. There was a rush order to do some front-end repair work, but nothing had been done yet."

"Was the right fender damaged?"

"It was. The TBI is sending a team down to get paint samples to compare with what they found on Percy Pickslay's car. They're also getting a search warrant to check out Keglar's place for fire accelerants."

Sid pulled his notebook from his shirt pocket and flipped it open to notes from the Bobby Wallace interview. "I have some new information for you. Remember back when we tried to make a case against Keglar for involvement with an auto theft ring?"

"As I recall, all you had were accusations by a sleazy informant with a shady reputation."

"Right. But now we have a witness who unloaded used auto parts that came in whiskey cartons from The Longbranch Saloon."

"I guess that's some consolation," Grizzard said, appearing totally unimpressed. "But it wouldn't matter if they came in a box with Hank Keglar's signature on it."

Jaz frowned. "Why?"

"It would probably be a Class C or D Felony. At most a Class B, which has a statute of limitations of eight years. That must have been fifteen years ago."

Sid slumped in his chair, his face twisted into a look grim enough to suit the Reaper. Was there no justice? He recalled a magazine essay by Ralph Waldo Emerson his mother had liked to quote that named such things as alcohol and strychnine but concluded: "the surest poison is time." Keglar hadn't ordered dumping of that TCE years ago, but it would have been his type of solution. Though he couldn't be held responsible legally, he had a moral responsibility as one of the owners.

Now he was off the hook for dealing in stolen auto parts.

Sid glanced at Jaz, then back at Grizzard. "If it turns out that one of Keglar's goons drove his car to kill Pickslay, can you get him as an accessory to murder?"

"Or a co-conspirator. But right now that's a big *if*. We'll have to see how it works out." He propped his elbows on the desk and leaned forward. "We have some new charges against the young man who set you up on that bribery sting. I guess you knew about that."

"Sheriff Emmons mentioned it, but he didn't give me any details."

"So far the man has refused to implicate Keglar in the drug transactions, but he admitted it was the bar owner who suggested he go to Sheriff Zachary with the tale about you trying to bribe him."

Sid almost leapt out of the chair. "The bastard! I should have guessed as much. I'll give that—"

"Calm down, Sid," Jaz said, springing out of her chair, reaching across to take a firm grip on his arm.

The DA stood behind his desk. "I don't blame you for feeling that way, Sidney. I'm sure I would, too. It's out of your hands now, though. Let the TBI take care of it. I recall you like to be personally involved in these things, but it would only get you into more trouble."

Sid took a couple of deep breaths to calm himself. It didn't help. He just wanted to get out of there. "Thanks for the information," he said. "Let's go, Jaz."

He hurried out of the office and didn't slow down until he was out on the sidewalk approaching his car. Dusk had come early, brought on by an ominous canopy of gray clouds that hid what was left of the afternoon sun. Along the streets he saw pairs of bottle-shaped lamps on tall stands that seemed to have a conspiratorial glow. Beyond them, a circular swath of grass surrounded a tall obelisk that supported a lone Confederate soldier who stood silent watch over Franklin's Public Square, his hopeless cause long ended. Sid knew the feeling.

The Surest Poison

"Are you all right?" Jaz asked as she caught up with him.

He unlocked the car and opened the door for her without answering.

She slid into the seat and gave him a guarded look as he climbed in. "Don't do anything stupid, Sid."

He sat behind the wheel and started the car. "I did something stupid three years ago when I let that asshole ruin my life in Lewisville."

"You've made a good start at salvaging your life. It's time to press on and show him that he didn't succeed. Sam Grizzard and the TBI will show him who's the real loser."

"I wish I could count on that." Sid's eyes scanned the traffic ahead, but his thoughts were elsewhere.

BEFORE THEY reached her house, Jaz took out her cell phone and called Bart Masterson.

"What's new with our friend Decker?" she asked.

"We got a fingerprint match. He's Tony. Must have kept his skirts clean. I guess nobody's taken his prints until now."

"Got a report on the gun yet?"

"They promised to get to it as soon as possible. He's denying everything, of course, but he has no verifiable alibi for the time of either murder. His Lincoln has the kind of tires they identified on Marrowbone Road."

"Shake anything out of his man, Vince? We thought you might get him to rat on his pals."

"I talked to Quincy from the fire department. We're working on it. A couple of our guys just got back from checking out Vince's apartment. Like to know what they found?"

"What?"

"A big file folder labeled First Patriots, Limited."

Jaz grinned. "Hold it for Arnie Bailey. He'll probably tell the chief to give you a raise."

"Yeah, I'll go order a new Corvette. Oh, another thing, while they were at the apartment, they got a tip on where to find his roomie, Shak."

"Thanks, Bart." She closed the cell phone.

"Hold what for Arnie?" Sid asked.

"They found the First Patriots file at Vince's apartment. Bart says they got a fingerprint match on Tony, and they picked up a tip on where to find Shak."

Sid remained silent the rest of the way. When he pulled up to her house, she turned to him. "Keep your seat. I'll let myself out. I suggest you go home and do some serious thinking about letting go of the past. You need to move on, keep your eyes on the future. You're a good man, Sid. Lots of talent, lots of ability. You can be the best PI in the business. Don't let a grudge from the past derail your career."

BACK HOME, Sid changed into white sweats and strode out into the night. Lights glowed warmly in the windows of the neighborhood. It was the end of another normal day for most people. It hardly looked that way to Sid. The black sky pressed down on him like a physical weight. A cold breeze brushed his face, raised the hair on the back of his hands. It sharpened his senses to a knife edge. He ran along lonely streets, in and out of occasional pools of light from a lamp post, picking up the pace as he went.

His legs pumped like pistons. Air rushed into his lungs. It felt like an attempt to suck in the whole of the night. When he hit his stride, a surge of power ran through his body. He was in his element.

What Jaz had said stirred about in his mind as if swirled by the force of the wind. "Let go of the past . . . keep your eyes on the future." He knew she was right, but could he let go? What if Hank Keglar weaseled out of this one the way he did nearly everything else, justice be damned?

"Go home and do some serious thinking," Jaz told him.

It would be a long night.

Author's Note

In some ways, this book was more difficult to write than my four Greg McKenzie mysteries. After I finished the first draft, with some critiques from my writers group (the Quill & Dagger Writers Guild), I realized I didn't like the way Sid Chance had turned out. I went back to the drawing board, recast his character, and changed a lot of the action. I also revised the relationship between Sid and Jaz. Who knows what may develop in future books?

I'm indebted to several other people for their help with the project. In no particular order, they include retired Nashville Fire Department Battalion Chief Billy Burgess, Maggie Lawrence of the Nashville Fire Marshal's office, Randy Moomaw of the *Ashland City Times*, Tennessee Bureau of Investigation Special Agent Dan Royse, and Chuck Head, Senior Director for Land Resources of the Tennessee Department of Environment and Conservation.

A special thanks to Nashville PI Norma Mott Tillman, who gave birth to the plot by telling me about a similar case she worked in West Tennessee. Thanks also for the patient editing work of Beth Terrell and the patient support of my wife, Sarah.